The Fae Wars

More Tales from the Occupation

J.F. Holmes, H.Y. Gregor & David Shadoin, J.R. Handley, Richard Cartwright, Lucas Marcum, Jonathan Shuerger, Claire Merrick, Jason Kyle

Table of Contents

In the Deed, the Glory

by H.Y. Gregor and David Shadoin

ELVES WEREN'T ANYTHING LIKE the stories.

Sometimes I hated the fairy tales I grew up with. The stories about friendly fairies and noble elves were a joke. None of them got it right, not even the Brothers Grimm. The real thing was way, way worse. I learned it the hard way.

I pedaled a little slower when I saw Husker Stadium, like I always did.

Technically it was called *Memorial* Stadium, but nobody I knew called it that. That's where the Huskers played. Dad took me to a few football games there when I was a kid. I loved how loud the crowd cheered, and made fun of how goofy the marching band outfits were. We ate Runzas and I got to drink all the soda I wanted. Back then, that was a big deal.

Of course, that was *before* the Elves.

I was a kid when I was twelve, maybe even when I was thirteen. Now I'm fourteen, and being a kid was *before*, too. *You grow up fast under the occupation, kiddo, or you don't grow up at all.* At least that's what Dad always said.

Sometimes even being an adult wasn't enough. I'd seen plenty of them die since Lord Halfast and his vassals took over. Dad said that wasn't normal for a kid, either.

My bike tires smeared through the soot on the sidewalk. This close to the stadium, everything was covered in grime from the smoke.

The smoke *from the dragons*.

Now *dragons* were exactly like they sounded in the stories. They were just as cool as they were scary. I always hung around downtown a little longer than Dad liked on my way home from school, just because I wanted a chance to see an Elf flying in or out of the stadium on a dragon. There were a few that lived here, but my favorite was a great big yellow-and-orange one. I saw it breathe fire once. Its scales flashed even brighter than the flames, and I could feel the heat from all the way down in the street where I watched.

Dad said that most people who got to see dragon fire don't live to tell people about it.

I think Lord Halfast got the idea to settle in here after a raid on STRATCOM — I could never remember what that stood for. A bunch of resistance guys had holed up in the old Air Force base. The Elves didn't stand for it. After they went in and kicked the humans out, I think the Elf lord liked the idea of an 'air force'. They took over the Haymarket — well, the whole world, really — and then Lord Halfast brought some of his greatest treasures *here*, to Lincoln.

Dragons.

It made sense that they'd turned the stadium into a dragon roost. Sometimes I even thought it was kind of a cool idea, even if it did mean no more football. I missed sports, but that wasn't anywhere close to the worst thing about the occupation.

I kept my head down when I crossed the pedestrian bridge into downtown. I rode past boarded up restaurants and shops. The boards weren't as bad as the new places — the ones *they'd* taken over. Some things almost looked normal. My favorite burger joint was still open. It was alright, if you didn't mind eating next to an Orc or something.

The Orcs freak me out.

Don't get me wrong, some things really were still the same. We had a police department, sort of. We still ate — mostly enough. I even got to go to school.

I used to fake sick to get out of class. Now faking sick gets you a beating, or worse — even for adults. *Especially* for adults.

It didn't take long to get through the Haymarket, past a line of other humans trying to get weekly rations, and across the old train tracks. The garage door was open when I pulled my bike into the driveway, and two big motorcycles were parked on the curb. My heart dropped into my stomach. We had company — I just wish it was unexpected.

Dad would have gotten rations while I was at school today. That meant Jack's rounds brought him over to our place.

I bit my tongue and went straight to the door leading into the laundry room. There weren't any sounds from inside the house. Sometimes that was a good sign. Other times... I smashed the button that closed the garage door. It screeched and complained, telling everyone in the neighborhood that I was home — and telling everyone inside, too.

The door opened before I could switch the garage lights on. Dad stood in the doorway, backlit so I couldn't see the look on his face.

"Hey, kiddo." He pulled me into a one-armed hug. *Uh oh.* Another bad sign. "You're home early."

"He's here?" I asked.

Dad hesitated, then nodded. "They're just leaving."

If I'd known Jack and his brother were going to visit, I would have come home sooner. Jack's less of an asshole in front of me. Dad stepped back. His knuckles were white on the handle of his cane.

"Wait here." He went into the living room, leaving me holding my helmet in one hand and my backpack in the other. In the small space, I couldn't tell if his limp was any worse than usual.

I tensed, ready to follow anyway, but Dad shut the laundry door. The lock *clicked*.

Damn. I'm not supposed to swear, but Dad does all the time, and I'm not a kid anymore.

Jack said something that sounded a lot like *"next time"*. The front door slammed shut. Dad didn't come back until Jack and Sean's motorcycles roared outside.

"I'm not scared, you know," I said as soon as he opened the door.

"I know, but you should be. Sometimes you should be brave, and other times you have to be smart."

"I can be both," I argued.

"That's what I'm afraid of, Devon."

I followed Dad into the kitchen. A pot of water boiled on the stove, and a lump of hamburger and an onion sat on a cutting board. The pantry door stood open. I peeked inside. It was never exactly full anymore, but there were a few new items. Not nearly as much as I'd have liked. We had a few boxes of noodles, some packets of mashed potatoes, and lots of canned veggies.

Jack never took the vegetables; he didn't like them. I was surprised he left the hamburger, but maybe he didn't like the fact that Dad had already opened it. Nobody could really afford to be picky anymore, but it was different when you were a bully like Jack. Then you had more choices. I didn't know how many other people Jack stole from, but our house couldn't be the only one. He hadn't lost weight like a lot of the other adults had.

Bully. That word was too childish. Jack was definitely an asshole.

"Are you okay?" I asked.

Dad's eyes tightened at the corners. I used to think he made that face when he wanted to lie to me. Really, it's when he wants to protect me from something particularly ugly.

"I'm okay." He tossed the hamburger into a pan.

Dad still leaned on his cane, though, and I could tell his leg was hurting him. It was easy to see which one he'd injured during the invasion. It was two or three inches shorter than the other one. Lately, Dad had stopped trying to fight when Jack and Sean came around. Mostly.

"Did you hide stuff before they got here?" I asked. We didn't always. Sometimes when there's less food than usual, they can tell.

"I told him you were a growing boy trying to eat me out of house and home." Dad's face pinched again.

That meant yes.

My stomach chose to growl at that exact second. The hamburger smelled good, and I hadn't eaten since breakfast.

"Do we have any fruit?" I asked hopefully. I never thought I'd miss fresh fruit and vegetables so much.

"Strawberries. They're in the usual place." Dad smiled. "How was school today?"

"We had to do math. And *vocabulary*." I made a face. Logarithms and vocab tests didn't feel very important when you lived within torching distance of a dragon nest. I thought we should be doing junior firefighting drills. For some reason when I told my teacher that, she didn't laugh.

"School is important. Even vocabulary." Dad chuckled.

I clomped down to the basement, which was really just a glorified storm cellar. Funny how tornadoes used to be the scariest thing around here. Now it was the only part of the house I knew would still be around if the Elves burned down the city — not that I'd want to be in the cellar when that happened. I probably needed to suggest firefighting again. Maybe to the gym teacher this time.

Old rugs covered most of the concrete floor. I rolled the biggest one up until I found the fake hiding spot. That one had some wooden boards over the concrete. The real one was in the wall, but I had to move the rug and the bookshelf to get to it. It was an okay hiding spot. Jack had stopped looking when he found the fake one. Sean had been too lazy to even look.

I pulled the bookshelf away from the wall and moved the loose bricks. The strawberries were there, and so was a piece of real chocolate cake. I could smell the frosting even though it was wrapped in plastic. My mouth watered.

"No way." I put everything back and took the food upstairs. "No *way*."

"Way. Save it for after dinner, though? Ten, maybe fifteen minutes." Dad added a can of tomatoes to the hamburger. I didn't ask how old they were.

I opened the box of strawberries; there were five. I gave Dad the two biggest ones. "Can I go to my fort?"

"Sure thing." Dad kissed my forehead. I tried not to grimace. He worked hard to keep *any* food safe from the gangs around here. I wasn't always a good kid, but I tried to be. I knew his leg hurt more than he ever let on.

Dad was in the Air Force, *before.* I was lucky I still had a parent at all. I knew how good we had it.

***

When I was six or seven, I took over the garden shed and called it my fort. Dad helped me hang blankets and flags from the ceiling, and I pretended they were castle tapestries. The shelves used to hold all kinds of emergency supplies. Most of those were gone, now. Either we'd used them, shared them with people who needed them more, or they'd been confiscated. We still had a few random tools and the odd assortment of chemicals you collect doing yard work and science fair projects. There were even some old holiday decorations — not like we celebrated anymore. There was another cache of food hidden under the floor, too. Mostly old military rations. They tasted okay when we didn't have anything else.

I took out my set of tin camping plates and used my pocket knife to cut two of the strawberries into tiny pieces, then opened the back window. I'd outgrown climbing through it years ago, but it was perfect for my visitors.

My watch alarm went off; five PM on the dot.

I didn't have to wait long — I never do, anymore. The buzzing of a half-dozen wings filled the air, and my friends flew through the window a second later.

Two of the Pixies landed next to the plate and started eating the strawberry pieces. The third one — I called him Hiss — waited on the windowsill. Hiss didn't trust me quite yet.

It was foggy the night I found the three of them near the pedestrian bridge. The big one, Hobbes, had been bitten by something. There was a lot of blood for a little body.

I knew we couldn't trust the Fae. Dad told me. My teachers told me. The little old lady down the road with the walker and the yappy dog told me.

He'd really needed help, though.

We watched each other from opposite sides of the sidewalk for a while. Then the third Pixie, Calvin, flew over to me and landed on my backpack. He was maybe eight inches tall, with blue-tinted skin and pointed ears like an Elf. Four dragonfly-like wings sprouted from his back.

I had no idea what he said when he'd started yelling at me. He'd sure said a lot, though. Loudly. Then he'd grabbed the collar of my jacket and practically dragged me across the road. He was a lot stronger than I'd expected. Just another thing to remember about the Fae; they were never what you thought they were.

I had a few band-aids in my backpack. Once I was sure he wasn't going to bite me, I wrapped them around Hobbes' leg. Calvin watched, but Hiss — well, you can guess how he got his name. He *really* didn't like me.

None of them touched the granola bar that I opened for them before I left. I guess they must have liked it, though. A few days later I saw them watching me from a lamp post.

I started leaving food for them.

Stupid, I know, but I felt for the little guys. It was obvious nobody else was helping them. Besides, Hobbes' injured leg reminded me of Dad's. After about a week, they started waiting for me in the backyard.

Most kids have stray dogs or cats follow them home from school. I got Pixies.

Dad didn't know about them. I didn't *think* he'd angry if he found out. Sometimes it's better not to know. Calvin and Hobbes finished their pieces of the strawberries. Hiss must have decided the fruit wasn't poisoned, because he finally came down and finished the last of the fruit. I unhooked the clasp on the chain necklace I wore and took off the coolest gift I'd ever been given; a stone ring.

At some point, I'd started talking to the Pixies like they could understand me. It was better than talking to myself. Then they'd showed up with this ring, jabbering and pushing it onto my finger.

Now I could talk to them. Even cooler, they talked back.

"Jack was here again today," I said once they'd all finished eating. I looked at the last strawberry in my hand and took a very small bite. "I hate him. If it weren't for Dad's leg, he wouldn't come around at all. Dad would have kicked his ass."

I didn't know exactly what Dad's injury was. Something had broken and not set right. A doctor could have helped him, once, but that wasn't likely these days.

"Like Orcs. White Hand." Calvin's wings blurred, he flapped them so fast. I called him that cause he seemed to be the one in charge. They'd told me their real names, but I couldn't pronounce them very well. They seemed to like the ones I gave them, especially after I showed them my old Calvin and Hobbes comic books.

Hiss, well. He just hissed. I had to give it to him; he stuck to what he was good at.

"Yeah." Most of the Orcs were bullies, too, though I'd come to learn that there were a few of them that were slaves. They hadn't come here willingly and they sometimes fought with the Elves and the other Orcs. That didn't make them safe. In fact, those ones were even more dangerous sometimes. You never knew what kind of fight they'd pick, or when. Or with who.

"Fight enemies." Hobbes nodded, agreeing with Calvin.

"Yeah, right." I slumped against the wall and finished my strawberry. It would be a few years before I was strong enough to challenge Jack's gang. "He'd squash me flat."

"You are small for a Human," Hobbes conceded.

"Hey…" I sat up straight as an idea came to me. "Elves can do magic."

"So can we." The Pixies had great big, blue eyes. They blinked them at me like I was crazy.

"Can you fix my dad?"

All three of their wings buzzed, filling the room with little wisps of wind. They were clearly upset — I just didn't know why.

"Small magic," Calvin hedged.

"Right." Healing Dad would be pretty big magic. If they could do that, they could have helped Hobbes after the dog attack. At least I *think* it was a dog. They never told me what bit him.

"Ainar heals." Hiss hovered a few inches in the air. "Ainar could heal."

I would have fallen over if I hadn't been sitting down. Hiss almost never talks, and he's *never* helpful.

"Who's Ainar?" I asked when my shock faded. "Why would he help?"

"Healer." Hiss landed on the ground with a soft *tap*. That was more like what I'd expected from him. I looked at Calvin and Hobbes, hoping they had a better answer.

"Ainar fights with Lord Halfast. There are talks of sedition," Calvin said.

"Sedition?" Maybe Dad was right about vocabulary tests being important.

"Some say he will kill Lord Halfast. Some say he will abandon his duties." Calvin crossed his arms. "Ainar is dangerous."

"But he could heal my dad?" I didn't want to get excited, but I couldn't help it. I was tired of being hungry, but I was even more tired of seeing Dad get pushed around by Jack. It could be years until I could stop Jack myself, and no matter what I said to Dad, the idea of fighting him scared me.

"Could?" Calvin nodded. "Will?" He shook his head.

"Elves do nothing for free," Hobbes told me.

"And they hate humans. I know." They hated the Pixies, too. At least *these* Pixies. I hadn't quite worked out why, but it was pretty obvious they were in hiding. They wouldn't need me to help feed them, otherwise.

Hiss hopped a little closer to me. His wings fluttered like he was ready to jet off if I made a wrong move. "Ainar hates Lord Halfast more."

I heard the back door to the house open, and Dad shouted for me a second later.

"I'll see you guys tomorrow," I told the Pixies. "Wait until the house door closes before you leave."

They knew the drill, but I reminded them just in case. It wasn't hard to forget the Pixies weren't some kind of pet, but they didn't always know a lot about the way humans did things. They'd barely started to trust me. I didn't think they'd keep trusting me if Dad found out and tried to run them away from the house.

I ate my spaghetti while Dad quizzed me on vocabulary words.

"What does 'sedition' mean?" I asked.

"Where did you hear that word?" he asked sharply.

"School."

Dad took a deep breath, and his eyes narrowed. "It's a word that people will associate with the resistance, if they hear you talking about it. I need you to be careful."

"Sure." We finished dinner in silence. All I could think about was the resistance. They had the right idea, even if the Fae had destroyed major cities during the invasions. Maybe we could go help them . Maybe *they* could help *us*.

Dad stood up with his empty plate. He winced, and his face went white as a ghost.

"I got it." I hopped up and took the plate, then dumped it in the sink. "You rest."

Once, Jack left Dad with a black eye. Another time Dad hadn't been able to walk for a few days after his visit. I started coming straight home from school most days after that. Jack was a monster, but he still seemed hesitant to do much if I was around. It was a small mercy, but the only one we had.

Dad's cane leaned against the fridge a few feet away. I handed it to him, then moved to wash the dishes. I hated washing dishes, but I could tell his leg was hurting him bad tonight. I grabbed the painkillers from the cabinet above the sink and handed them to him.

"Thanks." Dad shifted in his chair and grimaced. "Might be a rough night. Good thing I got that new book."

I gave Dad a big hug before I went to bed that night. I pulled the covers up to my chin and stared up at my ceiling. Most of the glow-in-the-dark stars we'd put up a few years ago were still there. They never glowed for very long anymore.

The floorboards creaked outside my door, and I knew it was Dad leaving his bedroom to go sit on the couch to read. He only did that when he's in a lot of pain. One of those nights where the painkillers didn't help. We'd tried to get him stronger ones, but they hadn't lasted long.

I bolted upright when I heard the *thump*. I threw the covers out and ran to Dad's side. He'd tripped on the stairs at the end of the hall.

"You're supposed to be sleeping." Dad couldn't even fake a smile. He used the stair rail to pull himself to his feet. His book was nowhere in sight. I put his arm over my shoulders. Part of his weight sagged onto me.

You're supposed to be walking.

I didn't say it out loud, though. That would only make him feel worse. I could be strong when Dad couldn't. That's what family was for.

We walked down one slow step at a time, passing his book where it had fallen on the landing. When Dad settled in his chair, I filled a cup of water from the sink and brought that and his book to him.

"Devon," Dad said, and I braced myself for a lecture about how sleep was important so I could focus at school the next day. It didn't come.

"Yeah?"

"You're a great kid, and I love you."

"I love you too, Dad. Do you want anything else?"

Dad shook his head. "Thanks, buddy. Get some sleep. One of us should, tonight."

My hands shook as I climbed back into my bed. I stared at the light spilling through the crack under my door, the one that always told me if Dad was downstairs or not. If the Pixies could get Ainar to pay attention to me, I wanted to talk to him.

The Elves couldn't hate humans as much as I hated Jack.

***

I didn't like Ainar.

We met at a coffee shop not far from my burger joint a few days later. I could hardly believe Hiss when he told me they'd set it up. It felt like a trap — but what was I really risking? Why would any of the Fae bother trying to kidnap someone like me? Dad didn't have anything they wanted. Even if he did, they'd just sweep in and take it like they had everything else in the world.

He looked the same as any Elf. Tall, pointed ears and long hair, and a face that the old stories would call 'fair'. His clothes weren't as fancy as some of the Elves I'd seen, but he dressed nicer than most Humans, and all the Orcs. I'd bet my next cache of fresh strawberries that his belt was made of real silver.

"What makes the Human beastie think I can help him?" Ainar's teeth glimmered. If he bit me, I was pretty sure I'd get rabies.

I pointed to Calvin, Hobbes, and Hiss.

"*Pixies*. They must be responsible for your translator as well, yes?" he asked.

The lump of fear in my throat wouldn't budge. I nodded.

"How badly injured is your father, boy?" Ainar sat back on the wall and pulled out a knife as long as my arm. He picked at a fingernail with it.

"Bad. He broke his femur, and he walks well with a cane. Some days he can't walk at all."

"And what makes his plight any worse than any other humans? I know men who lost limbs and sight. I know Elves who suffered worse. Your father was fortunate if he can still walk."

"Because of Jack."

"Who is?" Ainar grinned again, but there was nothing friendly about it. He was laughing at me.

"Jack comes around and steals our rations. He beats my dad if he tries hide food or stop him. Dad can barely walk right now because Jack came around yesterday." My hands balled into fists and heat rose in my face the more I thought about it. "Lord Halfast was supposed to be keeping humans *safe.*"

The lord had said that once, when he'd first come to Lincoln. He was here to keep us safe, to keep order, and make sure the transition went smoothly. Even I could tell it was a lie, but it wasn't like there was anything I could do about it. If the big cities and all the militaries in the world hadn't been able to stand up to the invasion, what was one kid supposed to do?

I can try to help Dad, though. That's one change I can make. Things can get better.

"What do you want?" I held my hand out, offering the stone ring that the Pixies had given me. Ainar laughed harder. I gritted my teeth. "Tell me. If you can help Dad, I'll do anything."

"Anything?" Ainar tilted his head to one side. His laughter died. "Stand up, little human."

The Elf stood, too. He circled around me with slow steps. My skin crawled when he walked behind me, but I didn't move. I'd said anything, after all. He'd never believe me if I couldn't even hold still.

"How old are you?"

"Sixteen," I lied.

"You're lying."

"Fourteen." How did he know?

"Better." Ainar stopped in front of me and put one long finger under my chin, tipping my face upward. "You know the Human gladiatorial ring?"

"You mean the stadium?"

"Painted in the red of your champions' colors." Ainar released my chin.

"Husker Stadium." I nodded. "Where Lord Halfast —"

"The new dragon roost, yes. Many of the great creatures use it as a waystation, but Halfast has three of his own. Do you know what else is there?"

I had a few guesses, but I shook my head. Ainar put my nerves on edge. *At least he's talking to me.* He even seemed to be interested in helping.

No, he's just interested in me, and what I might be able to do for him. I had to remember that wasn't the same thing. I had to be careful.

"Eggs," Ainar said.

It took me a second to realize he didn't mean chicken eggs. "You mean baby dragons?"

"I mean *eggs* that, yes, eventually will hatch and turn into baby dragons. Do you know what I want more than anything, human?"

I was getting tired of him asking questions. Who *didn't* want a dragon egg? I'd love one, and I didn't have a clue how to raise or train a dragon.

"Lord Halfast wouldn't just give you an egg?" I asked. Ainar's laugh was high and cold. *Okay, stupid question, I guess.*

"Dragons are not so common that anyone might have them."

"So, you want to steal one." That sounded dangerous.

"If you would do anything, Human, to help your father, how would you help me steal a dragon egg?" Ainar sat down on the wall again. His knife flashed back into his hands.

I wrinkled my nose. The only thing I'd ever stolen was some soda from my teacher's fridge a few years ago. She caught me.

"Can you fight?" Ainar prompted.

I shook my head.

"Can you destroy the protective wards on the stadium or blow off the doors? Can you carry an egg as large as you are, and safeguard it during the final days of incubation? No? Then you are useless to me."

"I know you don't do anything for free." I was getting desperate, but I didn't want to beg, either. "I've got to be able to help somehow. I can…"

"You can have three days to think of a plan to help me," Ainar snapped. "Three days to decide whether your father walks again."

"If I can help you, you *can* heal him, right? You promise?" I didn't want to risk making him angry, but I had to know.

"We will discuss it when you have an idea." Ainar flicked the blade of his knife toward me. "Begone."

He didn't need to tell me twice.

***

I pedaled a little slower when I saw Husker Stadium, like I always did.

I saw it differently this time. I'd thought there was a lot of security before the occupation, when there were just some guards and metal detectors on game day. Now it looked like it was in a warzone — which was at least partly true. Lord Halfast had ordered a new wall built all around the stadium, and there were guards at every gate I rode past. Sometimes they were Elves, other times Orcs, but they were never friendly looking.

Surprise, surprise.

"How the hell am I supposed to help steal a dragon egg?" I asked. My backpack shifted. I looked over my shoulder just as Calvin poked his head out of the gap at the top. He, Hobbes, and Calvin had somehow found a way to fit in there. They wanted to come with me to check out the stadium, and I wasn't about to say no to help.

"We stole ring," Hobbes said.

"That's a little different, unless you broke into the stadium to do it."

"We steal food." Calvin's eyes glowed inside my bag.

"Steal egg," Hiss said. "Use fire."

Fire? I was starting to think Hiss had a grudge of his own against Lord Halfast.

I circled the whole stadium twice, then took a break under one of the pedestrian walkways. The Pixies and I shared a bottle of water I'd brought with me. I shook it and the liquid inside spiraled into a cyclone for a few seconds.

A tornado would be a big enough distraction for Ainar to sneak in and steal the egg. Too bad I didn't have weather magic. Too bad I didn't have *any* magic.

Fire. Maybe Hiss wasn't so crazy after all. Lighting the stadium on fire would be really dangerous, though. What if it hurt the eggs? Could fire hurt dragon eggs? Probably not, but if they got damaged Ainar definitely wouldn't help Dad. He might even kill me for ruining his chance to steal one.

It would never work.

My brain jumped, then I did. I leapt off the stone wall and ran to look at the next road over. It was so simple, I couldn't believe I hadn't thought of it before. I definitely should have thought of it when Hiss said *fire.*

It didn't matter; I had it now.

"You guys will help me, right?" I asked. The Pixies glanced at each other. Their eyes were more serious than I'd ever seen them.

"Lord Halfast and his men are dangerous," Calvin said finally.

"But... Dad. Ainar was your idea."

"Ainar will not protect us."

I just stared at them. After everything we'd been through, I couldn't believe they didn't want to help. I couldn't decide if I was more angry or shocked.

"Ainar might protect us, if we help," Hiss said slowly. He looked up at me with narrowed eyes. "What does the Human want?"

I chewed on my lip. It was still beyond weird that *Hiss* was the one being helpful, but... there was some saying about gift horses I couldn't remember. Something that meant 'don't think too much about it'.

"Can you turn the stoplights on and off, and move traffic barriers? Change signs around?" That was a small way they could help. There weren't as many cars on the roads as there used to be, but there were still enough to make a good traffic jam.

Their job would be the easy part.

"Tell us your plans, Human," Calvin said.

They didn't think my idea was half bad. Once we worked it out a little more, they thought it was a pretty good idea. The Pixies agreed to go talk to Ainar about it. We came up with a code — if Ainar agreed, the Pixies would leave two rocks on my windowsill. They'd leave one if he said no, or if there was other bad news. If it all went according to plan, we'd assemble our war chest the next day and execute the attack in two.

When I got home that night, Dad's limp was worse again. There was no sign of Jack or his brother. The pantry looked the same, but there were always good days and bad days. I hoped today was just a bad day.

Dinner was leftover spaghetti. It was a little dry, but I ate it without complaining. It took everything I had not to burst out and tell Dad my plan. He wouldn't just think it was a bad idea, he'd get angry. He never wanted me to take any risks. If he knew I was preparing such a big one, he'd ground me.

Worse, if he knew I was planning this to try and help him, it might break his heart. I knew how much he loved me.

It was my turn to take care of him, for once. It would be worth it. *If it works.* I closed my eyes and imagined putting my fear into a box, then pushing it off the side of a cliff. It would never work if I was too scared to do it right.

"Would you quit fidgeting? What's going on with you?" Dad looked up from my math homework with a frown.

"Nothing." I clapped my hands together and tried to stay still while he quizzed me. I couldn't concentrate. "Can I go read?"

Dad sighed, resigned. "Sure thing. Don't forget to brush your teeth first though, okay? Your breath this morning could have killed a dog."

I rushed to the windowsill as soon as I got to my room. The Pixies had already been here. Two rocks waited for me.

Yes. I remembered to brush my teeth, then climbed into bed with a notebook and started listing out all the things I'd need to find the next day. I had most of the ingredients already, but some I'd need to find at the school. Warmth filled my chest as I wrote.

It took me a while to realize that feeling was hope.

***

I almost bailed when I saw the dragon.

If Ainar hadn't been standing right next to me, I probably would have. Suddenly all I could think about was getting roasted alive. A dragon that big could use my femur as a toothpick.

Ainar *was* here though. He said he had enough magic to do what I'd asked. I'd made a commitment, and I didn't like to imagine what he'd do if I quit on him.

Lying to an Elf wasn't a mistake I was going to make. I couldn't let him down, either.

Dragon and rider circled the stadium twice. It was the biggest, prettiest one, gold and fiery orange. His scales were so bright in the sun that he looked like a fireball racing across the sky. An Elf rider sat on his back. The dragon's silhouette blocked out the sun for a second, and I squinted to try and see what the rider looked like. I hoped it was Lord Halfast — not like I knew what he looked like.

No matter who the rider was, it was one less dragon to protect the eggs. That information would have been useful if I knew how many other dragons were still in there. It could be one or one hundred.

Well, probably not one hundred. That many wouldn't fit.

"How many dragons does Lord Halfast have?" I asked. Ainar's lip curled back. It almost looked like a smile.

Almost.

"Three. He is quite wealthy in this manner. Wealth breeds enmity."

Enmity — that was a vocabulary word I knew. A word almost as dangerous as *sedition*. I still didn't know what Ainar had against Lord Halfast, or why he wanted to steal a dragon egg.

Well, who *wouldn't* want a dragon egg? That part was obvious, but it didn't explain why he was willing to risk it. He'd be on the run as soon as he stole the egg. A dragon wasn't exactly easy to hide. I wondered where he'd go, and how far Halfast would be willing to hunt him to get his dragon back.

I had a dozen more questions, but I wasn't willing to ask any of them. There was something cold in Ainar's blue eyes. He was just as dangerous as the dragons.

Or the Orcs. That sent a shiver down my spine.

***

We hid in a parking garage near one of the stadium parking lots, waiting for the Pixies to give me the signal. I had one huge bag on my back and another strapped to the handlebars of my bike. They were full to bursting with fireworks. The Pixies had searched around the old state fairgrounds at my request. There used to be a seller that set up shop there when these things were allowed. Fortunately, it hadn't been cleared out — or someone was stocking up. Either way, they'd found them and I had a need for them.

The lighter — and the backup lighter — were in my pockets. I liked my arms and legs where they were, so I needed to be as careful as possible.

A car horn blared from a few blocks away, then another. The stoplight ahead of me switched off, then all three lights flared up at once. *Blink. Blink. Blink.*

Tires screeched on the road, and then there was a huge *crunch*. Honking filled the air.

It turned out we didn't need a signal from the Pixies. Regular old humans did that just fine. I poked my head around the corner. The accident wasn't bad — just a fender bender. It wouldn't be the last one today. The Pixies had already moved a bunch of construction signs and orange cones to the busiest parts of the city. I had to hope nobody would get too hurt in the chaos the traffic would cause.

This was the only way I could think to cause a big enough distraction.

Ainar raised an eyebrow at me as if to ask, *is that your big distraction?* The crease only deepened as a roar echoed out from somewhere deep in the bowels of the giant stone memorial. It was followed by another, as if they responded to the cacophony going on in front of us. Screams of pain answered.

The gate we stood near crashed open as several Elves and Orcs raced toward the streets, shouting over the horns and argument in an attempt to get the mess under control. I beckoned Ainar to follow me into the now open arch, tracing a path I had not walked in years.

"Crafty little Human, aren't you?" Ainar kept his voice low. I couldn't tell if his tone was mildly impressed or making fun of me. "What's next in this brilliant plan of yours?"

"Where are the eggs we need to steal?"

"Likely somewhere that can be heated and kept at that desired temperature."

I nodded, considering the options. While the dragons might roost in the open air of the field, I remembered the time Dad volunteered us to sell food to the fans as they watched the Cornhuskers take on the Buffaloes in a rivalry game. We'd been directed to a place to pick up Styrofoam containers and vests. The walls were lined with ovens and warmers full of the savory smelling Runzas, the melt-in-your-mouth Valentino's pizza, the juicy Fairbury hotdogs, and boxes of buttery popcorn.

"They're under the North endzone." I was so confident in my answer, Ainar didn't even respond with a standard Elven quip. We moved into the stadium, passing through a small labyrinth of tunnels and walkways as fast as we dared.

Sweat dripped down my brow; they had to be keeping the tunnels warm for the dragons. Giant eggs needed a lot of heat to stay warm. I wondered whether the dragons preferred heat, too. The stadium was so big, we didn't run into any guards. Finally, we reached the iconic carving: "Not the victory but the action; Not the goal but the game; In the deed the glory."

The words strengthened my resolve.

"I'm going to go out here. We need to draw the dragons out. Then we can sneak in behind them." Hoping I sounded more confident than I felt, I squared my shoulders and didn't look at Ainar. Would a mother dragon willingly leave her eggs?

It was time to find out.

I dropped my bags. Several fireworks and other effects spilled out as I unzipped them. Grabbing a handful, I then pointed to the remainder of the pile. "We set them up around the field, light them, and wait."

"Simple minds and simpler devices," the Elf remarked as he studied one of the displays.

"Do you have a better idea? I seem to remember that you asked me for this because you didn't have anything."

"True enough." He cocked his head at me. "Elven magic would be too detectable."

So, it would be obvious that this was Human-caused. If I got caught, I'd have more than Ainar's fury to deal with. Lord Halfast would probably have me skinned alive. *Great.*

I walked over to test the door. Stuck. It wouldn't budge even when I threw my full weight at it. Ainar paced it, touching the hinges and points of contact.

"I can open this, but it will make a terrible noise. It's been blasted a few times by dragon fire and seems to have partially melted the mechanism."

"Do it." I gritted my teeth. "It doesn't matter if they hear us now. We just need them to leave their nests."

Ainar gave me another bemused look, but felt for the crease between the doors. He pulled, his fingers whitening from the effort. A squeal of metal on metal rang out as he forced the door. It gave a few begrudging inches, then a few feet. Finished, he grabbed some of the supplies and stated, "We'd best hasten."

I ran out onto the field like I'd always dreamed of doing. Unlike in my dreams, I didn't run out to the sold-out seats and screaming admiration of a hundred thousand Husker-faithful. The stench of burned plastic hung heavy in the air. The turf had been torn up and scorched, the stands in charred shambles. The damage concentrated in places as if the dragons had marked their territory. The Elves — or probably the Orcs, under orders — had torn out almost all of the stadium chairs. Enormous, tiered platforms covered the north and west seating areas.

In the deed, the glory.

I took a deep breath and reminded myself why I was here.

For Dad.

Lord Halfest and his dragon were absent from the skies above. With no immediate threats, Ainar started placing his set on the ledge behind where the goalpost should have been. I turned to walk down the length of the field to set up my own fireworks. Despite the new layout and destruction, or maybe because of it, the stadium seemed bigger than ever. I hoped we had enough fireworks.

I linked the explosive to the safety fuse line as I went. It would only work if they all went off and I had time to get away. I'd just set up the last of them when a waft of sulfur and smoke drifted to me on the breeze.

A throaty growl rippled through the otherwise silent stadium. We weren't alone.

I turned to find a jet-black dragon with red splotches and a white underbelly staring me down from atop its perch over the gate we had opened. I'd never seen this one before. The creature was the size of small house.

Movement caught my eye. On the opposite corner, a deep purple wyrm slithered onto the field from an entry halfway up the stands. Smaller than the other, its green-tinted eyes followed me as it slunk toward the field.

Ainar was nowhere to be seen.

Shit.

The purple dragon roared a warning. Sparks flickered in the smoke escaping its fanged mouth. The jet-black huffed. It was a warning; the smaller froze at once.

Then the black dragon elongated its neck in my direction. Our gazes locked, and I knew it was sizing me up.

A million thoughts flew through my head as I stared down death. Who was going to take care of Dad? Who was going to ensure Ainar healed him? What would happen when he found out how I died?

The dragon let out a bellow that shook the stadium under my feet and unleashed a torrent of fire that reached the very tops of the press boxes. It dropped down to the field and stalked toward me, wings spread, and roared, gushing flames. The stands trembled, and the heat of the fire blasted at me as it lashed out over my head.

Something crazy overtook me.

Maybe it was the spirit of the warriors that had fought battles on this field decades prior, or of the men who the stadium was intended to memorialize. Maybe I just lost it. I screamed my defiance back at the monster, pulled out my lighter and lit the fuse. It paused as though curious, and our gazes locked onto one another again.

The whole world lit up with a dazzling display of sound and colored light.

I meant to make a finale that any pyrotechnic expert would envy. It did not disappoint. I yelled again, drawing courage from the explosion.

The dragon didn't even flinch.

The fireworks fizzled out. My will didn't fizzle. I held that stare, though every muscle in my body trembled. I took a few cautious steps backwards.

Then large black reared its head back and I could see the fire building again. I only had one chance. It leaned forward and let loose fire.

I turned tail and bolted. My heart raced as I scrambled up the nearest set of stairs, past the twisted metal and plastic of what used to be the crowd seats. I tripped over rebar, banged my knee into the chipped concrete, and went down with a curse.

Wheezing, I dragged myself to my feet. Pain shot up my leg; I couldn't put any weight on the injury.

I closed my eyes and waited for hot, fiery death. *Sorry, Dad.*

But the dragon's breath stopped just short of the tunnel. It roared, and I knew the second blast was coming. Forcing myself to ignore the pain, I darted down the tunnel towards the concourse. Unblocked, and unguarded — thank God. I shot straight for one of the gates to exit.

Then a mob of Orcs passed by the bottom of the stairs. I stalled in the shadow of a statue of two figures, trying not to breathe. How good was an Orcs hearing?

Their ears are pretty big. I plugged my nose. The small of ash and decay lingered there, and the last thing I needed to do was sneeze and give away my position. An Orc barked orders in a gruff voice. Their heavy boots thundered on the concrete as they ran by, heading toward the stadium center.

I held my breath and counted, just in case they turned around.

The statue was a familiar one: one figure was a player dressed in helmet and pads. He wore the number '18' and carried a football. The other was an older man with a hat and headset pointing towards my escape. That was the famed Coach Osborne who Dad always raved about when we went to games.

Behind him, scarred but visible, the words "Destiny is not a matter of chance, it is a matter of choice." I couldn't make out the last line of text, but it still sent a shiver down my spine. I'd made my choice. Now I just had to survive it.

Had Ainar escaped? I kept a careful eye out in case I was followed, but I was alone in the tunnels. There was something wrong about the strange emptiness of the place. Not a single Elf, Orc, or dragon barred the way. The Pixies must be doing their jobs well — and the fireworks inside the stadium had clearly drawn the other guards directly to the dragon roost. I winced at every scuff of my shoes on the concrete.

I ducked around a small group of Dwarves near the newly built wall. I got lucky — they looked bored. Once I escaped to the street, I circled back around to find my bike. Lucky again — nobody had stolen it. I only got one nasty look from a particularly perturbed Elf dealing with a traffic accident.

Dad didn't seem to notice that I'd returned late, or that I'd lost a backpack. He must've been in even more pain. I hoped Ainar had made it out and would get here soon.

***

Days passed. I went to school, I came home, Dad cooked and asked about what I was learning. Still no sign of the Elf. At first, I worried the dragons may have eaten him before I saw them.

The Pixies didn't return until the third day, either. Dad baked some zucchini bread while I was at school. I asked for an extra slice and excused myself to the fort. I tore the slice into three pieces, opened the window and waited, hoping they would return.

This time, Hiss was the first to poke his head in. Calvin and Hobbes swiftly followed. They landed near the baked offering and gave me a thumbs up.

"Where have you guys been?" I blurted out, unable to contain my excitement at seeing them.

They pointed at my finger. I raced to pull the ring off its chain and put it on.

"Too dangerous," Calvin stated.

"Hid," Hobbes chimed in.

"We distracted!" Hiss sounded really proud.

"Yeah, you did." I smiled. "You guys killed it. I'm glad you're safe and not in trouble. I haven't seen Ainar since we went into the stadium. I hope he's okay."

He better come back. But I was starting to think he never would.

The Pixies proceeded to explain to me what they'd seen that day. They'd caused chaos at several intersections around the stadium, and had a few close calls with the responding forces of Elves and Orcs while Lord Halfast had circled overhead. It sounded like everything had worked as I hoped. Until they mentioned Ainar.

"Ainar got egg!" Hiss exclaimed. "Escaped dragons."

"But have you seen him since?" I asked, angry that he was not only alive, but got exactly what he wanted — Dad was still not healed. I kept up *my* half of the bargain. "Where the hell is he?"

They all shook their heads, their smiles disappearing. Saying nothing more, they ate the last bits of bread and left. I sat back, wrapping my arms around my knees and trying not to cry. I'd faced a dragon and Ainar had just left us.

Dad would never be alright, never be healed, never be able to face down Jack and Sean. A hot tear slipped down my cheek. I wiped it away angrily, refusing to let any more fall. When my eyes dried up, I tidied up the fort and went inside.

"Are you alright, Devon? Did you hurt yourself?" Dad looked at me with concern as I tried to dodge past him toward the stairs.

"I'm alright, Dad. I'm going to bed. Really tired. I love you." I looked him in the eyes when I said it, willing him to know I meant it.

"I love you too, kid. You don't have to tell me, but you can always talk to me if something is bothering you."

I couldn't. Not about this. Not about helping to steal a dragon egg. Not about failing to get him healed. Not about feeding my Pixie gang.

"Okay, Dad. I'm fine. I'll see you tomorrow. G'night!" And I raced upstairs to the comfort of my bed.

A week had passed since I'd broken into Husker Stadium, with no sign of Ainar. Dad's limp got worse. Dread and hopelessness made my days gray and gloomy. I barely paid attention in school. I went to the fort only to deliver food to my few friends; scraps compared to what we should have gotten. Dad had picked up this week's rations two days ago, and the Elves had been stingy this time.

The next day when I got home after school, I saw the motorcycles. I didn't have to guess about the company. I reached the garage as a cry of pain came from inside.

"I don't care if you need to feed your kid! We're hungry and you owe us." Jack's voice echoed out of the front screen door.

I stopped short. They were here to get more food, of course. I thought maybe they would leave us alone this week since they hadn't stopped by at the usual time. Another shout of anguish meant they were hurting Dad this time.

Anger boiled inside my chest, and tears of rage blurred my vision. I parked my bike and instead of closing the garage door, I stomped out to the lawn. My fists were balled.

"Enough Jack! Leave him alone!" I shouted at the front door.

A sob escaped the house and the pleas of my dad as he begged them to leave me alone. "No, don't. You can't — I'll give you what you want."

I burst through the front door. A man with a bit of a pot-belly, a huge nose, and a mullet laughed. Sean. He'd pushed Dad up against the wall. Now he dropped his hands and took a step back. Beside him, his brother, gangly and tall, his brown eyes matched his cropped hair and five-o-clock shadow. Neither of them had lost weight from lack of food.

A cigarette glowed in Jack's mouth. I hated that smell.

"Well look here, Nathan. Your boy wants to challenge the order of things. Go on little bird. Squawk." Jack took another drag on his smoke.

The vision of two dragons standing in the stadium flashed through my mind. They had shown how terrifyingly magnificent they were. Creatures of death.

I had faced down dragons and *lived*.

Jack and Sean weren't dragons. They weren't even close.

"I said, leave him alone. You've got your own rations. You can't have ours anymore." I stared into their eyes. It may have been less impressive without the fireworks, but it didn't matter. I was afraid but ready.

In the deed, the glory.

For a second, no one moved. Then Jack burst out laughing, a wheezing, annoying sound. Sean followed with his own snickers. "What do you think you're going to do, kid? You think you actually grew up? That you scare us? Get back into the garage and I may leave your dad's leg mostly unbroken. But it's going to cost you some extra meat this time." He flicked his cigarette butt onto the couch. A thin trail of smoke rose into the air

My heart deflated a little. Had I really thought yelling at them would help? Not only had I failed but he was going to punish Dad more for it and take more food besides.

I'd let him down twice in two weeks.

I launched myself at Jack.

Sean grabbed me by the back of my coat, then shoved me down onto the couch. "You keep doing shit like this, kid, and the invaders might think you are part of the resist — Uhh, Jack?"

"What?" Jack stared at me, face full of rage.

"Look." Sean pointed at the door.

Jack rolled his eyes and dragged his gaze away from me. Then he choked on air.

I blinked away tears, trying to figure out what they were doing.

"We don't recruit them that young." That voice, smooth as a calm body of water, and familiar.

"Are these *Humans* the reason I am here to fix your father?" Ainar stood in the doorway. Contempt and disgust painted across his features.

I almost choked on air.

"Don't look so surprised child. I owe you a debt. I repay them." His gaze swept back to me. I swear it softened, if only slightly. "I had business that needed attending to. Dragon eggs don't hatch themselves." He took a step towards the brothers.

"I highly suggest you rethink your course of action before you take another step into that house." I watched as Jack pulled Sean in front of him.

"And what business is it to you, Elf? We have nothing against you. Your kind don't care right? We're just getting what's ours." Jack's voice pitched up half an octave. Sean put his fists up in front of his face as if he thought to box the Elf as he stalked closer. I imagined that this is what watching a lion hunt on the savannah looked like.

"No quarrel with me, you say? I think I have made it perfectly clear that you have a quarrel with me while I have business in this —" he waved his hand around, then scrunched his face when he said the word "— *house*."

It happened lightning fast. Sean screamed. Light flashed from Ainar's hands. Jack caught the second strike of flurrying magic. The brothers careened into each other, howling, and crashed to the floor. Scrambling over each other, they crawled past the Elf and out the door. Their bikes grumbled to life a second later.

"Now they will not undo the work I am about to accomplish. Show me where the patient is, Human. Then we shall consider our bargain completed."

Hope returned and fed my growing excitement. I was about to get exactly what I wanted. I had faced the dragons. I'd earned the treasure.

Now I just had to explain it to Dad.

Vengeance Is Mine

by J. R. Handley

HE'D BEEN A SOLDIER once, in his youth. That was back before the fall, back when life still made sense. He'd even waged war on behalf of his native land, of America, before she became the husk of her former glory. He'd traveled halfway around the world, seeing things that he wished he had not. But Jack Harlan was no longer the cavalry sergeant of his youth. The country he'd bled for no longer existed. And he wasn't sure that the Iraqi nation that he'd helped force democracy upon even existed anymore either.

Fortune returned the favor now in the cruelest twist of fate. It was his home that had been invaded. It was his land that had been pillaged. It was his friends who'd been killed. But the invasion was over now, and the dust had settled. His nation had lost and was now occupied by the elves and their slavish warriors. When it all went to shit, he'd shrugged off his duty to his ungrateful nation. The country that took his left eye and gifted him a lifetime of bad memories. And a Veteran's Administration that told him the pain was all in his head.

Instead, he hunkered down in the Appalachian Mountains with his kinfolk. He went to ground and protected his family and his neighbors. The rest of the world was on their own. He'd lived off the land with his wife and two little girls. They'd patiently waited for whatever the new normal would be as they eked out a living. That worked... until it didn't. The war came to him, eventually. He'd feared that it would, while hoping it wouldn't.

After the first year of the occupation their pantry was getting thin. He'd gone out hunting and foraging, while his wife and kids went to the Jenkins homestead. His neighbor was a widow from the war with the elves and about to give birth. His sweet Sarah was staying with her to help out. They'd tried to move Molly into their cabin, but she'd refused, so his wife went to lend a helping hand.

When he'd returned from his successful hunting trip to dress the deer and preserve the herbs he'd found, Jack saw smoke on the horizon. Without a second thought, he'd grabbed his rifle and took off at a sprint toward Molly Jenkin's place. It was already too late; he'd arrived to see her cabin engulfed in flames. His family hanging from the surrounding trees. Three orc soldiers stood around, turning the corpse of Molly's mastiff as they celebrated their victory.

Those bastards, he thought as he stood in shock. The occupiers murdered his family... his two sweet little babies. With a roar, he brought his rifle up. The targets were big... and distracted. Sighting down his scope, he fired two rounds into the eye of the furthest monstrosity. The orc staggered backward, stumbling. It fell into the raging inferno of Molly's house. The orc's primitive clothing caught fire and the beast screamed out in pain.

Swiveling his body, he aimed at the closest orc and fired. Jack kept firing until his extended magazine went dry. With a roar, he tossed it aside and drew the battered Ka-Bar knife from his belt. He prided himself on his attention to detail and the blade's edge was still sharp, despite years of use. The air was thick with the acrid stench of burning wood and flesh, the crackle of flames devouring Molly Jenkins' cabin. The sound drowned out the distant screams of the dying orc. Jack's vision tunneled, his single eye burning with rage and grief. The scar tissue around his empty socket, hidden by the patch his wife had lovingly made for him throbbed in pain.

The battlefield in front of him disappeared for a moment and he saw his wife, Sarah. He could picture her gentle smile and hear her infectious laugh. He remembered the touch of her calloused hands, worn by lovingly tending their garden to feed their family. And now she was gone. His girls, Lily Rose, and little Daisy were also gone. Their giggles were forever silenced, as their corpses swayed lifeless in the breeze. The sight seared into his soul, hotter than the inferno before him.

The roar of one of the remaining two orcs brought him out of his memories. They were startled, their grisly celebration interrupted by his bellow of rage. As one, they turned toward him. Their tusked maws dripped with spittle and blood. Their rune-etched armor clinked as the two demonic orcish warriors hefted crude axes, the metal glowing faintly with eldritch light. The closest orc, a hulking brute with a scar splitting its snout, roared, and charged at him. The beast's boots churning the blood-soaked earth in its haste to attack him.

Jack didn't hesitate. He didn't think or weigh his options; he acted on instinct and muscle memory. He lunged forward, the forest floor slick under his boots, and drove the K-Bar into the orc's throat with a wet crunch. Hot, coppery blood sprayed across his face. It stung his eye, but he ignored it. He watched as the beast gurgled and collapsed, its weight dragging him down with it.

"Get off of me, you bastard!" he roared as he pulled his knife out of the wound.

Then third orc swung its axe from behind him. The monster's blade whistled through the air, just missing him. The weapon was heavy with the stench of rotten flesh and dried blood. Gritting his teeth, Jack rolled, and came up in a crouched position with his K-Bar in front of him. Pine needles stuck to his sweat-drenched skin, giving him the look of a wild man.

"Mother fu —"

His roar was cut off as the remaining orc swung the weapon again, turning the initial swing into a back-handed assault. Jack dodged again, his chest heaving as the sudden burst of adrenaline flooded into his body. Hours of training, of muscle memory, saved him. Army training honed his instincts, and he effort-lessly attacked. He moved, striking out as he dodged the parry. He missed but kept the orc busy while desperately searching for another weapon.

Jack hit the ground awkwardly, his lost eye causing him to misjudge his landing. Scrambling on all fours, he grabbed a fallen branch, the large wooden ad hoc weapon in his hand before he regained his footing. The rough bark of the tree limb bit into his palm, but he ignored the discomfort. He used the branch to parry the orc's next swing. Despite his frenzied assault giving him a direct hit on the beast, the impact jarred his bones.

With a snarl, Jack drove his knife into the orc's side, twisting until he felt ribs snap. The beast howled, stumbling back, and Jack kicked it into the flames, its screams blending with the fire's roar. The motion knocked him off balance and he stumbled backward. Instead of getting back up, he sat there panting as he stared aimlessly at the carnage. The heat blistered his skin, but the physical pain couldn't touch his emotional anguish.

The silence that followed the brief scuffle was heavier than the battle's chaotic din. Standing again, he went to where his rifle lay discarded, picked it up, and slung it over his shoulder. He changed out its empty magazine and looked for a shovel. He saw Molly's barn, untouched by the fire and went inside. Stepping inside, he waited a few moments for his eyes to adjust to the dim light. He saw a shovel laying against one of the livestock stalls.

The air was thick with the acrid scent of smoke and the faint, metallic tang of blood. He smelt the flesh cooking, as the orc corpses roasted in the fire they'd started. Jack gripped the rough handle of the shovel tighter, the wooden handle biting into his palms. He stood in the dim, flickering light of the barn as waves of sadness and rage washed over him. He studied the shadows dancing across the weathered wooden walls as he contemplated the long march of time that he would have to endure alone.

Shaking his head to clear the emotions, he gritted his teeth for the grizzly work of burying his family. He felt their absence. A hollow ache in his chest that almost took his breath away. Then he heard it, the faint whimper piercing the emotionally charged silence. It came from the stall at the other end of the barn. It was where Molly housed her livestock during the biting winter months.

Should I switch to my rifle? I'd alert any nearby patrols... but it would be quicker than hand-to-hand combat. Shovel it is, he told himself. Moving cautiously, he brandished the shovel, its edge glinting faintly in the flickering sunlight creeping through the wooden slats of the building. His boots crunched softly on the straw-strewn floor as he rounded the corner.

There, partially covered by a blanket of week-old hay, was the last person he expected to see. It was Molly, his neighbor. She wasn't dead, instead she curled protectively around her newborn baby, the umbilical cord still glistening and attached. Her shallow breaths stirred the air, and the infant's tiny, trembling cries filled the space with fragile life.

"Okay, it's gonna be okay," Jack said, his voice low and steady as he stepped forward, the floorboards creaking beneath him. He leaned the shovel against the rough-hewn stall and knelt beside her. The faint warmth of her body radiated through the chill as he gently rubbed her shoulder, whispering soothing words that mingled with the distant howl of the wind outside.

"I know this has been a shock, but we have to cut the cord," he said softly.

Then he pulled his K-Bar from its leather sheath on his hip with a soft scrape. He'd originally cleaned it with dirt and wiped it on the orc's coarse clothing. *This isn't sanitary, I'll have to clean it, or it could lead to sepsis.* From his right cargo pocket, he drew a small flask of homemade whiskey. The sharp, oaky scent cut through the barn's musty air as he poured it over both sides of the blade.

"This might hurt," he told Molly as he worked carefully, cutting the umbilical cord. Then he went to work stabilizing the new mother, her skin clammy under his touch.

"Sarah hid me when we heard the patrol," Molly whispered, her voice breaking between shuddering breaths, her eyes glassy with tears that caught the dim light. "She was on her way back with her daughters, but she ran out of time. I was in labor and couldn't help. I couldn't help; I couldn't save her. They died to save me," she said, before collapsing into sobs, the sound raw and piercing in the quiet barn.

Jack fought the sting of his own tears, the grief a stone in his throat. He held himself together long enough to reassure her that everything was going to be okay. Only after he regained his Zen, could he finish the post-birth process. His hands were steady, despite the trembling in his heart. As he worked, he reassured Molly that her child was stable.

"Can you move?" he asked, his voice soft against the creak of the barn's timbers.

"I... I think so," Molly replied, her voice barely above a whisper. "I don't want to stay here anymore." Her words hung in the air, fragile but resolute.

"All right. You just rest here with your little girl," Jack said, glancing at the infant cradled in Molly's arms, her tiny chest rising and falling. "I'll bury my family. Then I'll take you to my cabin, where you can get cleaned up and rest. We'll figure out what to do next in the morning."

"I know what to do next," Molly whispered, her voice hardening. "We kill every single one of them."

Jack nodded, the weight of her words settling into his broken heart. He picked up the shovel and stepped into the smokey air. It took him a few minutes to find ground that was suitable for his family's eternal resting place. Most of the ground was rocky and would've taken too long to break up. It took him several hours to dig their graves, the shovel scraping against stones that had to be removed. Each strike echoed in the stillness, the clang of metal on stone.

"I'm sorry that I wasn't there," he said to his family.

Then Jack laid his family side by side, with his wife in the middle. He placed his wife's arms around their daughters. He positioned them in a final, eternal hug.

"I love you," he whispered. "Wait for me on the other side, I'll be there before you know it."

Jack wasn't a religious man, but he stood in contemplative silence, the heat from the fire heating his exposed skin as he tried to imagine a world without his sunshine. Tears streamed down his face, unashamed, evaporating on his cheeks from the heat. He ignored it as he gazed at the graves. They were the reason he'd kept living, despite the dark memories that clawed at him. Lost in thought, he didn't hear Molly approach, her footsteps muffled by the soft earth.

"You have to live," she whispered, her voice cutting through his pain. She was standing next to him; her newborn cradled against her. The fire had died down some, shelving his concern for the newborn. "That's what Sarah would've wanted. It's what your little girls would've wanted. We have to make this mean something."

Jack stood motionless for several heartbeats, then grunted his reply. The sound was rough in his throat, his voice raw from his primal screams of rage. He shoveled the dirt back into the graves, the earth thudding softly as it covered his family. He spent a few minutes piecing together a headstone, using two wooden planks ripped from inside Molly's barn. With his knife, he crudely carved their names, the blade scraping against the grain.

"I'll find you something nicer when this is over," he whispered to his family, his voice breaking as he caressed the makeshift cross.

Sound quieted around him; the forest itself was holding its breath. The wind stilled, the trees joining him in his mourning. Jack's knees buckled, and he sank to the ground. His hands trembled as they clutched the bloodied knife. His family was gone. His world was ash, bereft of beauty without the innocent love of his daughters. Without the comfort that his wife gave him, reminding him of his humanity in his darkest moments.

"Did you hear that?" he asked Molly.

"Hear what?"

Turning in a slow circle, he unslung his rifle and looked for the threat. The hair on the back of his neck stood up as he hunted for potential danger.

"Let's get out of here," he whispered. "We'll see if there is anything here to salvage when the fire dies out."

The journey through the dense forest of the Appalachians, with a woman who'd just given birth, took surprisingly less time than he'd originally thought.

The air was thick with the scent of pine and damp earth. The canopy prevented light from reaching them as they moved. What made it through cast long, eerie shadows across the uneven path. If it weren't for their circumstances, he'd have appreciated the beauty of the natural world.

They covered four miles to his homestead, getting there just as the sun dipped below the horizon. He couldn't see the sunset, but he felt it in his bones as he observed his surroundings. During their trek, Jack took the lead. His boots crunched softly on the fallen leaves and pine needles. His heart pounded in his chest. He still had the unshakable feeling that they were being watched — followed, even. The distant howl of a wolf and the rustle of other unseen creatures off in the underbrush heightened his unease.

They moved as silently as possible, stepping carefully to avoid snapping branches, and made every effort to conceal their tracks. Knowing the orcs had a keen sense of smell, Jack scattered crushed herbs and dragged branches to create confusing scent trails, in an effort to obscure their path through the darkening woods.

"Is this really necessary?" Molly asked, as her baby whimpered in her arms.

"We don't want those monsters to follow us to my homestead. So... yes, it is necessary," Jack replied.

They reached his cabin nestled on his homestead, its weathered wooden walls looming in the twilight. A wave of sadness crashed over Jack as they got closer to the building. There was a faint creak, as he pushed the door open, the sound echoing in the stillness. This cabin, once alive with love, laughter, and warmth, was now nothing more than wood, brick, and sadness.

Walking into his home, he stoked the fire he'd left and turned on the kerosene lamps. Then he turned to Molly and studied her. She looked defeated and broken, barely holding it together. Her face was pale and streaked with sweat under the dim glow of a lantern. She smelled of smoke and burned wood from the destroyed homestead. As he stared at the young mother and remembered the previous encounter, he fought back his tears.

"Search the cabin for anything you need," he said, his voice rough. "I don't know what baby supplies we have, but you're welcome to it."

"Thank you," Molly whispered, her voice barely audible.

His new companion hobbled toward his daughter's room, her steps uneven on the creaky floorboards. He followed her, unsure what to do with himself without his rock, his Sarah. When he reached the bedrooms, he noticed that the air in the small room carried the faint scent of lavender from forgotten sachets.

"Are you sure?" she asked, turning back toward him.

He couldn't respond, his voice catching in his throat. He nodded, watching quietly as Molly found cloth diapers and plastic pants. They'd once been used by Lily when she played with her dolls. The soft, worn fabric, offering a small measure of protection for her newborn daughter. He had to fight his urge to stop her from touching their rooms. His family didn't need them anymore. His wife had died saving this young mother, he owed it to his women to protect Molly.

"What are you going to name her?" Jack asked, as he tried not to focus on the looting of his daughter's room. His voice caught as he leaned against the doorframe, the wood cool against his shoulder.

Molly hesitated, her eyes glistening in the flickering light. "Would you... would you be okay if I named her after your little girls? Daisy Rose sounds like the perfect name for my child... if that would be okay?"

Jack couldn't answer. His throat tightened painfully, and he merely nodded as he fought back tears. After a moment, he steadied himself and titled his head towards Molly. Then he shuffled to the kitchen, the familiar clatter of pots grounding him. The two of them had spent all of their energy in their mad dash across the land between their homesteads. He knew that breastfeeding mothers needed calories like a flower needed the sun. That was a simple problem that he could solve.

The savory aroma of simmering stew filled the air as he prepared their meal. Molly finally descended the creaky stairs, carrying little Daisy Rose in a basket lined with soft, faded towels. He glanced over at her makeshift bassinet and had a bittersweet flashback to his own little girl's infancy. She placed the container gently onto the worn oak table beside their plates. The baby's soft coos were barely audible over the crackle of the fire he'd lit in the hearth.

"Thank you for saving me," Molly said, her voice weary as she settled into a chair.

"It's what she wanted," Jack replied, his gaze fixed on the flickering flames. "Sarah wanted to save the world one heart at a time."

"It's why everyone loved her," Molly said softly, her words mingling with the faint whistle of the wind picking up outside.

"Yes, well," Jack said, pausing as he stirred the stew, the spoon scraping softly against the pot. "I don't know what's next. But even if we want to go after the Orcish scum, we'll have to wait. They're going to be on their guard for a while."

"They will," Molly replied, her voice tinged with resolve.

The crackle of the fire filled the silence in the cabin, its warm glow casting flickering shadows across the rough-hewn wooden walls. The air carried the rich, savory scent of beef stew simmering in the iron pot, mingling with the faint tang of pine from the logs stacked near the hearth. He'd made enough to feed the two adults through a few more meals, using the fireplace to prevent overtaxing their solar panels.

Jack and Molly sat around the scarred oak table, their spoons clinking softly against well-loved ceramic bowls. They ate the rest of their dinner in companionable silence, the weight of their shared loss hanging heavy in the room. Jack's brow furrowed as he considered his next move. *I have to make them pay,* he thought, *but I have to be smart about it. Above all, I can't let Molly or Daisy Rose suffer. Not after my Sarah died to save them.*

Those conflicting mandates weighed on his conscience, threatening to drag him down and distract him. He didn't even realize he'd scooped the last of his stew into his mouth until his teeth scraped against the empty metal utensil. He found the spoon empty, the metallic taste lingering faintly on his tongue.

After carefully considering his alternatives, he came up with a plan. Setting his spoon down with a soft clatter on the table, he looked over at Molly. He waited patiently for her to look up at him. When she did, he noticed that her face was illuminated by the firelight. It was reminiscent of the lifetime of memories he'd made with his Sarah under these same lights.

"Tomorrow," he said, his voice low and steady, "I'll go back to your home. I'll see if anything can be saved from your house, barn and root cellar. Anything to help you survive the winter. Then we'll hunker down here and ride out the snow drifts. The first bout of icy crystals will be on us any day now. The wind's already howling outside, and Mother Nature won't be ignored."

"And then what?" Molly asked hesitantly.

"When I know you're okay, that Daisy Rose is okay, I'll leave my cabin to you. I won't need it anymore."

"Molly's spoon froze halfway to her mouth, her eyes widening. "What are you saying?" she asked, her voice trembling. She sounded brittle to Jack's ears, like she'd crack under the merest ounce of pressure. Her conflicting emotions played out across her face — fear, anger, and something fiercer. He saw the spark of God's light ready to ignite women by suggesting that they embrace femininity.

"No, I'm not going to kill myself," Jack said, his voice hardening, each word like a stone dropped into still water. "I'm going to kill them. Kill all of them. I'll drag as many of them to hell as I can."

Molly set her spoon down deliberately, the firelight catching the determined glint in her eyes. "I'll help," she said simply, her voice steady despite the weight of her words. "In the meantime, we can spend the winter preparing for the fight."

Jack leaned forward, the chair creaking under his weight. "Preparing how?"

Molly's gaze didn't waver, though her fingers tightened around the edge of the table, her knuckles turning pale. "I know I'm young, but I've been told I have an old soul," she said. "I liked studying history — watching documentaries, learning about the past. My grandpa fought in Vietnam, so I watched a lot of those old movies, documentaries, and read the histories. The Viet Cong were onto something with their booby traps. We can replicate that on our land. Make them pay for every inch they take."

Jack's eyes narrowed, the faint creak of the cabin's timbers punctuating the silence as the wind picked up outside. "That's a defensive move," he said, "and it leaves us nowhere to fall back to."

"If we plan it right, we'll have that too," Molly replied, her eyes blazing with resolve. She leaned forward, her shadow stretching across the table. "We can sketch out a plan this winter and scout for soft targets. If we travel far enough to hit them, they won't track it back to us."

Jack nodded slowly, the fire's warmth doing little to ease the chill. "It's decided, then," he said, the words sealing their pact with the promise of future battles.

They spent the rest of the day in companionable silence. Jack helped Molly care for her daughter, getting her situated on his recliner with their improvised bassinet securely propped up next to her. He watched over her while she slept, dozing intermittently throughout the night. He made regular patrols of his property, wary of a potential orc reprisal raid on his homestead. When the first rays of sunrise peaked through the windows, he prepared breakfast and waited for his companion to wake.

"Morning," he said, offering her a cup of hot tea.

"Morning," Molly replied, yawning and blowing on her beverage.

While she breastfed her daughter, Jack brought her a plate of food and fed her. After she ate everything on her plate, and a refill, he was finally able to eat and enjoy his coffee. Then he stood, stretching as he studied Molly's face.

"We don't have the supplies to last the winter. I was hunting to stuff our freezers and root cellars when the orcs attacked. I need to leave, but I will be back to take care of you and Daisy Rose."

"I'll come too," Molly said, as she stared down at her daughter.

"No, that wouldn't be healthy for your daughter. And I need you watching over the place," he said, placatingly. "I'll leave a shotgun by the front and back door, just in case. And a rifle in the bedroom upstairs, if you want to sleep up there."

"I think I'll man the recliner for a while," she said quietly. "Don't be gone too long."

He packed light, bringing everything he'd need to wage war on the invaders to his land... and to hunt for their freezer.

With grim resolve, he left Molly and his cabin behind. Killing three orcs wasn't enough, not by a long shot. It was time to pick up the rifle again; he had nothing left to lose. He moved out at a run, heading back to one of his nearby weapons caches. He was a shadow in the hills, a one-man resistance, scavenging ammo and explosives from his stores.

When he reached the closest location, he dropped to his knees and uncovered the dark grey Rubbermaid tote. Inside, he found enough weapons, ammo and explosives to start a war.

"They were my tax dollars that paid for it," he muttered, "might as well get it back with interest now that the country went belly up."

Re-armed, he rushed back toward Molly's homestead. When he was close, he slowed down and moved more tactically through the dense woods. He found no evidence that the orc skirmishers had returned to look for their missing kin. No new footprints or evidence of scavengers. The fire had mostly burned itself out, leaving a smoldering husk where a house had been.

As hot as the house is, the odds of anything useful coming from it are slim to none, he thought. *Let's check the barn and look for a root cellar.* He searched the area, until he found the detached storage building the locals had all built after the invasion to protect their goods in case of just such an event. It was disappointingly empty. *Then it's time to hunt some orcs and then find food for the winter.*

Jack followed the tracks of the orcs who'd raided the homestead, moving stealthily through the dense underbrush. The forest was alive with the rustle of leaves and the distant calls of birds, their songs sharp against the heavy silence of the morning air. His boots pressed softly into the damp earth, each step deliberate, honed by years of practice and relentless physical conditioning. The weight of his arsenal didn't slow him down; it felt like an extension of his body, as familiar as his own breath.

The trail led him to a rugged ravine, its steep walls cloaked in moss and shadowed by towering pines. Evidence of the orcs' passage was clear: broken branches, scuffed earth, and the faint metallic tang of blood lingering in the air. Jack crouched low, his fingers brushing over the disturbed soil where the orcs had scrambled up in their pursuit.

"You didn't even try to hide your tracks," he murmured. "Arrogance is a foible I can work with."

Standing, he followed, descending the rocky slope with the agility of a predator. His senses were sharp as he simultaneously searched for the orcish trail and paid attention to the threat of the enemy coming upon him. At the bottom of his climb, a narrow stream gurgled over smooth stones, its icy waters gleaming in the sunlight. If the situation weren't so dire, he'd have taken a moment to marvel at the natural beauty of his surroundings.

Looking around, he tried to reacquire the trail of his enemy… and then he saw it. The orcs had waded through the creek, making an effort to hide their trail. It didn't work; their heavy footprints pressed too deeply into the soft streambed betraying them.

"Nice try," he murmured, as he grimly considered his next move.

For two days, Jack tracked them, the journey wearing on his body but not his resolve. He stopped only briefly to rest, sipping from his canteen and chewing on strips of dried meat under the starlit canopy. His night vision goggles cast the world in eerie shades of green, revealing the orcs' trail where moonlight failed. The air grew cooler as the terrain shifted, the forest giving way to a small, secluded valley.

At the valley's heart, Jack found the orcs' crude encampment. The camp sprawled haphazardly across a clearing, a chaotic cluster of tattered tents circling a smoldering central fire. The acrid scent of smoke and charred meat hung heavy in the air, mingling with the faint musk of unwashed bodies. It was midday when Jack reached the clearing's edge, the sun high and unrelenting, casting harsh shadows across the trampled grass. He crouched behind a gnarled oak, its bark rough against his gloved hand, and surveyed the scene.

Only a handful of orcs remained in the camp, far fewer than he'd expected. *Must be out on another raiding party*, he thought, his jaw tightening. The monsters present were lightly armored, clad in patched leather and crudely made chain mail that clinked faintly as they moved. They carried swords and battle axes, their blades appeared to be poorly forged, glinting dully in the sunlight. Jack's eyes narrowed as he searched for the telltale aura of magical weapons, the kind whispered about in the Appalachian villages, artifacts said to shimmer with an otherworldly glow. But there was nothing. No trace of enchantment, no hum of power. Just a ragtag band of raiders, oblivious to the hunter watching from the shadows.

But then, he heard a rustle behind him. It was too soft, too deliberate, to be natural. His head snapped up, and he slowly turned around so he could keep an eye on both threats. He continued searching the shadows as he watched the orc camp. A deer on the other side of the clearing caught the orc's attention and he used their distraction to pull back into the foliage to investigate what was disturbing the trees.

At first, he saw nothing out of the ordinary. And then from the gnarled trunk of an ancient oak, a figure emerged. *It's like the tree is giving birth*, he thought in shock. A wooden feminine figure emerged, her form woven from living bark and vibrant vines, stepped into the flickering sunlight. Light danced along her skin, shimmering across her flesh. She looked to be made of polished mahogany and dressed in flowing moss, her hair a cascade of leaves that whispered with each movement.

"Shit, shit, shit," he murmured, shocked at her sudden appearance.

The feminine being cocked her head to the left, studying him. Her eyes glowed like emeralds as she watched him. As he studied her, he caught a strange smell in the wind. The air around her carried the crisp scent of spring despite the chill. The forest leaned toward her, their branches swaying in reverence to the special being.

"Jack Harlan," she said, her voice a melody of rustling leaves and distant streams, "your grief is a wound the forest feels. I am Sylva, the self-appointed guardian of these woods. They destroyed my home in their march across the dimensions. There is nowhere for me to go but here, so I stake my claim with Earth."

"Why are you helping me? Magical beings, non-earth entities, have been killing humans for a few years. Why here? Why now? And what are you?"

The creature studied him, her expression unreadable. "I am a dryad, something your legends speak of. As to the why and how? The elves and their orc slaves have desecrated my domain, twisting sacred roots. They choked the life out of the forest, poisoned our streams with their alchemical filth and decimated the wildlife. Your loss binds us, human warrior. The invaders know someone was stalking them. Flighted familiars observed the dead skirmishers and have prepared a trap."

"What trap?" Jack asked.

"They wish you to advance into the camp, to challenge those guards. When you do, they will encircle you. They will capture you and torture information out of you."

"A dryad? I remember reading about those in school. From the Greeks... right, tree dwelling tree spirits. I'd worry that I was going crazy, talking to you, but I already watched elves and orcs conquer my home."

"You are not crazy, good sir."

"Ok, the important stuff. So, the orcs seek to ambush my ambush? Then I guess I'm Sicilian today, because I'm going to triple flip the script. Have you ascertained their plans?" Jack asked.

"They plan to lure you into attacking the camp and swarm you. Whether they capture you or kill you is anyone's guess."

Jack's grip tightened on the handle of his weapon, his knuckles whitening from the pressure. "Tell me more of their trap," he said. His voice was raw, making speech painful. "Speak plain, spirit. I don't have time to lose."

Sylva's gaze softened, though her oaken form remained unyielding. "The elves know of your planned raid, of your defiance. They've woven illusions around the clearing, hiding archers in the cover. Worse, these beasts tip their arrows with strong venom. The kind that burns the soul. Your explosives, your ambush... their scryers have foreseen it. But there is another way. Lead them back into this ravine and prepare it to collapse in upon itself. Strike there, and the forest will fight with you."

He stared at her, as he contemplated what she suggested. Trusting a creature of myth felt like madness. His homeland was being invaded by such beings, aligning with this dryad felt tantamount to treason. *Is she even a dryad?* He was hesitant, the shimmer of elven illusions had fooled him before. He'd seen their treachery; trees that bled, shadows that killed. Despite that, this dryad's words rang with a truth his gut couldn't ignore.

"If you're lying," he growled, "I'll burn this whole damn forest down to find you."

Sylva's lips curved, a flicker of amusement in her verdant eyes. "The woods are not your enemy, soldier. Follow." She melted into the undergrowth, her form blending with the shadows, a mist dissolving into night.

Jack gripped his rifle tightly as he stood, slinging it over his shoulder. Then he followed, the weight of his pack dragging at his aching body. The forest parted for Sylva; brambles uncoiled, roots flattened, the air grew cooler and wetter, laced with the mineral tang of the nearby stream. His boots sank into loamy soil, the scent of damp earth grounding him. His grief was still the albatross around his neck, clawing at his heart. He moved silently, his training keeping his steps light despite the rage and exhaustion warring within him.

They traveled for several hours, until they reached a bend in the ravine. The curve was the perfect tactical location; the stream roared loudly, almost becoming a river with its waters frothing over moss-slick boulders. Mist sprayed everywhere, clinging to his skin as he looked for the best way to capitalize on the location and turn it into the perfect kill zone.

"This will do," he murmured, as he studied his surroundings.

He checked the surroundings, planning his attack. The banks rose steeply, choked with vines and brambles, forming a natural choke point. *Perfect*, he thought, as he considered where he'd place his claymore mines and the other explosives he'd acquired from the Army in the chaos after the elven invasion.

"This is going to be one heckuva fatal funnel."

He worked fast, planting C4 along the far bank, the plastic explosive's chemical scent sharp in his nose. The slightly sweet, plastic-like smell reminded him of almonds, which reminded him that he hadn't eaten yet. Pulling a strip of homemade beef jerky from his cargo pocket, he focused on his work. Jack rigged tripwires; their thin lines nearly invisible in the dim light that made it through the overhead canopy. Then he checked his weapons and magazines, all gifts from Uncle Sam. He'd left his hunting rifles in the cabin with Molly.

When he was done placing his explosives, he estimated how far back the landslide would be and set up his firing position accordingly. He set firing stakes to denote his sectors and built a defensive position for his M249 SAW. The squad automatic weapon wouldn't do a whole lot against an orc; he was counting on Mother Nature to do the heavy lifting for him. Then he placed his six grenades and four Molotov Cocktails in his position to add oomph to his attack.

When he was done, he pulled out his lunch and started eating. Only then did he stand and prepare to lead the orcs to their death. He followed his path back toward the opening to the clearing. Reaching it, he knelt and studied the situation. Upon finding it unchanged, he brazenly walked toward the enemy camp. The orcs didn't see him, or they pretended that they didn't.

He moved swiftly, darting between concealed positions, his boots sinking slightly into the soft grass. Each step was deliberate, silent, as he closed the distance to the nearest orc, a massive figure, easily seven feet tall, clad in weathered leather and clinking chain mail. The beast stood near the fire; a haunch of meat clutched in one meaty fist. The sizzle of fat dripping into the fire sent a savory, almost sickening aroma into the air, mingling with the acrid sting of smoke. Jack's stomach churned, but he had no time to linger on the sensation.

Dropping to his knees, Jack drew his K-Bar knife, the blade glinting faintly in the firelight. In one fluid motion, he slashed, first severing the orc's left hamstring, then the right. The creature collapsed to its knees with a bone-rattling scream, the sound tearing through the quiet night. The other orcs froze, their glowing eyes wide with shock, as Jack surged forward. He gripped the orc's neck, yanking it back, and dragged his K-Bar across its throat. Blood sprayed in a hot, coppery arc, hissing as it met the fire, adding a sharp, metallic tang to the smoky air.

As the orc's struggles ceased, Jack shoved the lifeless body forward, its weight thudding against the ground. He raised his M4 rifle to the low-ready position, the K-Bar still slick in his hand, making the grip awkward but manageable. His eyes locked on the second orc, its grotesque face snarling in the firelight. Jack fired controlled pairs, the sharp cracks of gunfire echoing through the trees. At first, the rounds seemed to do nothing, absorbed by the beast's thick hide. But Jack kept firing, his finger steady on the trigger, until several bullets punctured the orc's eyes. The creature roared, clutching its ruined face as it staggered.

The third orc charged from across the fire, its battle-axe raised, the blade gleaming with malicious intent. Jack dodged, rolling to the side. The pistol in the holster on his belt cut into his side, but he managed to avoid the orc's axe swing. It went wide, the whoosh of air brushing past his ear. He came up next to a tattered orc tent, the coarse fabric reeking of sweat and blood. Hastily wiping his K-Bar on his sleeve, he sheathed it and brought his rifle back up. The orc lunged again, its axe slicing through the air. Jack rolled out of the way, coming up behind the beast. Enraged, the orc swung wildly, its battle-axe inadvertently cleaving into its own companion, who crumpled with a wet, sickening thud.

The surviving orc stood frozen, staring at its dead ally, the fire casting long shadows across its stunned expression. Jack seized the moment, performing a quick magazine swap, the empty clip slipping into his cargo pocket. Then he slammed a fresh one into place. He brought his rifle back to the low-ready position, watching the orc's next move. *Wait for it, wait for it*, he repeated to himself as a mantra.

The remaining orc charged, swinging its axe in a desperate arc. Jack executed a combat roll, the grassy clearing cold against his back, and came up beside the orc. He fired several rounds into its neck, the beast's bellow of rage shaking the air. It turned to face him, mouth gaping, and Jack aimed deliberately for its eyes. Halfway through the magazine, he struck one, then the other, blinding the creature. To be sure, he emptied the rest of the magazine into the exposed sockets. The orc's roars faded into gurgles as blood poured from the ruined eye slots.

With no time to hesitate, Jack slung his rifle and drew his K-Bar again. He maneuvered around the flailing, blinded orc, its chain mail clinking as it thrashed. Leaping onto its back, Jack wrapped his legs around the beast's armored torso, the cold metal biting into his worn utility pants. He gripped the orc's head with one arm, the stench of its unwashed body overwhelming, and dragged his K-Bar across its throat. Blood sprayed, hot and sticky, coating his hands as the orc fought on, its strength fading but its fury unrelenting. Jack clung tightly, muscles straining, until the creature's struggles ceased, and the last orc in the camp collapsed, lifeless, into the dirt.

The afternoon sun blazed high, casting harsh shadows across the battlefield. The air hung heavy with the acrid stench of smoke and blood. Roaring into the sky, Jack's guttural stream of curses aimed at the fallen skirmishers cut into the eerie silence. He insulted and taunted the dead orcish warriors who were sprawled lifelessly in the dust. His words, sharp and venomous, echoed off the trees, ensuring anyone lurking nearby heard him.

Kneeling near the corpses, he started looting the bodies. His calloused hands rifled through their pockets, uncovering a handful of gold coins that glinted dully in the sunlight. Disappointment curled his lip; nothing else held value. No enchanted trinkets gleamed with arcane promise, no gear appeared worth salvaging for resale. Their packs, reeking of sweat and rot, held no food suitable for long-term field operations. With a grunt, Jack dragged the corpses toward the smoldering fire at the camp's center. He tossed their tattered tents atop the pile, the canvas flapping in the breeze, before settling over the orcs' twisted forms.

From his left cargo pocket, Jack pulled a battered flask, the metal cool against his palm. He unscrewed the cap, and the sharp tang of alcohol stung his nostrils as he sprinkled it over the heap of bodies and gear. Kneeling again, he plucked a dry leaf from the ground, its edges curling in the heat. Then he held it to the glowing embers until it caught fire with a soft crackle. With a flick, he tossed the burning leaf onto the pile. Standing, he watched flames leap up, licking hungrily at the orcish supplies. The fire roared, sending a plume of black smoke spiraling into the sky, thick with the stench of burning cloth and flesh.

Satisfied, Jack turned and strode deliberately toward the ravine, his boots thudding heavily against the earth. He made no effort to mask his presence, snapping twigs and kicking stones to leave a clear trail. The ravine loomed ahead, its steep walls cloaked in shadow and dotted with gnarled roots.

"God, please let them take the bait," he whispered in prayer as he walked.

Halfway to his destination, the air shifted and the hair on the back of his neck perked up. He heard a distant rumble that grew into the thunderous roar of boots. Orcs poured from the surrounding forest, their guttural shouts and the clatter of crude armor filling the air. They formed a ragged half-circle behind him, their silhouettes hulking and monstrous against the tree line, charging in his direction with weapons raised.

Jack didn't pause to count them. His pulse quickened, but his focus sharpened as he sprinted into the ravine, its narrow path sloping downward. The orcs' longer strides and added height gave them an edge, but he compensated with cunning. He needed to draw them deeper. Every few steps, he stopped, spun, and fired rounds from his pistol, the sharp cracks reverberating off the ravine walls. Each shot was deliberate, meant to taunt, to convince them he was a desperate man fleeing and fighting for his life, not a predator leading them into a trap. The orcs, snarling and relentless, took the bait, their heavy steps shaking the ground as they chased him into the shadowed depths of the ravine.

He continued running, only stopping inside the kill zone, allowing the orcs to catch up. When they were inside the death box he'd created, he scrambled up the incline and got into the fighting position he'd made. When the last orc entered the outside of the bracketed area, he clicked the clacker. The explosion reverberated the ravine, sending hundreds of small steel balls into the legs of the rear element of the orc charge.

While he prepared for the next part of the assault, Sylva the dryad knelt beside him. She sank her fingers into the soil, whispering words of power. Her magic unleashed a wave of pleasant feelings and the scent of the forest after a spring rain. The ground answered her call; vines slithered upward, their thorns glinting like obsidian blades, before coiling into natural snares. The air became oppressive, layered with the scent of fragrant sap and mulch. The forest was arming for war against the orcs.

The orc horde stalled, their boots pounding the earth as they shifted in place. The magic rippled off the ground at their feet, the vines trying to trap their limbs. There were more orcs than he'd originally thought, as a hundred orcs splashed in place in the stream. Sylva kept chanting and the water rose, water foaming around their waists. The panicked grunts of his enemies echoed off the ravine walls. As the panicked tension rose, Jack waited, heart hammering, until the middle ranks were mired in the current. Then he pressed the detonator, its click swallowed by the roar of explosions.

His claymores erupted, sending thousands of steel balls into the congregated masses. Then the C4 followed it, causing a deafening boom to shake the ground, hurling rocks, and mud in a deadly cascade. The air filled with the sharp sting of cordite and the wet thud of bodies hitting water. The secondary explosion caused a landslide, as Mother Earth began killing the outer layer of invaders.

"Get some!" he yelled, as he pulled the pin and threw a fragmentation grenade into the horde of the enemy.

Orcs screamed, their cries raw and animalistic, as vines lashed out, holding them in place to face the full impact of his grenade. Capitalizing on it, he threw the rest of his grenades. The explosive devices took out more trapped orcs, sending sprays of blood and flesh everywhere. More vines came out, as the dryad kept chanting, wrapping orc limbs, and snapping them. It almost sounded like twigs breaking, before they were drug beneath the frothing water.

Rat-tat-tat.

Rat-tat-tat.

Rat-tat-tat.

Jack fired with his M249, the squad automatic weapon's recoil pressing into his shoulder. Spent casings tinkled against each other, as the pile of brass beside him piled up. Despite the quantity of rounds, he ensured that each shot was precise. He aimed center mass, followed by headshots, his Mozambique Drill sending their blood spraying in arcs that smelled of copper and ozone.

"For Sarah!"

Arrows flew back toward him, some of the trapped skirmisher orcs managing to get into the fight. The bolts hissed past his ear, before Sylva raised a barrier of twisting branches. Creaks and groans from the impromptu barrier reminded him that the forest was fighting with him.

"Watch out!" Jack shouted at Sylva, as a pair of orcs charged toward them.

Before he'd finished his warning, thorns pierced orc flesh as roots tripped those attacking warriors. Their bodies fell backward, allowing the stream to swallow the invaders. The orcs broke, trampling each other in panic, their roars fading into gurgles as the water claimed them. The orc leader turned and fled, his bulk vanishing into the trees, leaving only the stench of defeat in the ravine turned battlefield.

"Never fear, human, the woods will handle the fleeing foe," Sylva said softly.

Jack lowered his rifle, nodding to the dryad as he waited for his ears to quit ringing. Taking a swig of his water, he washed down the bitter taste in his mouth. His chest heaved from the exertion, sweat and mist mingling on his skin. Looking down at the kill zone, he was awed at the destruction they'd wrought in the ravine turned graveyard. Orc bodies tangled in vines were piled in clusters. The stream ran red as the orcish blood pooled in the trapped water.

The silence drew on, until Sylva stood, her form half-fading back into the oak, her voice barely audible over the soft breeze. "The forest honors its allies, Jack Harlan. Your pain feeds its roots. Continue your fight, and we will stand with you."

He nodded, the weight of loss and vengeance settling deeper into his bones. Gathering his remaining equipment, he briefly considered checking the battlefield and looting the dead. Shaking his head, he decided against it and melted into the shadows, rifle in hand. The war wasn't over, but tonight, his family had started the slow process of claiming their due. For now, he had Molly and Daisy Rose waiting for him to bring supplies to last them through the winter as they prepared to kick things up a notch.

Medicine Wheel

by Richard Cartwright

"YOU'RE CUT OFF TILL you repay the house." Tsisdu McTavish was careful to mix a little regret in his firm delivery. The White Hand orc commander looked a little desperate.

"Just a little. I know my luck is bound to change."

If I had a dollar for every time I've heard that. "I'm sure it will, Gromick. But in order to play, you're going to have to pay." He thought the commander was going to cry. Not a good look for a nearly seven-foot-tall orc.

"What can I do?" the green-skinned warrior croaked out.

"Do you have anything that you could pledge to the Trading Post?" The wholly owned subsidiary of the casino was really a pawnshop, but the bands' marketing team thought the name resonated with the Indian casino theme better than 'pawnshop'.

The orc brightened, "I have loot rights to a bunch of old human weapons that we collected from... I think they're called armories. They're not really much use to us other than as trophies." He snorted. "Hardly any honor in weapons you collect from abandoned buildings."

"The Trading Post might do something with that. Did you get any ammunition with them?"

"Ammunition? Oh, the little projectiles that make the magic. Boxes and boxes of the stuff. The guide said they had '5.56' stenciled on them. There were a few cases of something called claymores, too."

"I know a lot of people like that ammunition so they can hunt for game to fill the stew pot. That would be worth something." He paused. "The claymores might be useful for pest control. Bring them along too."

"So, I can go back and play?"

"Right after you bring in the voucher from the Trading Post for the value of the guns, 5.56, and claymores."

"Okay, I'll get right on that." Without another word, the White Hand sub chief jumped up from his chair and rushed out of the room. A plump, gray-haired woman with high cheekbones stuck her head in the opened door.

"The pit boss called. He needs you to defuse some sore losers at the sandbox. Sam is managing a convoy from Ashville and is off the grounds. They need your gift."

"On my way Gola."

The Sandbox took up a corner of the games room. Dressed up to look like an American forward base from Afghanistan back when the world thought other humans were the biggest enemy, it was more popular with the orcs than the forest and urban combat settings.

Giant screens displayed desert combat, where players fought for cash prizes generated from entry fees and betting. Two sets of frozen screens looked down on a group of orcs with white hand tattoos that were tusk to tusk with a group of red arrow tatted orcs.

Tsisdu's grasp of the orc language was limited to phrases. The exchanges booming across the room to the entrance to the console games space were phrases he heard far too often.

"You cheated!"

"Fuck you, you cheated!"

"You're just crying because we handed your asses to you."

"Declare us the winners or we're going to cut off your members and feed them to you,"

The last came through in English as he came within the influence of the translator rings several orcs sported on their fingers. Both groups had hands on the hilts of their knives.

That was about enough of that. Tsisdu felt the undefinable something that his teacher called lifeforce or manna gathering in him. The lights slightly dimmed, and the screens flickered.

"Uruk-ki. What seems to be the problem?" A White Hand wearing the mark of a kezneg war leader spoke, cutting off the Red Arrow orc with identical rank marks.

"These memberless ones hid in the sand like snakes and popped up after we passed, shooting us in the backs like cowards! They should forfeit the purse!"

Tsisdu focused on projecting waves of calm and receptiveness from himself, like ripples from a stone tossed in a placid pond.

He could see it was working. Hands moved away from belt knives and the orc troops adopted attentive expressions like earnest pupils listening to a teacher.

"Now what the Lifereivers did was an old trick from the Plains Indians of Earth. It was considered an honorable way to deal with a vastly superior foe." The white hand orcs nodded their heads, a few preened with pride at being praised as vastly superior fighters. One of the red arrow orcs spoke up.

"I saw that in the moving pictures about the desert fighters on the worm planet, trying to throw off invaders with much better magic than they had." One of the white hand orcs nodded his head.

"The one with the floating fat human?"

The red arrow orc nodded. "Yes, all the humans had blue colored eyes."

Tsisdu smiled as he turned away from the now friendly group as they set up to play a double or nothing round while talking about the human movies they had watched.

Who would've thought that orcs could bond over a David Lynch movie?

***

A nondescript dark-haired man with the unique features and skin coloring that marked him as a Melungeon was sitting in his waiting room sipping a cup of coffee sitting ramrod straight. His well-worn clothes and scuffed work boots marked him as a mountain resident, what flatlanders would call a hillbilly.

"Mr. McTavish, this is Mr. Bitton. He's the new chief mule skinner for the transport company that is taking the consignment items to the Knoxville market." Gola said by way of greeting as he entered the antechamber to his office. She rested her chin on her right hand and said, "Did you get the problem on the floor sorted?"

Her hand was positioned so only he saw her fingers tapping on her pendant with the Cherokee symbol for strength.

He's late. "Come in, come in. I have the list of items that we're sending on my desk. Is Gola taking care of you?"

Bitton raised the mug as he smoothly rose to his feet. "Very much so. I haven't had real, honest to God coffee since I don't know how long."

"Bring it with you." A cup of honest bean coffee, not cut with dandelion root or chicory, went for more than top shelf single malt Scotch. Bitton followed him into the inner office, shutting the door behind him.

"Where's Blake?"

The man grimaced. "Fiddler's Green. An elf got handsy with his daughter and when Blake objected, the bastard ran him through like stepping on a bug and dragged Tess off." Bitton laughed mirthlessly. "Elf's catfish food now. He never saw Tess pull the knife from her boot as he pushed her to her knees in the alley behind the market. They're looking for a busty redhead in East Tennessee. You hiring?"

"I assume you dyed her hair already."

"Yep. She's got her daddy's high cheekbones. If she wasn't so fair, she could probably pass for Cherokee."

"Have Gatlin, the Trading Post manager, bring her up to Gola before you pull out. She'll find something for her to do out of the public eye. Why didn't you hide her out at your settlement?"

"Much obliged. She's good in a fight and easy on the eyes. If she wasn't a first cousin, I'd marry her. And that's the problem. She likes the boys a little too much and her looks have the boys liking her right back. With Blake not around to scare them off, the young bucks are going to be rutting. Too much of a distraction."

"I see. In other news, we have a line on a lot of 5.56. Plus claymores."

"Sounds good. Anything else?"

"Might be some rifles. You'll have plenty of credit. Your boys and girls cleaned up at last month's Madden NFL tournament. Here's your manifest for this trip." Tsisdu handed the muleskinner a sheaf of papers.

"I know. Orcs do love football. I just hope they never catch on to the nuances. The gamer company gave me a shopping list for controllers and console upgrades for the crew. Till next time." Tsisdu ushered him to a side door. "This goes straight to the back room of the Trading Post. Now that you're known to us, take that way if you need to see me. Saves time and you aren't showing your face in public as much."

"Good idea. Until later."

Gola's voice came over the intercom as the door was shut behind Bitton.

"Sam needs a word."

"Send him in."

Sam "You can't pronounce my real name" Bonecrusher strode through the office door. The black eyepatch, and metal left arm peeking out of the short sleeve dress shirt drew your attention. The casual observer would miss the slight limp caused by the artificial leg covered by the tailored suit pants. All Sam would tell people was that he had "done some stuff" during the first days of the invasion.

Tsisdu had heard that "some stuff" had earned him a large land holding between Waynesville and Cherokee, about an hour's ride from the casino, along with a generous annuity from the Elves. He had been playing blackjack a year ago when a troop of orcs had come in to make trouble. Fifteen minutes later, Sam had the orcs making good the damaged video slot machines and cleaning up the mess.

An hour and a comped meal with Tsisdu later. Sam was hired as the head of physical security. He was bored with life as a landed gentry. His first order of business was to arrange deals with some nearby Hauszwerg to magic the tables, slots and game stations to prevent El'diore using magic to cheat. The house had banned all magic users since the Invasion. Opening the casino to elves had nearly tripled the gross. The Fae liked to gamble. A lot of them liked it too much.

Sam wasn't one of them. But he missed being in charge of something that let him knock heads occasionally. The casino benefited from someone who knew how to handle the Fae races and had access to a limitless network of information and sources of items that were near impossible to find five years after the invasion but easily "fell off a truck" into Sam's waiting hands. It was an excellent arrangement for everyone.

"How was your trip?" Tsisdu asked, extending his hand as he walked around his desk.

The big orc never really quite understood the human shaking hands thing till Tsisdu explained it was to show that you did not carry a weapon in your hand and didn't mean the person ill will. Now he offered his good hand every time he met the casino manager.

"We have a problem." Orcs weren't much for small talk. Tsisdu raised an eyebrow as he resumed his seat and gestured Sam to the Orc sized chair across from his desk.

"Don't we always?"

"Indeed. Was Nen kri-krisur Gromick a problem? I saw the notice to cut off his credit."

"Not anymore. I gave him a way that he could pay off his debt to the house."

"Ah. Then none of my concern. However, Lord Ave'rll K'Rill, will be traveling from Charlotte in two days to examine this establishment."

"Do you know why?" The orcs had a back-channel network that put the E-4 mafa to shame. And Sam still had the connections.

"This area has become a playground for the El'diore especially... Biltmore, you call it. It reminds them of the estates in the old country. The Uruki-ki enjoy the hunting and the various sietchs that have been established. The tales of the skills of the pleasure slaves, especially the ones you have, are spreading far and wide all out of proportion to this backwater."

"They aren't pleasure slaves. We give them... employment... as housekeepers. What they do on their own time is none of our business." Sam snorted.

"As you say, 'whatever lets you sleep at night.' House K'Rill is concerned. It's an open secret that Spru'gil K'Rill was granted this area to get rid of him. From the court in Charlotte, Lord Jax'rill K'Rill thought that the chief virtue of the far western lands was as a distant dumping ground for the incompetent. And the crippled."

"We pay our tribute to Spru'gil K'Rill. He is a frequent and honored visitor to the Qualla Resort."

"That fool is not the problem. He's besotted with trying to win Call of Duty purses and the... charms of Daisy Miller when he fails to prevail even in pretend battle. Lord Jax'rill K'Rill is not stupid. He sees not only the possibilities, but the dangers of your establishment and your people. Jax'rill's sending Ave'rll K'Rill, a third cousin. He's young, but nobody's fool. Lord Jax'rill is, what's the human word? Mentoring him."

"Will he replace Spru'gil?"

"Probably not. His dragon is on the rise. Lord Jax'rill sees his protege soaring far beyond a simple picturesque holding. If I were to wager, Lord Ave'rll will have a year, perhaps two, of seasoning, after which he will be installed as the ruler of Ashville and the surrounding areas. Spru'gil K'Rill will be bending a knee to him."

"I understand what you are saying. I don't understand House K'Rill's interest in us. Are they not happy with the tribute coming in?"

"You're on the right path. Even with the amount of gold he throws away on gaming and pu... feminine companionship, Spru'gil K'Rill is doing very well for himself. His portion of your tribute is enough for him to curry favor at court. He has delusions of being installed in Asheville himself."

Sam's shrug and facial expression telegraphed to Tsisdu what he thought of the odds of that coming to pass. "El'diore with wit wonder how such a dissolute fool has wrested such wealth from the hinterlands. And so, we have Lord Ave'rll sojourning at the Qualla Resort and Casino in two days' time."

"So, we're the goose who laid the golden egg." Sam looked at him, squinting his good eye.

"Such a bird would be valuable."

"In the human tale, the goose was slaughtered and cut open to look for more golden eggs."

Sam was quiet for a few moments. "That could be an El'diore child's tale as well." Then he broke into a smile, showing tusks. "Then we need to be sure to convince Lord Ave'rll that we're more valuable as a layer than a dinner."

***

The rest of the day was spent making covert preparations for the impending visit. Sam had to protect his sources, so some things had to wait for the official announcement, which the orc said court protocol dictated to be twenty-four hours before Lord Ave'rll's arrival.

The Chief's suite was refreshed. It hadn't been rented out since before the Invasion. Lord Spru'gil K'Rill had always demanded the Presidential Suite, not realizing that the Chief's suite was twice the size.

Head of Housekeeping and Marketing, Loretta Swift, one of the few non-tribal members in management, called the spiffing up part of a "planned review" of the top tier accommodations. She hinted to anyone who asked, that the casino was hoping to pitch the venue for the conventions that were starting to come back on the market now that the insurgency had seemed to die down.

Tsisdu also met Tess Davenport, on the hotel mezzanine level. She was trailing after Loretta, taking notes. She was dressed in a black skirt and white dress shirt almost identical to Loretta. The twenty something apparently had a religious level of faith in the threads securing the buttons if the shirt that strained to hold in her assets was any guide.

Bitton was right. With the black hair and high cheekbones, the only thing that would keep her from being identified as a tribal member was her fair skin and freckles. Shockingly blue eyes were framed by the ugliest pair of glasses Tsisdu had ever encountered. The expression "birth control glasses" came to mind. *I wonder if it's an attempt to discourage attention. If so, she needs a way looser shirt.*

"Mr. McTavish, how good to see you. Tess Davenport, meet your new boss Tsisdu McTavish. He's the CEO of the resort and casino. Tess is my new assistant. She was studying resort management at UT when the Invasion happened."

He pulled back his hand as the girl curtseyed. "Pleasure to meet you, Mr. McTavish."

That's odd. "Welcome to the company."

"'Tsisdu' that's Cherokee for 'rabbit' isn't it? You don't look anything like a rabbit."

Direct and with a voice that sounds like sex

"Tess..." Loretta's tone was straddling amused and scandalized.

"You know Cherokee? Not many whit... Caucasians study it."

"I took a course at UTK before... some words stuck." Tess replied.

"In Cherokee folklore, the rabbit is a bit of a trickster spirit along with being wise. I was born nearly a month early, catching my parents walking in the woods unawares. So, they named me Tsisdu."

"Your mother tells a slightly different version of that." Loretta said dryly.

"Hush Loretta. So, what does she have you doing Tess?"

"I will be splitting my time when I'm not shadowing her between waitressing and housekeeping." Tsisdu gave Loretta a sharp glance. "And yes, Loretta told me what 'housekeeping' includes. I don't have a problem with it." Tess grinned. "Worst case, I can lay back and think of England."

"Strictly voluntary. I want you to be clear about that."

Tess dimpled. "Loretta made that plain boss. To be blunt, I enjoy sex. This will just let me enjoy it and make a little extra money on the side."

Tsisdu didn't have a response to that. He excused himself and headed back to his office with what was left of his dignity. Even otherworldly invasions didn't stop the paperwork.

***

The next morning didn't bring a herald announcing the visit. Loretta was in the middle of a report to Tsisdu and the rest of senior management when Chaske Reynolds burst through the conference room door, red faced and almost out of breath.

"Lord Spru'gil K'Rill is here. There's a Lord Ave'rll K'Rill with him. They both want rooms, and the Lord Ave'rll elf wants to talk to the liege holder. Is that you Mr. McTavish?"

"Close enough. Chaske, are you all right?" The boy was a funny color.

"Ms. Ghigau told me to get my ass to the executive conference room on the third floor and tell you what's happening. She specifically said 'don't wait on the elevator.'" He took a breath. "Sorry for cussing." the boy paused. "And sorry for not knocking." Another breath. "But Ms. Ghigau said to hurry."

Tsisdu rubbed his chin to hide his smile. The meaning of Ghigau's name fit her perfectly. "War woman can be a bit intense. But your message was very important. Go back and tell her that I am on my way. Take the elevator," he called to the boy as he left the room, A muffled "Yes sir" confirmed that Chaske had heard him.

"Early." Loretta said.

"That is very rude by El'diore standards." Sam observed.

"Rude or not, they're here. Loretta, continue the meeting." Tsisdu got to his feet. "Sam, you're with me. They didn't catch us completely flat-footed. We'll just have to make the best of it."

The pair rode the elevator down to the main lobby in silence. Sam had spent most of yesterday afternoon and early evening going over Elven protocols. He stressed several times that Lord Spru'gil wasn't typical of a House K'Rill lord. He had pronounced me ready last night and had nothing further to add. Sam wasn't big on pep talks.

Spru'gil saw us when we were about halfway to the front desk. A bellhop was standing behind a luggage cart with his usual mountain of bags and boxes. The elf's gesticulations caused him to turn, making eye contact.

"Liege man McTavish. Uruk-kuu Bonecrusher, how good to see you." One of the many, many things that Lord Spru'gil prided himself on was his command of the English language. What's challenging for those humans that have to deal with him is that he was apparently tutored by Stephen Fry. His vocabulary examples were based on the collected works of P.G. Wodehouse. The elf sounded exactly like Bertie Wooster, right down to word choices.

"Lord Spru'gil, what an unexpected pleasure. You called for me?"

"Yes. I would like for you to meet my cousin, Lord Ave'rll K'Rill. He came all the way from Charlotte to check out your fine gaming house and resort. Ave'rll be known to the human responsible for this wonderful establishment, Tsisdu McTavish of the Eastern Band Cherokee clan."

"Pleasure to meet you, Lord Ave'rll." The elf barely acknowledged Tsisdu, turning to Sam and saying something that translation rings couldn't interpret. Sam inclined his head and replied.

"I am humbled that Lord Jax'rill sends his greetings to an old cripple as myself."

"Tsisdu, I'm going to my room to freshen up. Can you send Daisy up the Presidential suite. That's a good man. Let's plan on dinner at six o'clock in the private dining room I favor. You should be done with all the tedious bookkeeping by then, cousin?"

The look Ave'rll gave his relative would have melted a Bradley faster than dragonfire. "At least far enough along to need a meal," the elf ground out.

"Capital. Tsisdu, be sure to have Uruk-Bonecrusher come. He has the best stories."

With that, he swept off, bellhop and luggage cart trailing behind. I caught the wink and nod of the desk clerk, so I knew the word had been passed for Daisy. I turned and made the slight bow that Sam had shown me for a lord, not one's own. "How may I be of service, Lord Ave'rll K'Rill?"

Lord Ave'rll was quiet for longer than would be considered polite. The El'diore looked remarkably like Spru'gil in the face, sharing the same Elven features. The eyes were the big difference. While Spru'gil conveyed joviality, Ave'rll's were as cold as the Blue Ridge in February.

The elf answered just before Tsisdu was going to repeat his question. "Lead me to wherever your account ledgers are kept."

Tsisdu was relieved to discover that Lord Ave'rll was fully aware of and comfortable with the idea of accounting software and computerized records. The initial review sessions with Spru'gil had been painful.

After setting up in the same conference room Tsisdu had started his day in, he acted as a go between and errand boy for Ave'rll. Initially, the elf demanded access to hard copies to spot check the online entities. After a while, he just focused on the networked laptop.

Four hours later, Ave'rll pushed the big screen laptop away and gave Tsisdu a sour look. "Your clan takes much out of Lord Jax'rill's property."

"Everything is in accord with the arrangement Lord Jax'rill' made with my tribal elders." Tsisdu cloaked his fury behind a bland expression.

"Perhaps the arrangement needs to be revisited."

I can't lose my temper. He reviewed recent tribal history in his head to calm down.

About eight months after the Invasion, Jax'rill and his retinue visited Cherokee. In an irony that wasn't lost on the tribe, Jax'rill treated with them as a vassal house rather than simply dictating terms. No one knew quite why, and no one asked. Tsisdu suspected that as a separate country within the United States that never formally took up arms against the Invasion, Jax'rill didn't see the tribe as a defeated foe, rather a new land to be annexed. He even decreed that additional lands would be added to that of the Qualla Boundary to be administered by the tribe, subject to the supervision of his appointee, one Lord Spru'gil.

Making the tribe the administrators and tribute collectors of the area was likely a move by Jax'rill to conserve his Elven and Orcish forces for more profitable parts of his territory. The area was historically poor, and its main source of revenue, tourism, had dried up after the Invasion. Jax'rill's expectations were low, and his tribute demands reflected that.

A group of Orcs has wandered into the nearly deserted casino while negotiations were going on. They discovered video slots. After a quick explanation by the floor boss on how the game worked, the off-duty warriors played. And played. By the time the agreement was hammered out, the casino had earned more revenue in three days than it had in the prior eight months. Profits grew as the word spread throughout the K'Rill territory and beyond.

By the time he mentally recited that bit of tribal history, he had formed a diplomatic answer. "Of course, the wise Lord Jax'rill can do what he will with his vassals. But being such a wise ruler, would he not wish to reward those who have so enriched his coffers making the best of this poor area?"

Lord Ave'rl gifted him with another icy stare. Then he cracked a slight smile. "Better your clan get the credit than my fop of a cousin." He paused. "Show me this 'Trading Post.' It seems to generate a lot of revenue."

The Trading Post was crowded with orcs, elves, and more than a few humans either browning the aisles, talking to staff, or standing in line with purchases in hand or items they wanted to pawn or sell. The decor was a little too cigar store Indian for Tsisdu's taste. The walls had reproductions of native American art, beadwork, clothing and weapons. Items from different tribes were jumbled together, especially the Plains Indians, that provided so much TV and movie fodder. *The marketers said this would appeal to a broad audience. The balance sheet indicates they were right.*

Ave'rll had wandered off toward the craft section of the store. He fingered a large medicine wheel that was hanging from a display. The elf seemed confused by the cross with red, yellow, black and white tips inside a stiff leather circle, with two eagle feathers dangling from the bottom.

"I thought the cross symbol was Christian. Are your people aligned with one of the White God sects?"

"The Cherokee people have many religions because religion is a matter of individual conscience. The religion of our ancestors is different from that of the various Christian sects. There are some principles that work in harmony. But to answer your question, no, we don't have any formal alliance with Christians."

"So what is this?"

"It's called a medicine wheel. The Cherokee use it as a symbol for our healers. Some use it as a focus for prayers or healing. The four spokes represent Earth, Air, Fire, and Water for many. It can mean many things to many Native Americans, it's not unique to my people."

The elf looked a little puzzled at first. Then his face moved into smooth neutrality. "Interesting. Perhaps we can discuss this further over dinner. I'm going to go to my room. I find myself a bit fatigued from travel."

An orc that Tsisdu recognized as one of Ave'rll 's guards came up to the elf and handed him a sealed envelope. "My lord. From your cousin." Ave'rll broke the seal and pulled out a bone white card. His eyes scanned the Elvish script.

"It appears that my cousin will be unable to attend dinner this evening. Probably for the best. Perhaps another time. Please have a meal sent to my room in about an hour or so." He and the orc walked away without another word.

Tsisdu swung by the kitchen on his way back to his office and updated the manager on the revised plans. He was a little surprised to see Sam sitting across from Gola. She normally left an hour ago,

The big wall monitor displayed security footage of a White hand orc that seemed to be doing unusually well with video slots. Sam suspected that the retired solider was cheating somehow. Gola and Sam regularly reviewed footage of players suspected of trying to rip off the house. She had started out as a dealer when the tribe first opened the casino and had a knack for catching cheats.

"Since your head is still attached to your body and you don't look like you have any grievous injuries. I assume the meeting went about as well as could be expected."

"Yes, although I think he has questions he hasn't asked me yet. Ave'rll and Spru'gil both canceled. I guess it's just you and me for dinner. I don't see any reason to waste the efforts of the catering staff. I want to go over some of the things Ave'rll seemed to be focused on."

"I am out of here. You two don't work so hard. Gola grabbed her purse and departed. Gola seemed to caress Sam's arm as she passed him. In turn, he seemed to pay an unusual amount of attention to the woman's backside.

No, no, no I will not think about the woman who raised me and my head of security being adults.

***

"He almost seemed disappointed that the books were clean. He made a crack about the percentage the tribe retained. He was amused to think that profitability was due to the tribe and not Spru'gil."

"Well." Sam went quiet as Tess came in with their desserts and to start clearing the table. Tsisdu could not help but notice the concerned look on her face.

"Tess, is everything okay?"

"Lord Ave'rll requested some additional food and dessert items. He also asked for me personally."

Tsisdu's blood ran cold. *Had he linked her to the death of the elf in Knoxville?* He dismissed the concern as soon as it crossed his mind. Everything west of the Smoky Mountains, at roughly the Tennessee, North Carolina border was House Cree'tip. The two houses did not get along.

"He asked for you by name?"

"Yes, I brought his dinner up to his room. He asked me to stay, but I explained that I had other duties including dropping off items at Lord Spru'gil's room. So, he let me go but asked what time my work would be finished."

"If you order her additional duties as Lord Spru'gil's sworn man, Lord Ave'rll could not override your assignment. That would protect her maidenhood." Sam interjected.

"Oh, I have no doubt he wants to have sex. I could see it in his eyes. Elves and humans are pretty much the same, telegraphing those kinds of emotions. I just don't know what to charge him." She smiled.

"The entire night. I would say that 10 pieces of gold or a thousand of your dollars would be fair recompense for a woman of your beauty." The ever practical Sam interjected.

"Thank you, Sam." Tsisdu restrained the urge to roll his eyes. "Tess, like I told you before, you don't need to do this. Tell him that you are under orders to be released no later than midnight because you have to come to my room."

Tess jerked back. Tsisdu smiled. "All you have to do is knock on the door. Tell me you're okay and leave. I just wanted to give you a way out."

"I'll bear that in mind." Tess smiled as she gathered the empty plates and departed.

"The El'diore are not as unified as they appear. I was watching one of your movies a few nights ago with Gola It was a story about a resort owner who also ran a gambling hall and tavern. I didn't understand all of it but factions that were nominally allies were actually enemies and enemies were actually friends. I think it was called 'Casablanca.' That the way the El'diore actually are. The rest of us Fae are not really much different. "

"I'm shocked, shocked to find that gambling is going on in here."

Sam looked puzzled. "I do recall that line being spoken by Captain Renault. Is there some significance to it? Other than it illustrated that the law enforcement officer was looking the other way at Rick's activities?"

"You're right. Although people today tend to say it to indicate that something everybody knows is going on. Wait a minute you were with Gola?"

He couldn't be sure because of the green skin, but Tsisdu thought Sam blushed.

"She and I are... companionable together. She takes me as I am, injuries, and all. I offered to seek the offices of the matrons, but she said that was not your way. I plan for us to be companionable for the rest of our lives."

"She's a wonderful woman. So long as your companionability doesn't interfere with your jobs. It's none of my business."

***

A loud knock on the door jarred Tsisdu awake. He had decided to stay at the resort while Ave'rll was here. The rooms reserved for staff in the event of bad weather were Spartan compared to guest suites, but the bedding was top notch. He glanced at the clock with sleepy eyes... 2:00 AM glowed in red numerals. Another knock, even louder.

Got to be Sam. No one else knocks like he's thinking about kicking the door in. "One minute."

He buckled his belt right as he got to the door. Flipping the security bolt, he opened the door to a grim-faced Sam. Loretta stood beside him, disheveled and face streaked with tears.

"We have a problem." Sam growled.

"It's Tess, she's in the infirmary." Loretta's voice cracked.

The cold tile of the casino infirmary reminded Tsisdu that he had forgotten to put his shoes on. Tayanita, one of the apprentice healers and a newly licensed RN waved them away from an area with a white curtain pulled around it. She spoke in low tones.

"Ms. Loretta brought Tess Davenport in about twenty minutes ago. She has a black eye, split lip, and bruising about her breasts, and... other areas consistent with sexual assault. She refused to allow me to do a pelvic exam. All she would say was she felt like she had been drained. I called Doctor Atsadi. He's on his way."

"She's still alive?" Sam asked.

"Yes, but barely. Her injuries are serious but not so bad to explain this kind of weakness. I did what I could. I am hoping Doctor Atsadi can explain it."

"It sounds like she was harvested by Lord Ave'ril. Normally that kills the living thing that is the focus. It's a vile practice, even by El'diore standards." Sam looked like he was going to spit.

"I should never have let her go to that bastard's room." Loretta injected in a choked voice. She was about to say more when a tall man who looked remarkably like the native American actor Graham Green strode in.

"Thank you for coming, Doctor Atsadi." Tsisdu greeted the MD and the most powerful of the tribe's medicine people. Tayanita looked relieved.

"No need to thank me for following my calling. Tsisdu, why don't you go and make some coffee in the break room. I will meet all of you there when I know something." He turned to Tayanita and asked her in Cherokee to give him the status of the patient as he moved to the curtained area.

"She's out of balance, like her life force has been drained. I did what I could to infuse her with mana, and encouraged her to rest."

Tsisdu got the message and moved Sam and Loretta to the infirmary break room before they noticed the language shift.

The hands of the break room clock had just moved to three thirty and Loretta was making another pot of coffee when Tayanita stuck her head in the door.

"Tsisdu, Doctor Atsadi would like a word. Ms. Davenport is resting. She won't be able to have visitors for a few hours. I would suggest that y'all get whatever rest you can till morning."

Sam looked displeased at first but regained his trademark impassivity. Loretta looked like she was going to argue but Sam gently took her arm and pulled her past the nurse. "Let the healers do their work. I suspect the dawn will bring some challenges and it is best that we are as rested as we can be to face them." The pair departed.

"Ms. Davenport insisted that she talk to you and only you before she would let Healer Atsadi encourage her to sleep." Shifting to Cherokee told Tsisdu that something important was going on. She led him back into the examination area where the curtain had been pulled aside.

"Here he is Ms. Tess." Atsadi said genially. Tess was sitting up in bed, dressed in an exam gown and gingerly eating a chocolate bar around bruised lips. She had the makings of a monumental shiner around her left eye. She looked exhausted.

"Tess I am so sorry." She waived him off.

"I knew what I was getting into. The sex was so-so. I guess the bigger the attitude the smaller the tackle works for elves too." Tayanita chuckled, earning her a look from the senior healer. "He didn't get rough till... he tried to drain me. Healer Atsadi tried to explain about it. And magic. He says I can do magic."

"With training, yes. We need to determine your gifts once you have regained your mana." Atsadi stated. You wanted to tell him something."

"Right, Lord Ave'rll said he needed me for a magic working in the morning. That you were more powerful than he thought. That's when I started to feel like he was sucking the life out of me. I struggled. He hit me. I was barely conscious when he tossed me and my clothes out the door of the suite. Like a guest leaving empty room service dishes outside the room.' She grimaced. "One of the other housekeeping girls found me as she was leaving a guest room and called Loretta. I work up here."

"Rest child," Atsadi touched her forehead and the young girl's eyes closed. He motioned for Tsisdu to follow him. They returned to the now deserted breakroom.

"Coffee?" Atsadi asked as he grabbed a white ceramic mug from the stack.

"No, dideyohvsgi. Thank you."

"Please Tsisdu. The resurgence of our ancient tongue gladdens my heart. But you have to admit 'teacher' is less of a mouthful."

"Will Tess be okay?"

"She will. Ironically the sexual activity probably saved her life."

"What?"

"She has magic. She also has an innate ability to draw life essence from the seed of sexual partners. The elf wasn't using a condom. He drained her, but her body was able to convert the sperm inside her into enough life force to barely keep her alive."

"You're saying she's a succubus?" Atsadi snorted.

"Does everyone play that game? No, as I explained to Tayanita after she relieved my concern about her pronouncement that she was a dungeon master, Tess is not any kind of evil demon. I gathered that she is rather promiscuous?"

"I've gotten that impression."

"A Wiccan could probably explain it better. I am just guessing here, but I suspect her desire for sexual encounters is the result of her body unconsciously gathering power. That will make her an asset to your sex worker intelligence gathering network."

"How do you..."

"Why do you think that Tayanita and I are the only ones who give the ladies their regular exams?" We're the only ones who know. I encouraged Daisy Miller to not talk to anyone about it, even those she thinks are on our side."

"She said you were going to train her. She's not Native American, much less Cherokee. The council is going to have a fit."

"The council has no sway over me or the rest of the medicine people. I don't limit my healing and other talents to the tribe. Magic is rising in all of us, not just the Cherokee. We need to conserve and train it wherever it can be found to have any hope of winning our freedom."

"That makes a lot of sense."

"That's why I am the teacher" The smile left the older man's face. "I take it there's nothing that can be done to legally balance the harm done to Tess?"

"Sam and I talked about it. Under Elven law the situation is no different from Ave'rll borrowing a hoe from Spru'gil's shed to tend his garden without asking first. Had he killed her, he would have been out the cost of the hoe. We can't push the magic drain because that would tip off the Elves that the tribe knows more about magic than the elves would be comfortable with."

"I understand. Perhaps there are other ways to redress the balance that would not expose us."

"I want justice for her. But I really want to know why he did it to start with."

"I have some ideas..."

***

Tsisdu was drying his hair after slipping on his medicine wheel pendant when his cell phone went off. Picking it up, he saw Gola's face. He punched accept. "Gola, I was just getting ready to call you." *To cancel my morning appointment so I can catch up on some sleep.*

"Come to the office. Now. Lord Ave'rll came through the door before I could make it to my desk, demanding to see you immediately."

"On my way."

He came through the door in six minutes. His hair was still damp and he hadn't brushed his teeth. He was wearing yesterday's suit. Lord Ave'rll wasn't there.

"He insisted on waiting in your office." Gola said by way of greeting.

Ave'rll was sitting in his chair, the chairs in front of his desk had been moved to the walls.

How juvenile can you be? "You wanted to see me?" Ave'rll was silent till the door shut behind Tsisdu.

"Yes. I am ordering changes to be made in the operation. You will reduce Lord Spru'gil's tribute by one and a half percent per month until you have reduced it by a total of ten percent. I will send an agent to collect the funds monthly. While I doubt the fool will even notice, if he does, then you are to lure him to visit and let me know when so I can arrange an accident to befall him."

As Ave'rll droned on Tsisdu felt his energy being drained away and the elf's words started making sense.

His own magic flared. The medicine wheel on his chest warmed. The drain stopped and his head cleared. Ave'rll frowned.

"That should have overwhelmed you."

The pressure on Tsisdu's skull increased. He felt like he was having the worst migraine of his life. The room lights went out completely. His pain eased.

The elf gritted his teeth. The pressure behind Tsisdu's eyes rose again.

My head's going to explode like some horror movie.

Two things happened just when he thought Ave'rll was going to overwhelm him. Power flowed over his body like a hot shower over chilled skin. The second thing was Ave'rll's attack buckled. Tsisdu's will steamrolled over the elf, leaving Ave'rll slack jawed, eyes glassy. Not dead, but his consciousness had taken a nap. Still there, but dormant.

He saw Ave'rll's plan. To weaken Spru'gil and eventually assassinate him. Ave'rll' would come in and 'expose' Tsisdu's embezzlement. The assassination would be blamed on tribal members acting on Tsisdu's behest, forcing the tribe to renegotiate the contract with House K'Rill to make reparations.

He even planned to eliminate Sam. Tsisdu took a grim satisfaction for Ave'rll's anger at his security manager for declining to be the elf's eyes and ears at the casino, citing the prior oaths to the tribe and Spru'gil.

Tsisdu's head ached. It was hard to concentrate. He rewove Ave'rll's memories, starting with him firmly abandoning the assassination and embezzlement schemes based on finding that the casino's accounting controls were too strong and the tribe's loyalty to Lord Spru'gil was too great.

He changed the memory of his encounter with Tess to be one of tremendous pleasure that he hoped she would grace him with again. In fact, he should tell all of his acquaintances about how wonderful the resort was to relax and have fun.

Finally, he left Ave'rll with the impression that he was exhausted from the prior night and was going to return to his room and sleep for the rest of the day.

"Mr. McTavish, I just wanted to tell you how pleased I am with your establishment. If you will excuse me." The pale-faced elf got up, stumbled, then righted himself and left the office.

"These aren't the droids you were looking for. Move along." Tsisdu muttered as he collapsed into his recently vacated chair. He looked up as Atsadi, followed by Tess entered from the side door.

"How many times do I have to tell you that our magic is nothing like the Force." Atsadi grumped good naturedly.

"Teacher, you cut it a little close there, didn't you?"

"Nonsense. Stretching like that strengthens you."

"You are looking a lot better Tess. I'm surprised that you are up." Tsisdu remarked. The black eye was gone as were the bruises on her face.

"I got here by the wheelchair in the hallway. Doctor Atsadi took the energy that he drained off Ave'rll and restored me. I'm as good as new."

"I just restored the balance child." The medicine man yawned. "Tsisdu can you get me a room? I need to get some sleep."

"Tess, are you up to getting a room comped to Doctor Atsadi?"

"Absolutely boss. In fact, I will personally ensure that he gets full housekeeping services." The woman almost purred.

She's certainly bounced back. "That's up to the doctor." Tsisdu replied mildly. Atsadi chuckled and moved toward the side door. As the door shut behind them, he heard his teacher say.

"Don't tease an old cougar child. You might find he can still bite."

Just as he was contemplating going back to bed himself, his intercom squawked. Signing, he answered. "Yes Gola."

"Sam needs to see you. After that I've cleared your appointments so you can get some sleep. I don't want to know what just happened, do I?"

"Probably not. Send him in."

Sam looked around, grabbed a chair, returned it to its usual location, and sat down.

"Lord Ave'rll tried to suborn me to betray my oaths. I refused. "

"I know."

"I have no doubt that he will have me killed. So... what do you mean, you know?"

The orc's proven that he won't betray his oaths. Plus, he's invested in Gola. Tsisdu told him everything.

By the end of the tale, Sam looked relieved. "Thank you for trusting me. Now I can aid your cause more directly."

"What?"

"I've known of your activities for some time. I did not swear allegiance to your tribe lightly. Those are to my last dying breath. My allegiance to Lord Spru'gil ends where my oath to you and yours starts. He never noticed."

"Why go against everything you know?"

"Because I know that everything I fought for was to further the people who enslave my people. I read the story of the Eastern Band Cherokee. Your ancestors rebelled against those who would uproot and crush them. Your people won a place for yourselves. I think the orcs and the other subject races can do the same if we all work together."

I extended my hand. "I think this is the beginning of a beautiful friendship."

New Model Business

by Lucas Marcum

Baltimore, Maryland
The Inner Harbor
September 15, 2020

"Why?"

"Because the point ears said so, and they're in charge."

"That still doesn't give them the right to…"

"I'm going to stop you right there." The heavyset man with glasses turned to the man beside him, facing away from the mist shrouded harbor they had been walking along. "It's because they're in charge and they told me that this was going to happen, one way or another. If you won't do this, they'll find someone who will."

"They never gave a shit about the orcs before, so why now? Also, why me? Even when the shop was up and running, we weren't anything special. Mitzer Bionics used to make thousands of them a year."

"That was during the Iraq war with the full power of federal funding and Mitzer's been out of business since the invasion." The big man sighed. "Look, Charlie. I know you're not happy about this. I know you don't like the elves. Hell, I don't like them either." He paused, then shook his head. "No. That's not the right word. I hate them and what they've done to our country, but this is the world now. Lord Denlin doesn't want any more riots here in Baltimore by disaffected Orcish veterans and their little gangbanger buddies and he really doesn't want Lord T'Mar to think he can't handle his business here and to send House troops, so he wants to try to keep the orcs happy." He paused for a moment, regarding the younger man. In the background, the squat black hull and masts of the USS Constellation could be seen, appearing like a vision out of the mist. The big man added reasonably, "Plus, you're my little brother and if I have to give this to someone, it's got to be you. You need the work."

Charlie shook his head and half-laughed at that. "Well, I won't deny that. I'm broke as shit, Mike." He regarded his older brother for a moment, then sighed. "Fine. I'll do it, but I'll need basically everything. The shop is closed, Dan was killed in the invasion, Stephanie has a couple of kids now and I have no idea where any of the machinists are. Hell, I don't even know if they make those mills and 3D printers anymore."

"My contact in the Imperial Authority says that equipment won't be an issue."

"What does that mean?" Charlie asked, skeptically.

"Well…" Mike hesitated, then sighed. "That's the catch. They'll give you everything you need to make the prosthetics and custom surgical instruments, but they want you to direct a team they have picked. I'll be your liaison to the local Imperial authorities."

"Elves?" Charlie's tone grew frosty.

"No, no." Mike added hastily. "Not elves." He hesitated, then added, lamely. "But not humans, either."

"Nope." Charlie turned and kept walking. "Not interested."

Mike said quietly, "Ten thousand Imperials now, plus a thousand every month to keep it up and running, with a commission for every Imperial subject treated for injuries sustained in the service."

Charlie stopped in his tracks and turned to face his brother. He regarded him for a moment, then shook his head slowly. "That is a lot of money."

"Yeah." Mike nodded, "A lot of people would jump at this."

"It is, but..." Charlie hesitated, then stated, "I don't want to be seen as working for the elves. Someday, this will be over and then..." His voice trailed off.

"Listen." Mike's usual jovial face was solemn. "I get it, but we gotta do what we gotta do to survive. We both got families to feed and this will help us both."

"Yeah." Charlie stuck his hands in his pockets and turned and glanced out over the Inner Harbor. The mist was clearing and the Constellation was clearly visible now, sitting in the dark waters of the harbor like a beast out of time. "Yeah." After a long moment, he turned back to his brother. "Okay. I'll do it."

The relief in Mike's voice was palpable, "Good. We're going to help a lot of people."

"Elves aren't people." Charlie stated flatly.

"We aren't working with the elves. We're working mostly with orcs."

"Orcs aren't people, either. They killed a shitload of people in the invasion."

"Yeah, but they don't want to be here — they were forced to come. They just want to be left alone. That by itself makes them better than the elves."

"I guess." The two brothers stopped and faced each other. "What's next?"

Mike pulled out a thick manilla envelope from his coat and held it out to Charlie, who took it. "We need to go get your 'experts'." He waggled his fingers in the air in quotation marks as he said the word.

"You can't be serious." Looking up from the envelope, Charlie asked skeptically, "The Baltimore City Correctional Center?"

"I wish this was a joke, but apparently these so-called experts are a real pain in the ass for the Imperium."

Opening the envelope, Charlie thumbed through several papers, frowning as he did. He held one up and read, "Garok Wargslayer of the Shattered Tusk Clan. Formerly a captain of heavy infantry, apparently fought in a bunch of wars back in the Old World. He was injured in the Battle of New York, deemed unsalvageable and discharged in 2020." He looked up, "Mike, this guy has a rap sheet like O.J. Simpson." Mike shrugged. Charlie continued, "Eighteen charges of aggravated assault, dozens of drunk and disorderly, multiple for breaking and entering, assaulting police officers, minor crimes against the Imperium, I mean — it goes on and on." He shook his head, "Whatever." He flipped the page, "And this one is a goblin gangster — literally. Apparently, he was arrested for and is awaiting trial on criminal conspiracy and racketeering. His record goes on for three pages, but the charges keep getting dismissed. That's not suspicious at all." He held up a glossy color photo. "He's got an eyepatch though, so at least he's got style."

"Charlie, I didn't pick them." Mike replied, tiredly. "I'm just a middle man."

"I know. I'm just giving you a hard time." With a frown at the last piece of paper, Charlie muttered, "This is interesting. This one doesn't have a criminal record." He read for a moment, then he looked up at his brother. "She's a dwarven artificer."

"So?"

"SHE is a dwarven artificer and apparently her crime is... insolence? I didn't know that was a crime."

Shrugging, Mike replied, "I saw that too. Maybe it is a crime for the elves."

Charlie held up the photo. The mugshot showed a plain but pretty woman with chestnut brown hair in neat braids. She had a slightly upturned nose, with a smattering of freckles on her cheeks. Her left eye had a large, dark bruise around it and her expression was of calm amusement, tinged with defiance. "She's cute." He shook his head. "I can't believe there's one here."

"She is cute." Mike replied. "She looks like our cousin Molly from Boston. And one what here? A dwarf?"

"A dwarven woman. Didn't you read the Imperial material on the dwarves? Their women are almost all held hostage back in some mountain fortress someplace and the men forced to work on pain of their death and extermination of their species."

"So..." Mike looked at his brother. "What does that mean?"

"It means that they're about as rare as anything we've ever seen and it gives us a huge advantage when working with the dwarves."

"And that's important because..." Mike gestured at his body. "Remember, little brother. I'm an overweight, middle-aged bureaucrat. I live in a world of paperwork and processes, not business."

"It means, you paper pushing tool, that her presence will almost by default get us access to the dwarven artificers and engineers and their tools and materials."

"Like what?" Mike asked, "I thought prosthetics were mostly plastic and carbon fiber and stuff."

"Before the invasion, sure." Charlie stuffed the papers back into the envelope. "But now we know there's a ton of stuff out there that we don't have access to."

"Like... raw materials?"

"Exactly." Charlie stuck his hands back in his pockets. "The stuff that the elves make their armor out of is called mithril. It's as light as titanium but twice as strong and not nearly as brittle. It's also way easier to work. They also use adamantine for weapons and rings and stuff. He regarded the older man for a few seconds and added, "It occurs to me that they're practically giving us a team that knows how to find it and work it. If we were up to no good, we could cause all sorts of problems with this."

"Yeah, the thought crossed my mind, too." Mike replied. "I don't think Lord Denlin is that subtle, though. Vicious and egocentric but not subtle." He frowned reflectively. "His old Spymaster would have used a group like this to set traps for the resistance, but... she's not with us anymore."

Nodding, Charlie thought back to last year when the discovery of the hated and feared elven Spymaster's horrifically mutilated body had been discovered in the harbor, shocking the city of Baltimore. The perpetrators of the gruesome murder had never been caught and the Imperial Authorities discouraged asking questions or discussing the incident, which merely led to more rumors. "Yeah."

After a moment, he shook his head. "Listen, for now let's just try to get the shop back open. If making a hook hand or two for an orc gets us back in business taking care of Americans, I can live with that." He turned back to his brother. "Ok. Let's do this. Sullivan's Custom Prosthetics will take the contract."

"All right." Mike grinned broadly, "I think this is going to be a very profitable venture."

***

-The Interview-

A Week Later
903 Greenmont Avenue
Central Baltimore

"What am I doing?" Charlie muttered to himself as he looked up at the grey stone building of the old prison. It dominated the run-down neighborhood, with its massive three-story granite walls, faux turrets and rings of razor wire at the top. Stone arches decorated the facade, giving the venerable prison the appearance of a castle out of antiquity. "Ok, Charlie. Maximum effort." Taking a deep breath, he looked at the letter in his hand, then stepped forward and pressed the buzzer for the visitor's entrance.

Several minutes later, he found himself following a young, slightly chubby corrections guard through a set of steel double doors and into a corridor. The walls had been painted white at some point in the past but time and moisture had turned them into a sickly yellow, compounded by the cheap fluorescent lights, which buzzed away high overhead.

84

The guard indicated a metal door with a mesh window. "This is the consultation room. You can talk to them here. The processing will be done probably tomorrow, and you can be here to pick them up at one or so." The guard eyed him for a moment, then added dubiously, "I hope you know what you're doing. There's a reason these three are in here."

"Yeah. Me too." Charlie straightened his jacket and stepped forward into the room. The guard said, "Just push the buzzer button when you're done and I'll come escort you out."

"Okay." Charlie moved into the room and sat down at a desk attached to the wall that faced a thick plexiglass window. Through the window was a mirror of the room he sat in, except there were three chairs and rings bolted into the desk for restraints. Speakers were implanted into the walls on either side.

He waited for several minutes, then looked up as the door opened. A guard entered, leading several figures, all manacled at the wrists and dressed in bright orange prison jumpsuits. The first was short, with light green skin, a sharply featured face and a casual, cynical air about him. His pointed ears had multiple holes, clearly for earrings and his jet-black hair was swept smoothly back. His right eye was covered with an eyepatch but the other was razor sharp, sizing Charlie up even though the glass.

Immediately behind him was a stocky, plainly pretty woman, standing about four feet tall. Her chestnut hair was in a thick braid down her back, stretching to her waist. Charlie recognized the dwarven woman from the photograph and noticed her startling green eyes, something he hadn't seen in the mugshot in the packet. He also noticed that she now had a second black eye to match the one from the photo and her lower lip was swollen. Upon seeing Charlie, she smiled; her eyes twinkling with amusement as if at some secret joke.

Behind her came the biggest orc Charlie had ever seen, standing at least eight feet tall with wide shoulders and rippling with muscle. The creature had to duck his head to clear the doorframe to enter the room. At first glance, he was a monster. The beast's eyes glittered malevolently from under a prominent brow. His face was covered in scars, with the most prominent being a black and green mass of healed burns that covered the left side of his face and extended out of sight under his prison jumpsuit, giving him an intimidating, monstrous appearance. His left arm was manacled to his waist and the healed stump of his right was bound to his chest with a glowing rope that snaked around his chest, waist and down to his feet, making him take small, shuffling steps.

After several curt commands from the guard on their side of the glass, the three were seated, and their hands manacled to the desk. The guard then departed, closing their door with an echoing boom.

The orc, the dwarf and the goblin sat and regarded Charlie. After a few seconds, he said, "I'm Charles Sullivan. I was given your contact information from the authority about a job."

The goblin replied, "First of all, we'd like to thank you for taking the time to meet with us." His voice was smooth with a tinge of...

"Wait. You invited me?" Charlie asked, astonished, "And why do you have a New Jersey accent?"

The goblin frowned and replied primly, "It's technically a 'Trans-Atlantic' accent not 'New Jersey, thank you." He then grinned slyly and winked, "And call it a tool of the trade."

"We're gettin' off topic here." The dwarven woman declared in an accented, slightly husky voice. "I hae some unfinished business in here before we get out and get ta work."

"Agreed." The goblin nodded and rubbed his hands together. "First, introductions." He spread his hands as much as the manacles would allow. "I am Rizlech Graflin Fazzort the Third, but I prefer to go by my adopted country's name, Reginald Edward Falkner." He grinned, suddenly changing his friendly countenance to one of hidden menace. The sharp points of his teeth glinted in the fluorescent light. "My friends call me Reggie."

"He's th' front o' out little business venture." The dwarven woman broke in. "And damn likely ta' cause ye equal shares o' gold and trouble, much like any goblin." Reggie grinned wider at this and shrugged nonchalantly. The woman continued, "I'm Fiona Stoneweaver, of Clan Dunhallow."

She leaned forward, folding her arms and resting her elbows on the table as she regarded Charlie with interest, "Ye dinna look like a healer."

"I'm not." Charlie replied. "I have a graduate degree in biomechanical engineering but I'm not a doctor or anything."

"Hmm." The woman regarded him for a moment, then shrugged, "Well. Wouldn't be th' first time th' elves hae given us a bit of a deal." She looked at him for a moment longer, her green eyes searching his face, then suddenly smiled mischievously, "I had a wee piggie named Charlie when I was a lass. I loved me that little oinker!"

Unable to help himself, Charlie asked, "Since we're clearly off topic, how'd you get the shiners?"

"Shiners?" Perplexed, Fiona looked at the goblin, who tapped his eye. "Oh, shiners! Aye, the black eyes." She grinned, "I met a lovely young lad who wanted ta marry me." She winked, "He dinna make th' cut this round."

The massive orc rumbled in the guttural orcish tongue. Fiona replied indignantly, "I dinna mean ta knock out his teeth. It's nae me fault he hasn't a strong jaw."

The orc rumbled again, and Fiona replied huffily, "No and I'll thank ye ta mind yer own business, ya cheeky bugger." She folded her arms defiantly and glared at the orc. "Yer nae me father."

"The big fellow on the end is our friend Garok." Reggie broke in smoothly. "Don't let his looks fool you. He's a big old teddy bear."

"Aye. A teddy bear who canna mind his own business," Fiona muttered.

The orc looked down at her and a deep bass chuckle rose from his thick chest. Fiona glowered as Reggie continued, "We asked ta be put inta the work program and Lord Denlin agreed." He frowned, "I dinna think it would be fer this, but this will work nonetheless." He gestured at the orc. "Garok here can be our first client."

"Wait a second." Charlie held up a hand. "Slow down. You know what I do, right?"

"Aye." Fiona replied, forgetting her monetary spat with the orc. "We were told ye make broken warriors whole again." She frowned, "But you're nae a healer and nae a priest so I'm assumin' ye make mechanical limbs." she leaned forward, her eyes suddenly intense, "Do ye use clockwork or enchanting? What kind of materials do ye use? Enchanted or nae? What kinda tools do ye have? I'd like ta see some a' them, if we can."

"Um." Charlie hesitated, then replied, "Well in the past, we've used a combination of hydraulics, plastics, stainless steel and carbon fiber. It depends — there's a whole bunch of factors we consider during material selection..." He paused, then looked at the three, "Way too much to get into now. Tell you what. I'm supposed to pick you up tomorrow at one. In the meantime, I'm going to get back into my old workshop and see what's left. We can go over all of this then."

"Sure, sure." Reginald replied, then added smoothly, "There's also the matter of our payment."

"It will be a fair market wage." Charlie met the goblin's eye steadily. "With a signed contract."

The two held each other's eyes for a few more seconds as the dwarf and orc watched silently. Then the goblin grinned broadly, "You aren't like the other humans I've done business with. Most are intimidated by the smile. You're not." He grinned, again the points on his teeth catching the light.

"Clearly, you've never done business in East Baltimore." Charlie replied, steadily. "When we go out there to establish suppliers and shippers, he's coming." He gestured at Garok. "It never hurts to remind people to mind their manners and Baltimore is a rough town."

The goblin nodded, "I think this is going to be a very good partnership." He gestured at the run-down prison around them, "Plus, we'll be glad to get out of here. This place is no picnic. Very little money to be made in here."

"Aye, but me and Garok hae a few bits o' business to finish tonight then we ken leave." Fiona declared.

The goblin rolled his uncovered eye dramatically. "The princess and the orc there are in a feud with a rather surly cave troll named Rocco from Philadelphia that is currently incarcerated here. Apparently, he and his goons were being disrespectful."

"Disrespectful about what?" Charlie asked curiously.

The goblin signed, "Young man, when you spend enough time around dwarves and trolls you'll learn they don't really need a reason to fight. They just do. It probably looked at her wrong or made a comment about her clan or some other esoteric dwarven reason to be insulted."

Fiona replied huffily, "I'll hae ye know that me clan hae defended th' Stone Mountain an' Dunharrow Hold for thirty generations again' th' bloody trolls and I'll not see their memories disrespected!"

"And why is Gigantor involved?" Charlie asked, indicating the hulking orc sitting quietly next to the dwarven woman. "Do orcs and trolls have a problem too?"

"Yes, but it's not that in this case." The goblin eyed Fiona, who glowered back at him. "In this case, he goes where she goes. It's a whole thing." He looked back at Charlie. "Don't ask."

"Okay..." Charlie replied dubiously, then put his hands on the desk. "In that case, I guess I'll see you tomorrow at one."

"Looking forward to it." Reggie replied. He smiled again, this time sincerely without a shred of the former menace. "I think we're going to make a great team."

***

-Hot New Startup-

Charlie pulled the van up to the side of the street and parked. He got out and locked the vehicle, then walked down the street. Carefully looking around him, he settled with his back to a light pole and waited across from the large gates to the prison. After fifteen minutes or so, the small door in the middle of the gate opened and the scrawny, green tinted frame of Reggie could be seen. He was followed by the dwarven woman and the hulking orc. They paused for a moment, looking around and blinking in the bright fall sunlight.

Charlie beckoned, "Over here." Seeing him, the three trooped over and paused. Eying them, Charlie frowned. "Maybe clothing and a meal is in order?"

The goblin was incongruously dressed in baggy gym shorts and a much too large T-shirt with Macho Man Randy Savage on it. The text read 'OOOOOH YEAH!' Fiona was dressed in a pink velour tracksuit with rolled up pant legs. The top of the track suit was zipped up as far as it would go but was clearly too snug in the chest. Charlie couldn't help but notice that the dwarven woman was not only bustier than he'd expected but that her biceps strained the upper sleeves. Shaking his head, he looked at the orc. He was wearing a bright yellow pair of extremely short, seventies style basketball shorts and a cut off Baltimore Ravens jersey, which exposed his muscled and heavily scarred stomach from the ribs down.

Seeing Charlie eying their clothing, the goblin scowled and replied, "Yes. I suspect the prison staff were intending to humiliate us. I was arrested in a custom-made three-piece suit. I had it made by a friend of mine in the East Harbor and it fit me like a dream." His scowl deepening, "The staff informed us that they 'lost it', along with the Princesses' clothing and the Brutes' armor. He's quite upset about it."

Charlie looked at the orc, who stood silently, eying him. "He doesn't look upset."

"Oh, he is, my dear boy. He is positively enraged." Reggie looked up at the orc. "He just doesn't have the emotional bandwidth to express it. He's rather impaired like that. Most orcs are, you know."

The orc spoke for a few seconds in the guttural language of his people, then Reginald nodded. "Yes, we can do that." He turned to Charlie. "You know of the dining hall with a purple bell on it?"

With a frown, Charlie thought for a few seconds. "No, I don't... Wait. Taco Bell?"

"They serve crunchy flatbreads with very low-quality pureed meats in them?"

"Yeah, I suppose." Charlie looked up at the orc. "Wait. He wants to go to Taco Bell?"

"That's the one. He's a fiend for it."

As on cue, Garok's stomach rumbled loudly. Charlie looked at the orc for a moment then sighed, "Sure. We can go by a Taco Bell." He looked at Fiona, who was attempting to draw the zipper on her track suit further up. "What about you? Food first or clothes?"

"Clothin' please." She scowled, "I'm about ta hae a structural failure o' this garment if we dinna."

"Okay. We can go by a department store, then go get food. After that we'll head to the shop and start getting ready to get it back in working shape." Charlie replied. "I have a van over here. You'll have to squeeze in back. We used to use it for deliveries back in the day."

The three Fae followed Charlie to the van and climbed in, Reginald in front and Fiona and Garok in the back.

As Charlie pulled out and into the street, Reginald said thoughtfully, "As I'm sure you know by now, the elves never do anything out of altruism. Their intent is to keep the orcish and human population content by caring for the war wounded and assisting the big house of healing in the city to make surgical instruments for orcish and troll victims. This is a good and noble goal — however, we were not selected for our dashing good looks and rapier sharp wit."

"Yeah." Charlie muttered, "I'm kind of getting that there's more to this story."

"Lord Denlin has a problem, you see."

"Apart from the riots and insurgents?"

"Yes. His problem is about four foot two, with eyes the color of smoked emeralds and cascades of curly chestnut hair."

Charlie looked at the goblin, who stared out the window at the run-down neighborhood as they drove. Abandoned cars without wheels, dilapidated homes with boarded up windows and litter predominated the landscape. Here and there a forlorn figure could be seen walking, bundled up against the approaching winter.

"What did she do?"

"She has incriminating materials on several powerful elven nobles."

"So, blackmail."

"In a manner of speaking." Reggie paused, thoughtfully. "I rather suspect she was thrown into that jail hoping her mouth would get her into trouble and someone would silence her."

"Doesn't seem to have worked."

"I should say not. She befriended the brute back there and was on the verge of organizing a large-scale prison riot when we were placed into a 'special work unit' together."

"So. She's a troublemaker."

"Royalty usually are."

"So, the term princess isn't just an insult?"

"Oh, quite the contrary. She's the sole surviving heir to the Granite Throne of Dunharrow. She's quite influential." The goblin frowned, "And since her mother is currently a sentient statue, I suppose she's Queen regent of her clan as well. Kind of a high value individual to be tossing into one of the most notorious prisons on the East Coast." He paused then added reflectively, "Then again, Lord Denlin isn't exactly known for being a strategic thinker."

"How did she get blackmail material on an elven lord?"

"Not lord. Elven lords — plural." Reggie grinned. "As in more than one. And... how shall I put this delicately... Males of all species are attracted to curves." He paused, then added meaningfully, "Even elven noblemen, if you catch my drift."

"She didn't..." Charlie replied in shock.

"Oh, yes she did." The goblin smirked, "And not only did she do it, she did it every which way you can think of, with multiple scrying crystals recording and a newfangled technology the elves don't understand called a webcam."

"Holy shit." Charlie shook his head. "And I thought royalty didn't go for that sort of stuff."

"My dear boy, you will find that above all other qualities; dwarves are immensely practical. She has a weapon and she used it. Her questionable means aside, she could topple the leadership of Houses Uridor, Tavor and Che'tin tomorrow if she chose to." Reggie frowned, "The fact that she hasn't means that she's waiting to use the information to cause problems for the elven leadership at a time advantageous to her people."

"Wow." Charlie muttered. "And to think we are going to have her making prosthetics for orc veterans."

"Yes, about that." Reggie responded, "How did you get in the business of making artificial limbs?"

"I'm not really sure. I like math and biology, and biomechanical engineering seemed to be a logical fusion of the two."

"And how did you end up taking care of human warriors?"

"I guess it was my way of giving back to my nation." Charlie was quiet for a few moments, then added, "My dad never made it home from Iraq. A lot of other people's dads did, missing arms and legs. I figured I could make their lives a little better, you know?"

The old goblin nodded somberly. "War is but a series of deeply personal tragedies." He looked at Charlie. "I'm sorry about your father, if the condolences of an old goblin mean anything."

"It's okay. It happened when I was six. I don't remember him as well as I want to." Charlie replied simply, "My big brother Mike had a hard time with it for a long time but we got through it."

"I understand." Reggie replied, gently. "My little sister Clarissa was the captain of a destroyer in the campaign against the Ironfist Clans in the Western Reaches. She and her crew were killed when the last of the great dwarven warfleets destroyed the Fleet of the Eternal Moon. They say her destroyer went down with its guns blazing and flags flying." He was silent for a moment, looking out at Baltimore harbor as they drove, "That was nearly three hundred years ago and I remember her and her razor-sharp wit like she was here yesterday." He shook his head and added with a bite in his tone, "I will give the elves this — they excel at making others do their dirty work for them."

Charlie nodded silently, then slowed the van. Ahead of them, several Baltimore police cars were pulled over, their lights flashing. Four human and two orc officers had five or six orcs handcuffed on the ground and were pointing rifles at them. As Charlie and Reggie watched, one of the orc policemen delivered a vicious series of kicks to one of the cuffed prone figures. He was soon joined by several of the humans, raining blows on the restrained orc.

"Seems best we continue on our business." Reggie observed soberly. "This city remains as tense as when I was arrested."

"There's a Target about fifteen minutes ahead. You guys can get clothes and sleeping bags and stuff. We're going to bunk you in the shop until we get up and running."

***

"This is it." Charlie announced, shutting off the van. "Or what's left of it, anyway."

Climbing out, he made his way towards the nondescript building in the industrial area. The smell of rotten fish and seawater reminded him how close they were to the harbor and the litter blowing in the streets silently told the story of a dying part of the city.

"'Tis a cheery area." Fiona remarked, looking around. "All we need are a few corpses strewn about and it would look like a proper sacked city." She looked at Charlie, who had stopped in front of a set of sturdy double doors, reinforced with steel and wire mesh on small windows. "What happened here?"

"Baltimore was in rough shape even before the elves came." Charlie replied, sorting through his keyring. "Our industry moved overseas in the eighties and with them went the jobs. That started a cycle of job losses, which increased crime and when crime increased people left the city. Eventually, the only people left are those who can't leave or have enough money to where it doesn't matter how bad the crime and economy are."

"So why did you stay?" Reggie asked, his one good eye locked onto Charlie's face.

"I grew up here," Charlie replied, his tone growing defiant, "My family has been here since before the War of 1812 and I'm not about to leave now."

"Well, I guess I'm nae one ta talk about defendin' a lost cause." Fiona replied with an uncharacteristic, sad half smile.

"Baltimore isn't a lost cause." Charlie replied stubbornly. "All cities have cycles. We'll come back from this. We always do."

The big orc rumbled in his guttural tongue. Fiona translated, "He says no one is defeated until they choose to be." She looked up at the towering creature, fondly. "He's surprisingly inspirational, fer a walkin' nightmare."

Shaking his head, Charlie unlocked the door and entered. Passing through a small room with an empty receptionist desk, he unlocked another door, this one of reinforced steel.

Running her fingers over the reinforced doorframe, Fiona raised an eyebrow, "These fabrication' machines o' yours — dangerous or valuable?"

"Both, but only really valuable to the right people." Charlie indicated the city outside with a nod of his head, "The people hanging around in this neighborhood wouldn't see the value." He grinned wryly, as he worked the second set of locks. "They would strip the copper out of them to sell."

"Aye." Fiona nodded, "Barbarians always strip technology fer the components. 'Tis seen throughout history."

"They aren't barbarians." Charlie replied giving the dwarf a hard look. He entered the large, dark room ahead of them. "They're regular people, just poor and desperate — like most these days." He found a large switch in the dim light and pushed it up. As the banks of overhead lights powered on, he added, "And poor and desperate are two subjects I know more about that I ever wanted to." He gestured at the now illuminated workshop. "Here we are." The cold fluorescent light revealed dozens of machines under dusty tarps, shelves of boxes neatly labeled. Dozens of tools were hanging on the walls at several stations near carefully posted warning signs and safety equipment. "This is where we machine and manufacture the prosthetics." He pointed at machines in turn. "That's a 3D printer that we use to make sockets. That's a lathe to trim carbon fiber rods." Pointing at a door on the far side, he continued, "That's the machine shop. We inherited it with the building and actually found it really valuable to be able to make our own components." He frowned, "We don't have a machinist anymore, though. Our machinist Jonah moved to Arizona right before the invasion."

"Oh, I'm sure we ken make it work." Fiona's eyes were shining looking at the workshop. "What do we hae in the way o' raw materials?"

"Stainless steel, Carbon fiber, injection moldable plastics. Stuff like that."

"Oh, no. That'll nae do." She turned to the goblin and said thoughtfully, "Do ye think ye can set up a supplier fer a few things fer me?"

"That's what I'm here for, your majesty." Reggie replied smoothly. "I'll start first thing tomorrow. What did you need prioritized?"

"Iron." The dwarf replied promptly. "Lots and lotsa iron. Also, I'll need the materials ta make a forge." Fiona looked at Charlie, "Charlie, my dear. Do we have any outside space? Will need ta be fenced in, I'm afraid."

"Um... We have a loading dock. It's gated."

"That'll work. I'm goin' ta need it for the forge." Fiona rubbed her hands together, happily. "Now, if you lads will get ta work on that, I'll be takin' a look around." She wandered off into the workshop, humming happily. Occasional exclamations of excitement could be heard as she explored the abandoned shop.

With a sigh, Charlie turned to Reggie and eyed him for a minute. Now dressed in a polo shirt and khakis with dockers, the goblin looked like a short green banker on a business trip. "Why does she need iron?"

"Because she knows her customers." Reggie grinned and indicated the orc. The orc grinned, his horribly scarred face splitting to reveal large tusks. He held up his stump as if to say 'See?'.

Charlie shook his head. "That's gonna weigh a ton. Won't they want something lighter? Carbon fiber or stainless steel?"

"See, you know orcs, but you don't really know orcs. Their style is..." The goblin hesitated, searching for the right words. "Well. Let's just say if brutalism was a fashion aesthetic, that would be the orcish sense of style. Plain, heavy, usually made of iron and preferably with lots of spikes."

"So, we're making weapons." Charlie stated flatly.

"No, we're making prosthetics for orcs." Reggie corrected him, "The fact that they like to use them as weapons is entirely beside the point." He eyed the man next to him, then asked suddenly, "How are you in a fight?"

"What?" Startled, Charlie stammered, "I don't... I mean..."

With a sigh, the goblin waved his hand. "Never mind. We'll take the orc and the dwarf." He produced a small notebook and jotted something down. "We can start day after tomorrow. Friday night most of the longshoremen will be out drinking anyway." He frowned, "We'll need a prototype first." He looked up from the notebook. "What are you waiting for?" He indicated the orc. "Start measuring him!"

"Um." Charlie replied, "I can do that but for what?" He stopped, "Also — let's try to remember this is my business."

"Yes, yes." Reggie replied, soothingly. "I haven't — it's your business, it's your equipment and you're keeping us out of prison." He gestured around them, "You're also the only expert we have in these things and we need to get a prototype fast, so we need you to apply those talents of yours."

Staring at the goblin for a moment, Charlie thought about this then relented, "Fine. I'll measure and make an initial socket." He pointed at the goblin, "Tomorrow, I'm going to have a contract for you three to sign."

"That's fine." Reggie replied, "Tomorrow, we also start the fun part."

With trepidation, Charlie asked, "What exactly is the fun part?"

With a sharklike grin, the goblin replied, "Advertising."

Staring at the goblin for a moment, Charlie sighed. "I have a feeling there's more to it than mailers."

"Oh, there is but it'll be fun." Reggie returned to his notebook, then looked back up, "Incidentally, do you know how to suture?" In shock, Charlie stared at the goblin, then saw the slow smile creeping across the goblin's face. "Just kidding."

"Jerk. You almost had me."

With a laugh, Reggie pointed at Charlie, "You should have seen your face!" He shook his head chuckling and bent back to his notebook, "I will do the suturing. Your job is to get good video."

"Of what?"

"What do you think?" Reggie looked back up. "The violence, of course. How else do you sell stuff to orcs?"

"I guess I hadn't really thought about it." Charlie admitted, "So we're going to go out and pick fights?"

"We?" Reggie scoffed, "No. We are not going to." He gestured at Garok's towering figure. "He is and he's going to do it with a prosthetic — 'purpose built for the orc who has everything'."

"Wait." Charlie held up his hands. "So let me get this straight. We're going to build an improvised prosthetic hand of some kind, then we're going to have Gigantor here go beat the shit out of someone with it, capture it all on tape and use that video to advertise?"

"Well, that's sort of the general gist, yes." The goblin admitted, "It would be better if it were several someone's getting beaten and if he was clearly using a purpose-built appendage designed for an orc to do it but... yes. That's basically it."

Charlie stared at the goblin for a few seconds then slowly shook his head. "And this will bring in clients?"

"Oh, you'd better believe it." Reggie indicated to Garok, "Right, big fella?" The orc nodded and chuckled, again his scarred visage splitting into what was his smile. He rumbled for a few seconds in the harsh orcish language. The goblin laughed, "He says if we kill a couple people accidently it would be even better, but he understands how you might not want that." Reggie grinned and added, "He says he wants to be respectful of you and your business."

"Thanks for that." Charlie replied sourly.

"Anytime!" Reggie replied cheerfully. "So, I'm going to start making some phone calls. Let's get busy — we have a lot of work to do before Friday night!"

With a sigh and a scowl, Charlie nodded and looked up at the orc, "Follow me."

***

-Aggressive Advertising-

Later That Week
Hacksaw Sally's Bar and Music Hall
1300 Russel Street

Charlie eyed the building dubiously, then looked at Fiona and Reggie next to him. He then looked at Garok, who was dressed in battered denim jeans, a flannel shirt that was rolled up on the forearms, exposing his new iron right hand strapped onto the stump of his arm. The crudely shaped, flat metal fingers were curled into a fist, giving it the impression of the flat blades of an excavator.

"Is that going to work?" He asked, nervously. "I mean, after he starts using it for... whatever."

The orc looked down at his new hand and flexed his forearm. The metal claws snapped open and shut menacingly, then looked up and grinned — a broad, toothy grin.

"Oh, it'll work." Fiona said confidently, "I'll be honest, 'tis a wee bit of a slap-dash job but it came together nicely. Might even become a best seller." The orc rumbled and she snapped back, "I had ta work with that I had dinna I? Ye need to be patient, ye great green wretch."

"What did he say?"

"'Tisn't what he wanted." Fiona replied with a dark look at the orc. "He wanted, in his words mind ye, 'A hammer that has a blade that retracts and can also be used as a fork'."

100

Bursting out laughing, Charlie replied, "He wants a hammer-knife-fist that's also a fork? That's amazing."

"Aye." Fiona replied, "Tisn't th' hammer bit that's hard. 'Tis fittin a fork inta it where it will nae bend when he hits people with it."

"Remind me to show you my Swiss Army knife after this."

"I will." Fiona replied. She turned to the orc, "Now, ye great lunk. I made it plenty strong, but it's nae indestructible. It ken break so bear that in mind." The orc nodded silently. Fiona frowned and muttered to herself, "Then again there is nae a stress test like a blottered orc usin' somethin' as a cudgel." She reached up and patted the orc's massive bicep. "Ye know what? Dinna worry about breakin' it. Have fun."

The four approached the door through the parking lot filled with motorcycles, battered pickup trucks and worn looking older model cars. The muted thumping of base and guitar chords could be heard through the walls. Painted on the brick wall next to the door was a large mural of a buxom redhead in a saloon dress. She had a cheeky smile and a shotgun resting on one of her provocatively cocked hips. The sign over the door read '*Hacksaw Sallys*'.

Next to the door stood two bouncers; a human and an orc. The human was very large, almost as big as the orc next to him. The orc bouncer eyed Garok for a moment then wordlessly jerked his head. He then pointed at Fiona and rumbled in a deeply accented voice, "Thought you was locked up. No trouble from you again or you're out. Mizz Grazlock's orders."

"I'll be as mild as a wee lamb." Fiona replied, her eyes sparkling. "And let Miss Grazlock know that I won't be causing trouble tonight."

The human interjected, "Seriously, Fiona. She threatened to call the Imperial Authorities if you did it again." He pointed at her sternly, "I mean it. Fighting is OK, but no fire this time."

Fiona rolled her eyes and replied huffily, "That was an accident, Thomas."

"Tell that to United Mutual insurance."

Fiona rolled her eyes, "I will nae be starting anythin' tonight. Ye hae me word."

"Then welcome back and have fun." Thomas and the orc stepped aside and waved them in. "We got a couple new bands in the lineup." He handed Charlie a flyer and added, "Welcome to Hacksaw Sally's, man. Any friend of Fiona's is a friend of ours. Just stay behind the brass rail." Charlie looked at him quizzically, "You'll see. Trust me on this one."

Nodding, Charlie followed the orc, dwarf and goblin into the dimly lit bar. The inside of the bar was a single large, rectangular room. One end was a wall spanning bar, with multiple bartenders and a large brass bell hanging behind it. Charlie noted with interest that one of the bartenders was an orcish woman. Orc women were not unheard of in Baltimore but definitely not common. The music had stopped temporarily. At the other side of the room was a large stage, with bright spotlights aimed at it. Three orcs, a dwarf with a short mohawk and a heavyset, muscular Samoan with long hair in a thick braid down his back were setting up instruments. About a dozen feet away from the bar there was a waist high, polished brass rail, with periodic spaces for people to walk through, separating the bar area from the band and the tables. There was a mixed crowd of humans, orcs and dwarves seated around the bar, mostly sticking with their own kind. Fiona and Garok led the way to a table close to the brass rail. He noticed a small sign with orcish and dwarvish runes on it, then underneath in English: '*Enter at your own risk*'. He indicated the sign with a raised eyebrow.

Reggie grinned, "That, my dear boy, is why we're here."

Under his breath, Charlie muttered, "Oh, brother." The four sat down. Charlie looked at the flyer in his hand. The painting of the woman from outside was on the front, as was the address of the bar. He flipped the flyer over to the lineup. He read them aloud. "So, this is tonight's lineup: 'Bloodtooth, Soul Devourer, Baby Faced Timmy and the Cannibals, Hammerfall, The Goulash Boyz, Wolfhound, and apparently a dual headliner of Warmother and Iron Teeth Mayhem." He looked up, "I've never heard of any of these."

"Well, no offense Charlie — but you look more like a smooth jazz type of fellow." Catching Charlie's dark look, the goblin grinned, "Joking, joking! But… this is a biker bar that caters to the rougher elements of the city. Some of these bands are orcs."

"You're kidding."

"Not at all. Apparently, they've developed quite a taste for it. Reminds them of their ancestral music, apparently."

The orc woman from the bar stepped up to the table and stood there silently. She was easily over six feet tall, and wore a low-cut black tee shirt and jeans. Her biceps rippled under the shirt, and she had tattoos on the sides of her neck, extending down to her shoulders and arms. Her skin was a lighter shade of green than Garok, who Charlie interestedly noted wouldn't meet the orc woman's eye.

Fiona slapped the table, and declared, "I'll hae a bottle o' the McCallen twelve and my handsome but silent friend here will hae th' house swallie." Fiona looked around the bar, which had started to fill up with more humans and orcs. She held up two gold pieces, "And ye keep those drinks flowin'. Me boyo here is havin' a wee celebration'." She slapped Garok on the forearm. The orc maid took the gold pieces and vanished without a word.

"We didn't order drinks though." Charlie remarked, watching the crowd respectfully part and let the orc woman through.

"Oh, we're going to stay sober tonight." Reggie replied. "This is not the night for our types to drink. We need our wits about us and you need to keep your phone ready to film."

"Speaking of…"

Charlie broke off when the Samoan at the microphone stepped up and shouted,

"GOOD EVENING HACKSAW SALLY'S! IT'S A GREAT FUCKING NIGHT FOR SOME METAL!!!" The crowd roared in reply. The big man yelled, "WE ARE BABY FACE TIMMY AND THE CANNIBALS! ONE,

TWO, THREE, FOUR!!!" The dwarf on the drum set hit a steady, aggressive beat, then the guitars of the orcs behind him burst into life and he let out a long, guttural scream into the microphone. The harsh, rhythmic music hit them like a tidal wave. Charlie could see the orcs and humans bobbing their heads to the racing beat and heavy chords. He looked at Reggie, who grinned and gave him a thumbs up. Fiona was leaning back on the rail, eying the crowd. She saw something, then nudged Garok and pointed at the biggest orc in sight, currently sitting several tables over. Garok looked at him for a long second then nodded once. The orc woman returned, set Fiona's bottle of scotch on the table and a glass, then slammed down a massive mug that looked like it had been carved from stone. She then turned and left silently. Charlie caught a whiff of the drink and coughed, his eyes watering.

Seeing this, Reggie laughed and leaned close and yelled, "Orcs don't go for complex flavor profiles. That's probably fermented in the back in an old drum and cut with rubbing alcohol."

"It smells like gasoline!" Charlie shouted back.

"That might be in there, too!" Reggie replied, "Here we go." He indicated the other orc, who had seen Garok staring and was staring back, his eyes hard. Garok slammed the eye watering brew and imperiously waved his new iron hand in the air, signaling for another. The two orcs continued this for several more songs, staring at each other and drinking. There was a pause in the music and a sudden moment of silence descended onto the bar. The two orcs' staring match had gotten the attention of most of the patrons. Garok suddenly and deliberately leaned over and spit on the floor in the direction of the other orc. The other orc's face darkened, and he leapt to his feet, hurling the stool he had been sitting on out of the way. Shouting in the orc guttural language, the challenge was clear.

Remembering his task, Charlie pulled out his phone and started to film. Garok stood up slowly, towering a full head over all of the other orcs in the bar, including his challenger. He stepped forward, towards the smaller challenger.

Seeing the fight about to begin, the orc on the bass guitar started playing a low, fast and ominous bass riff, cutting through the bar adding to the tension.

The Samoan front man leaned into his microphone, "Well, we don't come here for the food, do we folks? RING THAT BELL, BABE!" He pointed across the room at the orc woman behind the bar.

The orc reached up to the large brass bell behind her, grasped the rope and gave it two hard pulls. The clear tones of the bell swept through the bar. The Samoan screamed, "LET'S GO!!" The band once again erupted into the pulse pounding heavy metal and the two orcs leapt at each other.

The challenger swung a massive fist at Garok. He casually leaned out of the way, letting the wild swing sail harmlessly by then returned a contemptuous backhand with his iron fist. It struck the orc in the jaw and sent him flying backwards into his tablemates, bowling them over. The other orcs struggled to their feet and looked down at their now unconscious friend lying in the wreckage of the table. They looked back up at Garok for a split second, then all four of them charged. Garok met the next foe with the iron hand again, sending him flying into a nearby table full of dwarves. There was an angry stream of dwarven expletives, and a mug flew from the dwarven table over Charlie's head and hit a table full of human bikers behind them. Suddenly the room erupted into violence. A half dozen brawls broke out with Garok fighting three orcs simultaneously, while the group of dwarves divided between assaulting the single orc tangled in the wreckage of their table and the rest charging the enraged human bikers. Charlie stood up just as a furious dwarf tackled a human and blasted through the table, landing in a heap of broken furniture.

Reggie yelled to Charlie, "Get to the bar!" Charlie nodded and ducked as Garok threw one of his opponents at another of his foes, missed and knocked down three dwarves that were kicking the prone biker. His eyes wild, the biker popped up and pulled a knife and approached a dwarf from behind.

Seeing the weapon, Garok turned his attention from his battered orc foes and reached over and with his mechanical hand. He caught the biker's wrist and twisted casually. The snap of bone was clearly audible over the din of the brawn and the heavy metal and the biker fell to the ground, moaning.

From the darkness, a figure that even dwarfed Garok emerged and roared like an angry dragon.

Charlie looked up, his jaw dropping at the sight. The beast was eight feet tall at least, with slate grey skin, deep sunk eyes and snaggled teeth visible through the snarl. He was wearing ragged shorts and a black shirt with the sleeves ripped off. The front of the shirt had the word 'OBEY' on it in large white letters. It took a deep breath and let out another bellowing roar. Unphased, Garok stood to his full height and roared defiantly back and raised his fists — iron and flesh.

Feeling someone tug at his wrist, Charlie looked down to see Reggie with a shocked expression on his face, shouting, "THEY HAVE A CAVE TROLL!"

Seeing an opening, Charlie dashed for the rail and dove over it, landing hard on the suddenly open floor space. A few battered combatants of multiple species lay on the bar side of the rail, all either panting for air, unconscious or bleeding. The orc woman stood in between the rail and the bar with a large axe handle on her shoulder, calmly watching the fight evolve. Clearly, this was her area and there would be no fighting on this side of the rail. The doorman's instructions suddenly made sense. Turning, Charlie focused the camera on the now devastated table area of the bar. The smaller fights had stopped, with orcs, dwarves and humans scrambling for cover, their enmity apparently forgotten as they hurriedly helped each other out of the way of the pending clash.

The band frontman called out, "Oh shit! Here we go, it's the main event! Yo, Mikey give me fifty on the orc! HIT IT BOYS!!!" The orc on the bass guitar again began to strum a fast, low two tone beat, quickly picked up in a counter melody by the dwarf on the drums. With a roar, Garok leapt at the troll as the lead singer let out another primal scream and the heavy metal once again erupted.

As the two massive creatures traded blows, Charlie noted with amazement that the fighting around the bar had all stopped — replaced with a furious series of side betting between former combatants, with money changing hands and odds being placed on a half dozen aspects of the fight. The orc and the troll rained blows on each other furiously for several minutes. Suddenly, there was a metallic CLANG as of a trash can being hit with an iron bar and Charlie saw something skitter across the floor in front of him and stop by his foot. He noted with shock that it was a bloody tooth the size of a golf ball. There was a massive THUMP and Charlie looked up in time to see the cave troll hit the ground twitching, then slump unconscious.

Garok stood alone in the middle of the ruined bar, surrounded by smashed tables and chairs, blood stains and spilled drinks. His shirt had been torn away, and his heavily muscled body was covered in bruises. His already scarred face was a mass of blood, but his eyes blazed fiercely. He suddenly roared and shot his prosthetic hand in the air in triumph.

The Samoan metal singer yelled, "HAIL TO THE CHIEF, BABY!!!! THIS ONE IS FOR THE IRONFIST!!"

The bar erupted in cheers and the band broke into the familiar notes of 'Iron Man'. Fiona appeared out of the gloom, sliding off a bloodstained pair of brass knuckles off of her right hand. Her lower lip was swollen but her green eyes sparkled with excitement.

"I hae got us a machinist and a master smith contract lined up. They'll be by tomorrow ta' get ta work." She looked at Garok, who was still roaring and shaking his fists in the air like a prizefighter. "He seems ta hae enjoyed himself, hasn't he?" She shook her head in amusement. "Let's collect him before she lays claim ta our lad." She jerked her head at the orc maiden, who was watching Garok impassively.

"She doesn't seem interested," Charlie replied, fascinated despite himself.

"Oh, dear boy." Reggie chuckled, "That stare is the orc equivalent of practically panting with desire. That performance he put on alone would be enough to get the attention of any orc maiden." He perked his ears up, "And also apparently the attention of the cops. It's time for us to go." The faint wail of sirens could be heard outside. Fiona bounced over to Garok and seized his hand, dragging him towards the rear of the bar towards the kitchen exit. Reggie paused long enough to thrust a heavy bag of gold at the orc maiden and said, "For Madame Grazlock. Do give her my regards." The orc woman nodded and took the bag, her eyes not leaving Garok's hulking figure as the four fled through the back door of the bar and into the night.

***

-New Business Model-

Later the next week
The Workshop
2237 South Clinton Street

Charlie entered the front room of the building and stopped. Reggie had been busy the past few days. There were now three more desks, two of which were manned by goblins, both currently on the newly installed telephone extensions and tapping on computers as they did. A third goblin was scrutinizing paperwork, then filing it carefully. None of them looked up as Charlie came in. Reggie was leaning over one's shoulder, watching the screen intently. He pointed suddenly. The goblin nodded and started tapping keys. Reggie looked up and saw Charlie.

"Charles, my dear boy. How are things?"

Taking of his jacket, Charlie replied slowly, "Fine. I see you've been busy." He indicated the desks and the goblins, "Where did you get this and who are they?"

"Ah! Yes." Reggie rubbed his hands together in a satisfied manner. "Those two are old associates of mine. We worked together on a previous business venture. I think the one on the left is the brother of my cousin's husband on my sister's side but I could be mistaken." He looked at the goblin scrutinizing the paperwork. "That one — unfortunately — is a direct blood relation of mine; a third cousin, twice removed. He's got a particular set of skills that we don't need at the moment, so he's making sure all the 'I's are dotted and 'T's are crossed." He smirked, "Literally. I have him double checking every paper in this place for them."

"What are his skills?" Charlie asked, "Can we put him to work?"

"Well..." Reggie hesitated, then sighed. "His skills involve getting into and out of places that he's not supposed to be."

"Like... buildings? Safes? Locked doors? What are we talking about here?"

"Erm... Yes, all of them." Reggie frowned at the young goblin, "He's a genius with all of that stuff but an absolute idiot when it comes to everything else."

"You think we're going to need a safecracker?" Charlie asked, carefully.

"One never knows." Reggie replied reasonably, "Plus, one thing I know for sure is that he's not is a spy for the elves."

"Aren't most goblins willing to do whatever it takes to make money?"

"That's a very hurtful stereotype, Charlie." Reggie replied reproachfully, "And while not entirely untrue, my extended family are no fans of the empire. We've paid far too much in both blood and gold to them over the millennia." He regarded the goblin scrutinizing the paperwork with his tongue sticking out of the corner of his mouth. "He's also far too stupid to be a spy." He looked at Charlie for a moment, then shook his head. "Anyway, you said you had someone lined up to run the business end?"

"Yes. Her name is Zuri. Her brother and I were friends in college."

"I see. And her experience?"

"She ran a chain of Kinko's here in Baltimore before the invasion. Now she delivers food to make a living and hates it."

"What is this 'Kinko's?"

"Office supplies. Paper, desks, pens. Things like that." Charlie replied, "They also do services like copying and printing." He indicated the empty human sized desk. "It's a very similar skillset to Susan, our last office manager. She'll be fine."

"Very good. She'll handle the legitimate business side of this enterprise." The goblin grinned, his teeth again glinting. "I'll handle the rest."

"Yeah, about that..." Charlie replied, "I really don't want to get arrested."

"Nobody's going to get arrested, Charlie." Reggie rolled his one good eye. "We're legitimately making prosthetic limbs for disaffected veterans here." He eyes Charlie for a moment, then added, "As for my side ventures, you'll find yourself more than adequately compensated. We're already working with our colleagues in the shipping industry to start facilitating sales of high value goods and services into and out of Central America. High risk, very high reward. I'll fill you in on that later." He jerked his head at the workshop. "In the meantime, the Princess and the Beast are in there working on that iron claw again. They had a few ideas for a better fit they wanted you to work on."

"Yeah." Charlie shook his head and started for the door. "I put some more of the video of the fight online last night. I'll do more today but I can already see it floating around social media."

There was a heavy hammering on the outer door of the building. Charlie and Reggie traded a look, then Charlie moved to the small screen that monitored the exterior doorway.

"Oh shit." He looked up at Reggie. "We have a problem."

Reggie scurried over to the monitor and peered at it. The powerfully built young orc from the bar was outside, accompanied by three, much larger orcs. They stood facing the door, calmly. "This..." Reggie started, then paused, "Hmm. Something isn't right about this. The orcs usually take their lumps and move on. They don't really go in for vendettas. We'd better get the big guy. He'll know how to handle this." He turned and snapped in rapid fire Geblish at the three other goblins. The one with the paperwork dropped what he was doing and scurried off to the rear of the shop. The orcs outside hammered on the sturdy door again, the blows ringing through the building.

Moments later, Garok's hulking figure stepped through the doors from the workshop with the chestnut haired dwarven princess behind him. Without a word, he stepped to the door to the exterior. Charlie eyed the big orc. His battered face seemed to have healed already, leaving him just as scarred and intimidating as before. On his right arm, the metal tongs of the prototype had been replaced with a large, clenched fist made of iron. In between the forged fingers were dark slots. Garok slammed the double doors open and strode outside. As he did, he snapped his right arm towards the ground in a flicking motion. A foot long black blade slid out of the iron fist and locked into place with a menacing 'click'.

The four orcs outside watched him approach, motionlessly as Garok approached and stepped right into his former opponent's face. The orcs were dressing in work clothes, with one of them in a longshoreman's coverall. The younger orc stared back for a moment, then placed a fist on his own burly chest and began to speak. He spoke for several minutes, then gestured to the three orcs behind him. Garok listened, his scarred face seemingly set in stone. When the smaller orc finished speaking, he nodded once then turned and walked back inside without a word, retracting the blade into the iron prosthetic with a snap.

The four orcs looked at Fiona, Reggie and Charlie expectantly. Charlie suddenly noticed that all three of the new orcs were missing their right hands, exactly in the mid forearm.

"What the hell just happened?" Charlie whispered.

"We just got our first clients." Reggie whispered back. To Fiona he said, "My dear, it's time to work. You keep me about a week ahead on supply and material requests and I'll do my best to fill them. If these gentle folk are to be believed, there's going to be several dozen more coming this week alone."

The dwarf sighed theatrically, and beckoned the orcs to follow her. "Come on, lads. Let's see what kinda' mad ideas ye want fer yer arms." The orcs obediently followed the stocky woman into the shop, the menace suddenly gone.

"Why are they missing all their arms in the same spot?" Charlie asked, "That doesn't seem like a statistically likely accident." He shook his head, "And also weren't Garok and that guy fighting like two days ago? Do they just let that go?"

"Yes, they were fighting but Garok definitely and undisputedly won, so by rights he's in charge." Reggie shrugged, "It's an orc thing." He shut the double doors and carefully locked them behind them. "There's a lot of leaderless orcs in Baltimore. The Great Houses have been using it as a dumping ground for unsalvageable wounded orcs and troublemakers. Garok's performance against superior numbers and then that master class fight with the cave troll made him very noticeable."

"Okay, but what about the missing arms?" Charlie persisted.

Reggie's lips twisted distastefully, "There are elven houses that punish disobedience among the orcs by removing their sword hands and banishing them from their clans. It's to humiliate and break them psychologically."

"What do they do when that happens?"

"Drink and fight, mostly. It's why Baltimore has the problems that it does. Thousands of maimed, humiliated orcish veterans unable to bear arms or be warriors anymore, all drinking themselves into a stupor every night and causing trouble. It's why we were sent to you — to give the appearance of helping with the problem."

"So, we weren't meant to succeed."

Reggie looked amused, "Heavens no, my dear boy." He shook his head. "No, the elves don't care at all. To them, this is a public relations move."

"So, it doesn't matter, really."

"Ah, but it does." Reggie replied. "Think about it." He pointed towards the workshop. "Those three warriors in there were once stripped of their clans and their sense of self. They were deemed worthless and cast off, so they spent their nights drinking their sorrow and fighting out their rage... but what do they have now?"

Slowly Charlie replied, "They have a hero."

"Yes." Reggie replied with a twisted smile, "And just as importantly, they have a symbol."

"The iron hand."

"Yes." Reggie replied. "The iron hand, clenched into an unbreakable fist, wielded by a fearless, unbroken leader. Just the sort of symbolism an orc would be drawn to."

"Clever." Charlie muttered, then fell silent thinking. After a moment, he looked up, "Was this your plan?"

"The prosthetics, no. Getting into the orc market to make money, yes. I did not think they would make a particularly good consumer base, truth be told. Orcs don't really go in for high value consumer goods." Reggie replied, sounding slightly regretful. "That demonstration in the bar for advertising was the Princess and the Brute's idea." He frowned, "But after hearing that conversation, I suspect it might end up more than just a product."

"What do you mean?"

"The disaffected orcs in this city now have a symbol and a leader." Reggie replied, thoughtfully, "They work at every dockyard, warehouse and factory in this city. They're cops, bouncers and security guards. They outnumber Lord Denlin's troops by a dozen to one." He indicated the orcs in the workshop, "Even the unmaimed ones will respect and follow someone like Garok."

Slowly, Charlie said, "That's a lot of orcs…"

"It is thousands of orcs — at the very least." Reggie looked at Charlie and stated with a serious look, "We may have just accidentally formed an army and definitely affected the political power structure here in Baltimore City." He shook his head and said as if to himself, "Not an army — and we didn't form it, we just gave it a nudge." The goblin paused, then said thoughtfully, "No, this is a clan — but not like the old-world clans, bound by ancient tradition. This one is a clan born of the New World, with the help of the people of the new world. A clan that owes no allegiance to the elven houses and has no hostages belonging to the elves." He looked Charlie in the eyes, his face somber, "This is the beginning of something new."

"But what?"

"That, my dear boy, is the question." Reggie turned and watched the orcs speaking with Fiona and Garok in the workshop, "To whom will the first new clan formed in America owe its allegiance? To whom will they swear their blood oaths? More importantly, for what and for whom will they fight and die?" His eyes wandered to the massive shape of Garok, his arms folded on his thick chest, the iron fist clearly visible. The powerful orc stood slightly behind and towered over the stocky figure of the dwarven princess as she spoke animatedly to the young orcs, who listened intently as she talked. The human and the old goblin watched for several long moments, then Reggie murmured, "To whom indeed."

The Ruin of Kaliban

by Jonathan Shuerger

I AM CALLED ALBARETH, though that is not my name.

I serve as equerry of House Ravenna, banner bearer of the Eighth Legion and warrior of the Way. My tale is not as interesting, though later you may find it so.

Today I lay quill and ink to page to create record of the Demon. He was not known as such when he arrived on this little jewel in the void they call Terra. By many epithets and slurs was he recognized amongst his elven brethren, thanks to his family's cataclysmic fall into shame.

But he is now so known, and as the skull piles grow, I wonder if, in the infinite lines of fate, he might have been just another spoiled princeling jockeying for favor with his fellows, had they but accepted him.

No, I suppose not. Captain Sevarion Kaliban has always had the cold edge of steel in his gaze. When he looks upon you, you can feel his mind piercing through you like a spear tip, revealing your secrets to him. He was never one for the silly games of court intrigue played by bored elites. He had power to amass and enemies to slay, and not these pathetic mortals that claim ownership of Terra.

The lives of orcs and humans, he spends as currency to advance his own position. His rivals vanish or retire, unwilling to fall beneath the dread gaze of Kaliban the Black, Demon of the Eighth.

The end of the world lies in those eyes. I've always said so.

***

The arrival was ordinary, as such things went. The portal in Briarthrone Keep cast its light throughout the stone chamber, washing the marble stones with flickering beams of luminance. The other equerries gasped, always impressed with the dramatic show of radiance.

I did not. It was another turn of duty for me, another elven noble to serve, another ego to massage and feed until the humans somehow slew this one, too. I had lost three thus far. Three arrogant lordlings striding down the stairs with cocky smirks, as if they owned the Portal and all of Terra already.

I had laid all their house gems at the feet of their shocked parents and seen to the disposition of their effects. No one respected Earth as they should, and on this merciless battlefield, the unwary died swiftly.

Which was why today, a pale Houseless surprised me.

A group of five elves, minor princes of very thin royal blood, strode down the steps, chattering and laughing animatedly to one another. They were beginning their grand adventure, their voyage to glory and renown. None had expected the chance to be here; the glory of the Terran Invasion was to go to the highest and most noble of the elves. They did not know how many casualties we had suffered to allow their graceless entrance.

Only one remained at the threshold of swirling energies, sharp and black against the backdrop of writhing energies. I watched curiously as this elf lowered himself to his knees on the marble floor and pressed a hand to it, his fine white hair falling like a curtain across his shoulders. His weapon, a glaive of fine make, he laid on the cold stones, its face shimmering with reflected light.

I was so shocked by the unprecedented behavior, I missed all but the last of his words, spoken low. A whisper of a promise to himself, stolen by an equerry's lip-reading skills.

Walk not in the footprints of others, my son. Carve the road.

He rose to his feet, taking up his weapon to tuck behind him, and those cold eyes knifed into me like chips of ice as I passed the chattering lordlings.

I knew this was my new lord. The one for whom I had waited for many years.

I held a scroll with his details on it, but I did not unfurl the parchment. I knew all I required.

"Lord Sevarion Kaliban, I presume?"

He inclined his head slightly toward me. "Yes?" he asked quietly, his tone considered and refined, yet with the promise of violence behind it.

I bowed shortly. "I am Lieutenant Albareth of the Eighth. I have been assigned to serve as your equerry."

"Excellent," he said, glancing about. The other new arrivals swept out of the portal chamber, already babbling about glories to be won as their servants chased after them.

"Lord, there is an informal gathering for the new officers in the mess, and —"

"Captain."

I stuttered to a stop. "Apologies, my lord?"

Kaliban did not look at me, taking in the chamber, cataloguing it as he spoke. "My rank is captain, Lieutenant. Use it."

I realized my mouth hung open an instant, and snapped it shut. "Yes, Captain."

"And this informal gathering — is it a tactical briefing?"

I shook my head slowly. "No, my l — Captain. It is a chance to welcome new arrivals and make introductions."

His lip curled, and he sighed. "I had hoped, fool that I am," he said, "that elves in an active war zone might conduct themselves differently."

I had no idea how to respond to this, so I said nothing.

Captain Kaliban marched forward. Rather, he uncoiled, his movements lithe and predatory.

"I have command of a company?" he asked, his boots clicking against the marble.

"Yes, Captain," I said, adapting to his preferred means of address. "2nd Company, Ghidoran Tribe."

"Are they black orcs?"

"Sergeant Ulkhtar is, Captain, but the rest have yet to darken."

"Hm," he said. "Take me to meet them."

"N — now?" I asked. "But Lord Commander Vaerion ordered —"

Kaliban stopped so abruptly, I almost ran into the back of him. I sidestepped quickly, narrowly avoiding the very sharp blade of his glaive tucked behind his shoulder. He did not turn to face me, but lifted his chin.

"Hear me now, Lieutenant Albareth of the Eighth Legion. I have not passed through the portal to this barbaric world to lick some pissant's boots immediately upon arrival. Nor have I come to drown my cowardice in cheap wine while hiding amidst the laughter of equally cowardly fellows."

He turned to me, and his sapphire eyes fairly burned with intensity. "I have come to conquer, to tear glory from the Terrans' corpses, and I will suffer no delay nor countenance any hesitation in that pursuit. Have I made myself clear, Lieutenant?"

I nodded shortly. "Inescapably, Captain."

"Now take me to my command."

***

The interior of an orc barracks is a rank assault on elven sensibilities. We have refined senses of smell and hearing, as compared to other races, which is why our art and music are so much more subtle.

Orcs, on the other hand...

Loud pulsating booms blared from a stereo system, accompanied by some kind of screaming lyrics. Warriors in various hues of green lounged in the barracks or fought one another amidst cheering circles. Testosterone clotted the air, so thick I could chew it.

Elves never entered the barracks, and to do so would be seen as an invasion of the tribes' privacy. Therefore, I hesitated at the threshold.

Captain Kaliban did not.

He swept the cloak to the Ghidoran tribe's barracks aside and strode within. I swore to myself and trotted after him.

This was going to be... interesting.

Kaliban walked several steps within and stopped, again considering his environs with that intense focus. Learning, I realized.

One orc, a female in a black sleeveless top and pale green skin, glanced over at us. Her eyes widened, and she smacked the orc next to her on the arm. The orc snapped a glare at her, but she straightened and bellowed, "Good day to you, my lord!"

The orcs within froze and turned to us. Someone flicked off that atrocious blaring music, and my aching temples thanked the dead gods for small mercies.

Kaliban took a single step forward, his arms loose beneath his black cape. He did not cross them; he did not square up before the tribe to appear larger with his hands on his hips, as so many officers before he had done.

"Which of you," he asked, "is Sergeant Ulkhtar?"

A giant, black-skinned orc stepped forward. I knew him well. He had also lived through three previous commanders.

An orc's skin darkens as it ages, but also as it battles. The hormones within its system tints the pigment of its skin as battle rage flows through its veins. You could tell how deadly an orc was by how dark his skin was, and Ulkhtar was black as coal.

"My lord," the orc rumbled.

Kaliban waved a hand dismissively. "Captain," he corrected.

Ulkhtar snuffed, standing awkwardly. He did not know what to do. That was alright; I did not know, either.

Captain Kaliban knew exactly what he wanted, however.

"I am Captain Kaliban of the Eighth Legion," he announced to the room. He did not raise his voice, yet every orc in the barracks stayed locked onto him. "I come to spill the red blood of the humans and stack their skulls."

Orcs grunted in surprise. Elf lords did not speak this way.

Kaliban glanced around. "Your previous commander died to his own stupidity, against the advice of both Lieutenant Albareth and Sergeant Ulkhtar."

He pointed at Ulkhtar. "I read they punished you for his failure. The lashes have healed well."

Ulkhtar shrugged, but his eyes burned at the memory of his humiliation.

Kaliban looked around. "I come to conquer," he said, repeating the words he told me. "You are my weapons. We have not chosen one another, yet now our fate lies woven as one cord."

He pointed at Ulkhtar, then tracked the finger across the room. "I know you are strong. You are Ghidoran. Your kill marks outnumber the stars in the sky."

More approving grunts. The testosterone in the air spiked.

Kaliban patted his chest. "You deserve to be commanded by one worthy. I come to be tested of you."

The room fell silent.

Ulkhtar stepped forward. "Captain," he rumbled, "orcs not hurt elves. We get punished."

"Lieutenant Albareth," Kaliban said.

I snapped to attention, uncomfortable at being singled out amid beings I normally only shared a battlefield with. "Captain?"

"Make record that should Sergeant Ulkhtar draw my blood in single combat, the grog rations for the Ghidoran tribe shall be tripled for the evening."

Intakes of breath. Orcs glanced at one another, their eyes widening in anticipation.

"Should he kill me," Kaliban said, not taking his eyes from Ulkhtar's, "he may claim my father's glaive as his own inheritance for all time."

Even I jerked at that. An orc, bearing not just an elven weapon, but an heirloom? It was unprecedented. It was inappropriate. It was —

"Done," Ulkhtar said with a wide grin. "Here?"

Kaliban nodded. Then, somehow, he shocked me again.

Around orcs, elves do not remove their armor. The lesser races resent us, and often seek to plunge a dagger into our backs when the opportunity presents itself. We have not become the masters of the universe by embracing foolish habits.

Therefore, when Kaliban unfastened the shoulder clasps of his breastplate, I did not move to take it. He removed the entire piece of armor and turned to me, one eyebrow raised.

"Vocalized commands should not be required for this, I think," he said, and I lurched from my stupor to take the armor.

Piece by piece, Sevarion Kaliban stripped down to his black breeches, bare feet and bare chest. While the skin of his torso was porcelain, perfect as a young god's and lean with muscle, the scars behind stole my breath. A vicious crosshatch of lines, the edges knotted with thick callouses, etched across his back, and the orcs fell deadly silent at the sight.

I knew the work of an arthro-whip. I had seen the punishment administered rarely, for few elves had the stomach to watch the victim eject their intestines through their mouths. The whip itself was tipped with the spines of great centipedes, and the toxins induced savage hallucinations before they stopped your heart.

It was a cruelty reserved for the basest traitors of the lower races, and they rightfully dreaded this fate. To my knowledge, no elf had ever suffered its poisoned lash.

No being had ever even *survived* it.

Yet here Kaliban stood, hands loose at his sides as his hair hung down the sides of his face, his cold eyes boring into Ulkhtar's, who stood solemnly, looking down at this strange new officer. The orcs looked to their sergeant now, uncertainty in their eyes, but the chieftain did not move.

The elf chucked his chin once, and Ulkhtar nodded in a show of respect before attacking.

There are few things more terrifying than a black orc whose blood is up. The roar shook the barracks room. My heartrate accelerated and I had to repress an instinctive rush of fear. Elves were never on the receiving end of a war chief's charge. This was all new to me.

Ulkhtar crossed the few yards between him and his prey in a blur. His massive knuckles, pitted and warped by decades of hand-to-hand combat, rocketed toward the captain's head. He did not pull the punch, and Kaliban did not move.

The strike nearly pitched Kaliban off his feet. With a surprising grace, Kaliban rocked with the blow and flipped over, bleeding off the thunderous power of the strike. The captain reeled a couple of steps before righting himself. He put a hand to his lip and looked at it, grunting at the red painting his fingertips. He glanced at me, and the entire room held its breath.

"Lieutenant," he said. "See that they get their grog."

He did not wait for my stuttered response. Instead, he lunged forward, transforming from cold elf into feral wolf in a heartbeat. Ulkhtar tried to crouch down, but Kaliban swung a clawed hand at his eyes. As the orc instinctively blocked the blow, the elf kicked out his front-facing leg and crunched a knee into his gut. Without hesitation, Kaliban sprang up in a quick hop and slammed his other knee into Ulkhtar's jaw, pitching the war chief's head backward.

Kaliban twisted in mid-air and delivered a perfect kick, striking like a snake. Ulkhtar staggered back a step, driving his weight into the floor to regain his balance.

It was already too late.

Kaliban leapt on him full-on, teeth bared like a goblin. For a horrific instant, I thought he might emulate the vampiric princes of legend and bury his fangs in the orc's neck, but Kaliban instead slammed the great orc into the floor. His fingers clamped around the chieftain's throat, and I saw black blood sprout from around his fingertips as he penetrated the skin.

Ulkhtar froze, his hands raised to try to stop Kaliban, but he let his heavy limbs flop to rest on the floor.

Every being in the room heard Kaliban's hissed words.

"I am your captain. You are my weapon. I hold your life in my hand, and even when I release your throat, it will remain so. Strike my enemies with the same force you struck me, and I will suffer no hand upon your tribe, be it elf or no. Swear to me now, Ulkhtar, chief of Ghidorah."

The black orc slammed a fist into the floorboards. "I swear, my Captain," he rumbled.

Like a cobra, Kaliban withdrew his hand from Ulkhtar's neck, and I saw the lines of blood dribbling down the orc's neck. The elf glanced at his hand, and without further thought, dragged the bloody fingers down his face, striping his visage with Ulkhtar's black blood.

A savage grin split Ulkhtar's features, and he punched a fist into the sky. "Glory to the Eighth!" he roared, "Glory to Captain Kaliban, Kaliban the Black!"

The room erupted with bellows.

***

Kaliban did not turn to the healers for the blow to his skull, as I recommended. Nor did he make his way to his quarters, where the meal I had ordered even now cooled and congealed upon the table.

No, the young captain barely waited long enough to replace his clothing and armor upon his person. Now he stalked through the interior of Briarthrone Keep, his robe swishing behind him.

"Captain?" I asked, lengthening my strides to keep pace. "What, then, is your destination?"

"Tactical," he said, and turned down the corridor to his left. "I wish to see the current state of the battlefield. The last report I read was a month old."

My eyebrows raised as he turned another corner, perfectly guiding himself to a room he had never visited.

"You know your way well," I observed.

Kaliban grunted. "This structure," he dragged his hand along the wall for emphasis, "was built according to standard specifications. Though superbly gifted in fortification, the dwarves are not known for their imagination. What works in one location works well in another. I studied their blueprints in depth to prepare for my eventual assignment."

I cocked my head at that. "'Eventual', Captain? Even as a Houseless, you expected assignment?"

He chuckled. "Do you always remind your lords of their piss-poor social standing? Seems unwise."

I ducked my head. "Of course, apologies, my l —"

He raised a hand to forestall me, but did not stop walking. "Your question is good, and worthy of answer. Yes, I am aware of my status as a Houseless prince. I assume you did your reading on your own assignment to me?"

I nodded once. "Of course, Captain."

"Then you know the circumstances of my House's fall from grace?"

Again, I nodded. The subject itself was too sensitive to speak aloud with so many passing through the halls.

Kaliban did not seem to care. "My father retained lofty ambitions for his House, and my mother stoked those flames no end. Denied initial entrance into the Terran invasion, denied glory due him as a House patriarch, he sought power through other... more *proscribed* avenues."

"Summoning," I said.

He glanced at me, his eyes glinting like sapphires as they considered me. "Yes. My mother discovered a record, buried in the crater that remains of Zadok's Folly. Within it were the process and incantations to summon and bind a demon of the Outer Void to a House's service. It was a lengthy ritual, requiring many days and much sacrifice. My father sent me away then, for if the ritual should fail, an heir should survive of his House."

Kaliban did not break the edict on his lips and speak the forbidden name of his disgraced House.

"I am told the ritual failed. Seconds from success, the Tower Council struck, and their mages incinerated everything and everyone in the chamber, including my parents. The secret police sought me out soon after. As you can see," he patted his back, where the scars of the arthro-whip were now hidden, "I was... tested to see what I knew of my parents' actions."

I inclined my head. "And you passed."

Kaliban chuckled darkly. "I passed. For this reason, I hold little in common with other elves of similar rank. I am the heir of disgrace, a prince of the ruined. My heritage is that of abomination and witchcraft."

He gestured around him. "Then the call was made for more warriors, and I saw my chance to wash away the stain of others' sins in the blood of conquest."

I nodded, suddenly understanding. "Hence we go to Tactical, rather than the social gathering for the new lords."

He smiled and walked on. "Hence we go to Tactical."

"You are not where you should be."

The words dropped with contempt from the mouth of Lord Commander Vaerion Ecthelad, master of Briarthrone. The elven lord, his golden hair falling down his armor, lounged on his throne, swirling scarlet wine in a crystal goblet.

He took a sip of the liquid and leaned back, his jade eyes bored as he took in Kaliban and myself.

Kaliban inclined his head. "Lord commander," he said. "I came to acquaint myself with the tactical situation."

Vaerion's lip curled for an instant, then his features returned to their placid serenity. "How we have fallen," he murmured, "that we must entertain even the Houseless among our ranks. I would ask why you are not with your betters at the welcome ceremony, but I see you realize no one wants you there either."

I glanced at my captain, but no anger rippled across his face. He said nothing, waiting.

At last, Vaerion waved his hand. "As you please, *Captain*."

He said the last word with a raised eyebrow, as if he could not believe he had to say it.

Kaliban saluted, fist to chest, and moved into the tactical circle. Runes lit around him, and a map of the area projected before him. With practiced hands, Kaliban tapped floating sigils and began to tailor his tactical readout.

Briarthrone Keep was an outpost in what the humans called the Sonoran Desert, in the south of what was the state of Arizona in the United States. After the Legion's invasion, it was decided that the highway system would be preserved to facilitate transport of supplies from the portals in San Diego and Los Angeles to eastern Texas and the southeastern ports. Briarthrone held three battalions of orcs and Vaerion's household guard to keep the Tenth Way open and free of raiders.

I stepped to the captain's side as his cold eyes searched through recent reports. "This image is recent?" he murmured to me, keeping his voice low.

I shrugged. "We have a scrying mage in Briarthrone who says he updates the map regularly, but he is most often drunk in his chambers. As he says, the desert never changes."

Kaliban sighed, a quiet hiss of frustration. "Understood," he said.

He cupped an area of the projected map with his hands and drew them apart, expanding that sector. "Ajo Pass," he said. "This is where the raiders usually strike?"

I nodded. "They call themselves Rodney's Raiders, Captain. Leftovers of the American military, commanded by a human they call Colonel Rodney

Callaghan. He is cunning, this human, striking swiftly like a falcon and vanishing into the desert."

"And we have no thought where his base might be," Kaliban stated flatly. "Still."

"That is correct, Captain," I said.

He glanced at me. "How has this intolerable situation been allowed to persist?"

I shrugged. "Lord Commander Vaerion believes the matter shall resolve itself. In his words, no human can hope to match the perfection of the elves."

A small sigh escaped Kaliban. "And so, he does not engage, lest this Callaghan prove otherwise."

I nodded slowly, unsure of how much to say. "The lord commander is of low station, Captain, and considers himself... slighted by this assignment. He thinks it beneath him."

"Hm," Kaliban said. "And High Command?"

"Frustrated. Many resources have been lost to the raiders, and they strangle this route of supply."

Kaliban's eyes grew shadowed as he considered the display, and I saw him sink into his thoughts.

"Houseless."

At Vaerion's voice, we turned. "Yes, lord commander?" Kaliban asked, rising from his contemplative state.

The elf lord leaned forward, a trifle unsteadily. I kept a schooled expression of neutrality on my face; there was little to do in this wasteland of brown and most elves passed the time and intolerable heat in their cups.

"You wish to see our tactical situation?"

Kaliban considered the question for a breath, then answered, "If I may."

Vaerion stood to his feet. "Come, then. A shipment of dwarven weapons passes on the Tenth Way, and Command has decreed that I am to escort them personally. You and your company shall join me."

He glanced down at the floor, his lip wrinkling as he beheld himself. "This is not home," he said. "This is Earth, where even the basest born may prove himself worthy of glory. See how true elves conduct themselves in war, and perhaps even you can be elevated above your trivial station."

Kaliban nodded. "It would be my honor."

"Oh, save it," Vaerion muttered, stepping down from his throne and sweeping past us. The reek of wine blasted our nostrils. "You command the rearguard, where you belong. Eat dust and watch highborn cover themselves in glory."

"As you say," Kaliban said, his eyes glittering, "lord commander."

***

I had traveled much of the territory known as the United States in my time on Earth. In many regions, the coming of autumn heralded a drop in temperature, where the chill of the wind grew crisp as winter neared. The colors of the trees changed, the leaves fading from uniform green to yellows and reds before falling to the earth in a carpet of whispering foliage.

Not so in this dismal dung heap called Arizona.

In the privacy of my helm, I sighed. The autumnal equinox had already passed, well on the way to winter, and yet the heat still baked us in our armor. Unending brown stretched out before us, with no water or change of color in sight.

Kaliban and I sat astride wyrm-steeds. For every dragon that reached full maturity, a dozen more grew no further. Some became wyrms, little better than guard dogs of the encampments. Our steeds were not even that. These creatures barely grew at all after hatching, practically non-intelligent, and they were given to the least of the elves.

Us.

I sighed again.

I don't know if you know what the heat does to the smell of orc. It intensifies it as their sweat glands over-produce to cool their massive frames. The wind, *when* it blew, blasted the noxious reek into my nostrils, and it dizzied me.

"A weapon in its own right," I muttered, and Captain Kaliban's helm twitched toward me.

"Something to offer, Lieutenant?" he asked, a touch of a smile in his voice.

"No, Captain," I said, fighting the urge to wipe the offending stench from my nostrils.

"Our patience shall soon be rewarded," Kaliban said.

I grunted. "I have little confidence in that, sir. First the lord commander assigns you this demeaning position, then orders you to take an inventory of and *load* the convoy, as if you were a mere scribe or laborer. It is insulting and meant as such."

Kaliban shrugged and took a swig of water from a skin at his hip. He was the only elf lord I had yet seen who did not drink wine.

"We do what we can with what we have, Albareth," he said. "And that I have done."

I squinted at that and faced him, but he leaned forward, suddenly focused.

"Sergeant," he said, his voice intense, and Ulkhtar strode forward. The black orc seemed no worse the wear for the loss suffered at Kaliban's hand, and in fact the experience seemed to have solidified his trust in his new captain.

"Make ready the tribe," Kaliban hissed. "The enemy approaches.

I searched the desert. Before us, the convoy toiled away on the great highway the humans called the Tenth. Eight great hoversleds passed over the baked asphalt, escorted by Lord Vaerion atop his drake and surrounded by the elves of his household guard. Lord Vaerion appeared bored, and he had compelled one of his retainers to hold a shade over him to protect him from the worst of the heat. His mount basked in it.

"I see nothing out of place, my Captain," I said.

"And is therefore," Kaliban said, "the perfect time to strike."

He glanced at me and Ulkhtar. "Do nothing until I command. Respond."

Both the orc and I exchanged glances, but we answered, "Yes, Captain."

"Good." The pale elf turned back to the convoy below. "Let us see what we see, then."

***

The first strike, when it came, shocked me.

One moment, the hover sleds hummed along the road, with bored elves and orcs trudging alongside. The next, missiles rose from the desert on tall plumes of smoke and slammed into the convoy. Dwarven steel shredded into storms of deadly splinters as armor-piercing warheads punched through the first and last hover sleds to blow them into raging infernos. Orcs bellowed in pain and rage, staggering from the blasts and clutching wounds inflicted by the shrapnel.

"There," Kaliban said, and I saw what he did.

Dust rose in a trail from behind a ridgeline, and I saw American armored vehicles burst from cover. Heavy machine guns, primitive in design but no less deadly, pivoted on their swivel mounts and opened fire. Lines of tracer fire stitched through the ground around the convoy, and I saw orcs and elves torn to bloody pieces in sprays of gore.

"Now they concentrate," Kaliban said, and I saw his eyes had unfocused, as if he listened to music rather than witnessed a battle.

"Hrgh," Ulkhtar grunted. "Look."

The lines of tracer fire converged on Lord Vaerion's drake. Sparks sprayed from the creature's thick armor, and the beast roared in anger. Vaerion hauled on its reins and dug his heels in.

"Predictable," Kaliban said, as the elf lord soared above the battlefield. The drake became a dot in the sky, then banked for its return. At this point, the slaughter usually began.

"Tell me, Sergeant," the captain said. "How does one slay a dragon?"

The orc shrugged. "Don't know," he said. "Never killed one."

Kaliban glanced at him. "Dragons are supremely dangerous upon the ground, within its cave."

He gestured back at the battlefield. "So you must flush it out and blow it out of the sky."

I opened my mouth to ask what he meant, then more contrails of smoke blasted from the ground. Two missiles, then two more, leapt into the sky, arrowing for the drake. The creature did not see the ordnance incoming, caught up in the thrill of its first dive.

Four more missiles launched, again in two pairs, just as the first pair hit.

Vaerion suddenly twisted in his saddle, his helm's proximity runes no doubt warning him of the threat. He hauled on the drake's reins, and the beast rolled to the side just as the first missiles dove in. Its wing swatted the two warheads to spiral away into the air, where they exploded.

The twin blasts threw Vaerion forward in his saddle, no doubt dazing the elf. The next two lanced in, and the drake spun in mid-air, presenting its armored belly to the missiles to protect its master. The missiles punched into its armor and the drake screamed as fire consumed it. It lost altitude, its smoking wings struggling to keep it airborne.

Four more missiles arced toward the drake. Vaerion yanked on its reins, and the beast twisted toward the weapons. Fire sprayed from its mouth as Vaerion cast an illusion spell of his drake. A second drake appeared in the sky, launching itself away from the elf commander and his mount.

The first missile lost its tracking in the fiery stream and tried to follow the illusion, exploding in empty air. The second exploded within the torrent of dragon's breath, and the shockwave was enough to break Vaerion's concentration, shattering his illusion.

The third and fourth missiles roared in, and in desperation, Vaerion forced his mount into a deep dive. My mouth fell open at the tactic, because Vaerion was not far enough above the ground to pull up.

The third missile streaked over Vaerion's head, missing the drake's core by mere yards. It impacted in the desert and blew a spray of sand and rock fragments into the air with a boom that shook my chest.

The last buried itself in the drake's weakened flank armor, broke through and detonated. The explosion blew its hind leg and wing off of its body and launched it into a death spiral, throwing Vaerion free. At the last moment, before the drake's body slammed into the desert and the furnace in its core exploded, I saw the flash of a shield spell activate around Vaerion, the magic laid into his armor activating to save his life.

All around the convoy, humans in camouflaged fatigues sprang from holes dug into the sand, rifles barking non-stop. Orcs and elves pitched into the dirt, blood spurting from their chests and mouths, and I saw the first weapons thrown to the sand.

In the distance, I saw raiders with weapons raised surrounding Lord Commander Vaerion, who tried to struggle to his feet. A soldier slammed the butt of his rifle into the elf's helm and knocked the lord commander flat.

"Captain?" I asked. "Do we engage?"

Kaliban remained motionless in his saddle, watching the massacre below with unblinking focus. "No, Lieutenant," he said in a dangerously low voice. "We do not."

***

For an hour, we watched as the humans rounded up the battlefield. They looted the bodies of fallen warriors, taking weapons, ammo and trophies. They loaded the cases of dwarven weapons onto their trucks, ready to take them back into their mountain fastnesses.

Despite the rampant spoiling of our dead, Sevarion Kaliban did nothing.

Ulkhtar and I shared concerned glances. No longer were we elf and orc, separated by station and rank. Now we were both subordinates observing a disaster that would see us all punished. An elven lord commander, a shipment of elven weaponry in the hands of humans, and a marked lack of response upon our part — there would be no forgiveness for this.

Kaliban did not so much as send a message to High Command. He straddled his wyrmsteed, eyes unwavering through the slits of his helm.

At last, he spoke. "Sergeant."

Ulkhtar stepped forward. "Captain," the scarred orc answered.

"See that the company is prepared to strike when the throat is bared."

Ulkhtar looked to me before answering, "Aye, Captain."

"Ulkhtar."

The orc looked at his master. "Captain?"

Kaliban looked down upon him coldly. "Mercy is the weapon of the weak. Wield none."

Ulkhtar slammed a fist into his chest. "Aye, Captain."

Kaliban turned to me. "With me, Lieutenant. And tie this to your spear."

He pulled something out of a saddlebag and handed it to me. It was a long strip of white linen, its tail blowing in the wind. It appeared to be one of his bed sheets.

I blinked and looked from it to him. "My lord?" I said, forgetting myself.

He clucked his tongue and his mount moved forward. "Know the ways of your enemy, Lieutenant. Come. We go to bare the throat."

***

Two more elves, two more trophies to take, rode out in full view of the enemy with naught but a strip of white cloth fluttering overhead. Yet Kaliban swerved to neither the left nor the right.

Rifles trained upon us but did not fire. Heavy machine guns, capable of shredding even our armor, tracked our path, but remained silent. Humans in desert pattern fatigues surrounded us, their eyes narrowed and cold.

One lifted a hand. "Hold up there, elf. What do you want with that flag of truce? Y'all never used that before."

Kaliban did not look down at him, but kept his eyes focused on the main trucks, where a human male with gray in his severely cropped hair stared at us.

"Tell Colonel Callaghan that I have come for the life of Lord Commander Vaerion Ecthelad of the Eighth Legion."

The man glanced at his compatriots, then hooked his thumbs in his webbed vest. "And what if we don't have no Lord Commander Vaerion Egg Salad of the Eighth Legion?"

His men chuckled. To my surprise, I saw a smile touch Kaliban's lips as well.

"You do, staff sergeant."

The man's head twitched, surprised at Kaliban's identification of the rank insignia on his chest.

"As a matter of fact, I will wager a substantial sum that he has divulged his full name, rank and over-estimated value to you many, many times."

The staff sergeant grinned ruefully. "Well, seems like you *do* know him. Let me take you over to Colonel Rodney."

He waved his arm, and a path opened through the raiders. Kaliban slid from his wyrm-steed, and I did the same.

"And your weapons, too, elf."

Kaliban nodded shortly, and I slid my sheathed sword from my back and hung it over my saddle horn. Kaliban left his glaive where it lay hooked to his saddle.

"Lead on, staff sergeant."

***

Colonel Rodney Callaghan had a forceful presence up close. I stared as we approached. This small man, clad in the same fatigues as his men with no medals, honors or banners, had humiliated the Eighth Legion at Bri-arthrone for months.

Nearby, the lord commander kneeled with his back to one of their trucks, his hands ziptied behind him and a black canvas bag over his head.

"So," Callaghan said as the captain came to a halt a few yards away. "Who might you be?"

Kaliban stood with his hands loose at his sides. His carriage bore no arrogance, none of the spiteful superiority an elf might normally display in the presence of humans. He kept his helm in place; again, an oddity. Most commanders I knew bared their heads that their enemies might behold their faces and recognize their foe.

"I am nothing but a servant of the Eighth Legion," Kaliban said quietly.

"Hm," Rodney said, grimacing as he scratched at the stubble on his neck. "That's different. This one hasn't stopped telling me all about him-self so I won't kill him. Finally put a gag on him."

He gestured at our escort. "Sergeant tells me you're here to negotiate for him. Some kind of ransom?"

Kaliban's helm tilted to the side. "That is not what I said."

One of Rodney's salt-and-pepper eyebrows arched. "That so? Well, go check him out anyway. We haven't hurt him since shooting him down, despite my inclination to the contrary. Then we'll talk terms."

Kaliban inclined his head. "My thanks, Colonel."

Rodney squinted at him. "Huh. You're the first elf to use my rank... *ever*. Most of the time, I get some high-and-mighty insults. Something different about you."

Kaliban ignored him and stepped toward Vaerion. When he slid the bag off of the elf's head, Vaerion's green eyes blazed up at him, and a stream of muffled curses and orders poured into the gag in his mouth. Vaerion launched himself to his feet, shouting incomprehensible gibberish.

Kaliban waited patiently for the tirade to cease, and once Vaerion fell silent, his face red and his eyes wide with fury, Kaliban put his hands on the elf's shoulders.

"The price of failure, Vaerion Ecthelad," Kaliban said quietly, "paid in full."

Before I could even blink, Kaliban rammed a spear hand into Vaerion's throat. The elf's eyes bulged in shock and choking sounds emitted muffled from his gag.

Kaliban swept the lord commander from his feet with a sudden kick to the shins, and Vaerion fell on his face to the earth. Kaliban finished him with a brutal stomp on the back of his neck, and I winced at the audible crack of the elf's spine splintering beneath Kaliban's boot.

The surrounding humans shouted and drew their weapons at the sudden violence, but Rodney held up his hands. "Wait!" he bellowed. "Hold your fire!"

Kaliban twisted from Vaerion's corpse and stalked back, his gait now the rolling slink of a great cat.

Rodney stood with his hands on his hips, his face hard. "That," the man spat, pointing at Vaerion's body, "was a valuable prisoner. I let you check him in good faith. I can see that I will not be making that mistake again."

"And I said," Kaliban hissed, "that I came for his life. Do not blame me for your man's error in reporting."

Rodney's eyes did not blink. "What *was* that?" he asked quietly, his voice intense. "You came here under flag of truce just to kill your own man?"

Kaliban stood tall, even surrounded by dozens of angry humans with weapons trained on him. "Vaerion Ecthalad humiliated his command, his Legion and his species for the last time today. I came to deliver sentence and execute justice upon him."

Rodney considered him, tapping his knuckles on his body armor. "You *are* different," he said finally. "Haven't met an elf like you. How long you been on Earth? Where'd they transfer you from?"

Kaliban gave the smallest of shrugs. "First day."

Rodney barked a short laugh. "Is that *so*? Well, your kind might have benefited from someone like you, but sadly, this is also gonna be your last day. Staff Sergeant!"

Rifles came up, aiming at Captain Kaliban. He did not shrink from the dozens of weapons trained on him.

"I had not finished speaking, Colonel," he breathed.

Rodney grinned. "Well, by all means, finish what you were saying, kid."

"This," Kaliban said, indicating the ruins of the convoy, "was not your ambush. It was mine."

Rodney glanced around, hands on his hips. "Well, you did a bang-up job. I got a dead lord commander and some high-quality weapons out of it."

"That I," Kaliban said, placing his hand on his chest, "packed."

Rodney blinked. "What? What does that mean?"

Something lit up under Kaliban's hand, and the first truck exploded. A geyser of flame sprouted into the air a dozen yards away, hurling American soldiers from their feet. Another cooked off, this one closer, spilling soldiers into the dirt. Even I felt to my knees from the shockwaves, and I saw our gaolers suffered the same.

Only Kaliban kept his feet, braced for the impacts. He extended his hand, and from thirty yards away, his glaive hummed and launched itself toward him from the saddle. The weapon slapped into his hand, keened with almost predatory glee and Kaliban the Black flourished it once in a savage flash of silver.

Rodney reached for his comm unit, but Kaliban blurred forward and cleaved him in half, splitting the man from shoulder to pelvis in a single stroke. Scarlet sprayed across Kaliban's armor, painting him in gore, and Rodney's pieces flopped to the ground, his eyes wide in horror.

Rifles barked from the few raiders still upright, and Kaliban danced to the side, dodging the volley of hot lead. He lunged forward, striking like a serpent, and blood gouted from severed necks and lopped limbs as Kaliban fell upon the reeling raiders.

I had left my weapon on my wyrm-steed, but I still bore the standard with the flag of truce. I swept the staff about, smashing rifle barrels aside and sending shots wide.

Almost no one paid attention to me. Roars sounded from the desert, and I turned to see Ulkhtar, war chief of the Ghidoran tribe, slam into a soldier and lift him bodily from his feet. The black orc hurled the screaming raider a full twenty yards to slam into a truck, which exploded as another of Kaliban's rigged crates detonated.

Then the rest of the tribe crashed into the reeling humans, and the true butchery started.

***

Six hours later, the representatives of High Command arrived, signaled by Eighth Legion communications with a new signature appended.

Kaliban received them from his throne, and my heightened senses could hear their heartbeats quicken in their chests as they beheld him.

Sevarion Kaliban sat upon Lord Commander Vaerion's high-backed drake seat, taken from the slaughtered beast's back. He held his glaive in one hand and the skull of Rodney Callaghan in the other. Dog tags, taken from the slit throats of the fallen, jangled in his fist. The throne itself was lifted from the ground by the skulls of Rodney's Raiders, ripped from their necks by the now-fanatically loyal Ghidoran tribe of orcs and stripped of their flesh til only the white bone remained.

The representatives, nobleborn elves all, stepped uncertainly toward him. "What is this barbarity, Captain?" one of them snapped, but his heart was not in it. His gaze was that of an elf who understood what he saw, and yet did not think such a thing could be true. This was a tableau of much older days, when the elder elves tore dominion from the hands of cruel gods.

Kaliban's cold eyes fixed upon him. "Take this message to the lords of High Command," he said. "In the wake of Vaerion Ecthelad's death, I, Sevarion Kaliban, Houseless of the Eighth, hold his seat."

He stood, and the gesture emphasized the throne at his back. Drenched in human blood, standing upon a pile of grinning skulls, Kaliban the Black stared down at them with unblinking eyes.

"The human resistance here has been crushed. The Tenth Way has been opened. I shall hunt the remnant of their raiders in the mountains, and their skulls shall join their fellows here."

"This —" an elf sputtered, "this is most irregular. To assume command as a mere *captain* —"

His voice trailed off as Kaliban fixed him with that gaze. No life stirred in those eyes. "The lord commander took months to fail completely. I arrived this morning and broke them by sunset."

He looked up, his eyes unfocusing. "Tell your masters that Sevarion Kaliban the Black is the Demon of the Eighth Legion; by atrocity defined, by mercy unswayed, and by fools unhindered."

He raised a bloody hand, holding Rodney Callaghan's skull to the sight of the heavens. "Victory is ours."

He said it tonelessly, but as the orcs of the Ghidoran tribe roared, the messengers of High Command paled.

***

Only when we returned to Briarthrone and I stood in the silence of my quarters, did I allow myself, at last, to laugh.

It started as a breath, which became a chuckle and finally a full-throated roar of laughter, barely muffled by the thick tapestries on the walls.

The Demon of the Eighth, he said.

By the murdered gods, the irony was nearly enough to peel the skin of this disguise I wore.

I took a deep breath through the nose. I found the abattoir stench pleasant, actually, much like the incense true elves might burn in their quarters. Old blood and rot were my aromas of choice, and the half-devoured corpse of the original Albareth provided both in pleasing amounts.

My laugh was low and guttural, powerful enough to damage the fragile vocal cords of this frail body. I would repair the damage later.

With a wave of my hand, I opened a scrying and beheld the elf Kaliban in his quarters, silently washing the blood from his armor. I could sense his focus; his will clad in steel that his campaign of conquest had only just begun. How remarkable, that he turned the symbol of his father's failure into the avatar of his meteoric rise to greatness.

"Your father did not fail, little demon," I breathed. "He did indeed summon one of the old ones to serve House Ravenna. Now I am bound to the success of his heir."

Kaliban glanced up, his gaze sharp as though he heard me. I held my breath, even one such as I held rapt by the lethality, the *hunger* in that unblinking stare. So odd, to see a look one of my brethren might sport in the eyes of a mortal. Disquieted, I closed the scrying, lest somehow he see me.

I am called Albareth, though that is not my name. I now serve as equerry of house Ravenna, banner bearer of the Eighth Legion and warrior of the Way.

My smile split my cheeks at the thought of the look in Kaliban's eyes. The end of the world lay in those eyes, though he knew not how. When I finished using him to summon brothers banished in ages past, I would devour him as I would the rest of his damned kind.

Until then, the laws of my summoning held tight around me like chains, and I am compelled to suffer undignified servitude beneath Kaliban's boot.

A chuckle shook my chest at the parallels between us. An elf pretending to be a demon, and a demon wearing an elf. How novel.

"Glory to the Eighth," I snarled, and took another bite of the last fool I had betrayed.

House Built on Sand

by Claire Merrick

University of Pittsburgh's Holland Hall, Pennsylvania Protectorate

One month since the southwest "storm"

The overcast night sky lit up red, then a frigid shade of blue. The sonic part of the explosion hit a half-second later, shaking everything inside the high-rises lining the Allegheny River. It was not intense enough to break the windows of Zach Bourassa's dorm two miles to the east, where bleary-eyed college-age men bolted out of bed. No one turned on any lights; those who had electricity knew better. The elves would not deem their curiosity a valid exception for their weekly power allotment.

"Shit, that's in the Strip," a student muttered.

Zach joined his three dorm mates in the one-room pad angling for a view of the river, waiting to see if there would be a cascading effect or a retaliatory strike. If it was an attack by human rebels, then the dragons would be on the horizon in seconds.

Thankfully, the glow receded with a residual crackle. Zach collapsed onto his mattress and fell back to sleep.

***

The first woman who came to the shop in the morning was a new customer. Zach needed little more than a glance to tell that she had never done this type of 'shopping' before. But every human who ever wandered into All-Seasons Outdoor Surplus on Darragh Street was new at this. Given her age, he figured her breaking point had to do with children, and she proved him right the moment she opened her mouth.

"Just wondering if something will help the food last longer." Her sleeve muffled her next sentence while she wiped her eyes. "Dad... my daddy walked out in the middle of the night; left behind his coat and his pistol. Just took his old hunting knife. He thought it'd make it easier to feed the kids."

She kept talking, which was another sign she was new. Customers quickly learned not to make small talk. The less information shared, the better if anyone got scooped up. "It's not as many mouths as it used to be. My oldest boy went east with his cousin a month ago. They wanted to get to the Alleghenies before it got cold." She cleared her throat and tried to correct herself. "I mean, the Iron Hills."

As if that would keep the El'dori from hauling her downtown for insubordination, he thought. They both knew the only reason to flee into the Alleghenies was to join the human rebel groups.

With a dispassionate shrug, he plucked an elegant silver ring of keys off a peg beneath the counter. He took it to a wooden chest just out of sight from the showroom, while she kept chattering.

"The boys were being sent to the refinery anyway, so if their lives were going to be in danger, I guess they figured it didn't matter. But it does leave us without the pay they might've got. So, now I'm going back to work. My oldest daughter is watching the kids during the day. She's twenty-four."

The key fell from his hand. "Fuck me," he hissed and dropped to his hands and knees to seek out the key on the dark, dusty floorboards, and to suppress his own instinct to sniffle.

Thoughts of Mom chewing him out always came to him when he used certain words. Then he imagined his sister, like a demon on one shoulder, mouth twisted in a suppressed chuckle while mother-angel tut-tutted on the other shoulder. It was a trivial thought, but with their voices permanently silenced, he clung to imaginary arguments.

Just find the key, he told himself. The more time it took doing business with her, the more time for someone to come in and notice that what he gave her was certainly not outdoor recreational gear. Someone who did not care that the food supply was low, who might even take sadistic glee in exposing the lack of legality in their transaction.

Abandoning the chest of fake artifacts and panaceas, he grabbed a different key and took it to a cabinet further back in the storage room. The spoon he picked out was covered in rust. Someone without his gift might figure it would poison any food it touched.

He brought it back to the counter. "You're lucky it's the only one we got. These are hard to find. But I'm willing to cut you a good deal for four-hundred."

"Hundred!" The woman's hands dropped dejectedly.

This is where you're supposed to haggle, he thought to himself. But, of course, a year ago, she would have bought whatever her kids wanted from Kuhn's, probably with a loyalty card. He had heard that rationing was not so bad in other parts of the conquered United States and was not sure why Pittsburgh drew that short straw. Allegedly, Pennsylvania's El'dori lord was a fairly decent dude if you got to talk to him, though that could be the propaganda at work.

"Duplication spells don't come around here often. I'm not expecting more like this for at least six months." It was a canned line. He said it with no emotion.

She said, "I got sixty dollars on me. I don't know. I might have a couple hundred in cash back home. I can go back and look."

Zach hung the key ring back in place. "Give me the sixty now, and I'll get you an I.O.U. for another sixty next month. When you come back, we'll work out the rest."

Hopeless eyes brightened. "I'll make that happen."

He handed it to her without a word.

***

Two hours later, he was being pummeled across the face by a wizened, green-tinged hand. Gyo'neri was frighteningly strong for someone so short and wiry.

"Why'd you let her pillage the good stuff?" Did all goblins have voices this screechy? Zach had wondered that many times.

"It's been in that cabinet for months, and no one bit yet. I don't think we'd get more for it."

Gyo'neri caught a fistful of brown hair and swung him sideways. His face smacked hard against glass.

He was more bothered by a sharp sting that coursed through his thigh, but he bit the inside of his cheek to keep from showing it.

"Sixty. Sixty! Did you even haggle? What am I saying? You didn't haggle, 'cause you gone soft."

"Trust me, I know people. She'll be back to pay. She's honorable in that way."

"Pfah!" But Gyo'neri backed off. He pulled a case out from under the cashier counter, clawed out a cigar, and stuck it in between his teeth. "Oughta send 'er a Black Hand," he said in between chomps. "Won't even wait to see if she pays up. Just send her a note tonight, so she won't fuck with us, y'know?"

Zach pushed himself off of the vending machine that had painfully broken his fall. Well, Gyo'neri called it a vending machine. Zach knew it was an ancient cigarette machine. Someone—an asshole hippie artist, probably — had gotten ahold of it at one point and painted it in rainbow swirls, so when Gyo'neri saw a colorful box with knobs on the front, he assumed it was a vending machine.

It didn't even hold cigarettes or sodas anymore, but the goblin had indulged himself in mobster movies not long before entering the 'entrepreneurship' scene. And since the mafia used to money launder with vending machines, he wanted one for aesthetics.

Zach limped into the back room and mentally practiced all the arguments he'd make out loud if he were stupid. "Why'd you expect someone to pay top dollar for a food duplication enchantment? Our customers are families. The ones with the money aren't the ones going hungry."

Few collaborators of the elves lived within walking distance of the University of Pittsburgh. The El'dori ruling this Protectorate were in Philadelphia. Human bureaucrats gobbled up estates in the traditional rich neighborhoods like Edgeworth and Shadyside. The lesser elves preferred the scenic views near the Point, or perhaps wanted the rivers to put some distance between themselves and Mayor Mel'kuan. At least one family of pointy ears turned the Drury Plaza Hotel into their home because they liked how the skyscraper looked.

Only Philadelphia's vassal lord, Mel'kuan, lived close to Darragh Street, having chosen the Cathedral of Learning for its imposing facade. Zach had seen what happened to the Cathedral's international room committees who complained about the elf's disrespect for its cultural significance. Mel'kuan summoned Pitt's remaining student body to the stadium so they could witness the executions. Even compared to the horrors of the invasion, that was the atrocity that stuck with Zach.

Safe in the back room, he focused on the stabbing in his leg. Gyo'neri had knocked open an oversized safety pin he threaded inside his pocket. He shoved his hand into his jeans, less worried about bleeding and more worried about losing what that pin secured to his person.

To his relief, no blood had marred the paisley swirls in a bolt of pashmina fabric. Its greenish-blue hue and fringed edges reminded him of a peacock feather. The same design on the shawl Agnes liked to wear. She might have had it when she vanished in the chaos of the invasion, somewhere on the side of Route 22.

***

Zach did not see the goblin again until noon. He was about to slip out for lunch when Gyo'neri shoved him into a coatroom. "Don't let 'em see ya."

Anticipating another beating, he covered his face before registering the real fear in his boss' voice. He cracked open the closet door for a glimpse at the new and dangerous guest strutting about the showroom. The black leather coat complemented his acid-washed jeans. He was so tall, his pointed ears nearly reached the top of the doorframe.

Gyo'neri greeted the elf with a flurry of bows, adjustments to his suit-coat, and massaging of his own knuckles. "How might Gyo'neri serve Lord Deriyan?"

"They found Bretti's body," the elf sneered. "However much of it that they could scrape off the back wall. I may have lost a year's profit to a pissant who didn't know how to store magic."

"Losing him and the shop last night is all the better for Lord Deriyan, and Gyo'neri, too." When he got nervous, the goblin's mafioso accent flickered on and off. "Gyo'neri can send strong boys from the Pitt to salvage it. Perhaps his lordship would like to consider a discount for the labor and risk of sending them into the danger zone."

Deriyan batted away a fly irritating him. "Your bargaining power's not what you think. If you want my business, it won't take you long to recoup what you pay me. We'll likely see another rationing cut. Even our allies will see their gifts spread thin. That's right, *Tereilen*?"

147

Zach shifted for a better look; he had not noticed the second elf. He didn't need the emphasis Deriyan placed on the name to recognize Tereilen. Elves in the Nurianel family shared a uniquely dark shade of red that looked plum when the lighting was right. They made appearances on TV more and more as rebel ambushes picked off other nobles. Everyone knew Tereilen's father was gunning to fill the vacuum. What would jeopardize Tereilen's future more — getting blown up in a Fianna booby trap or running a side gig in the black market?

Tereilen looked around, twitching. "That's true. Last month's... observation... emboldened the rebels, and they're attacking more supply routes."

The observation. Was that what the elves called the purple lightning show?

The smug college kid side of Zach wanted to joke that they shouldn't have snatched up Dr. Saadoun if they were so worried about supply chains. The commerce professor had initially charmed the elves into keeping Pitt open, newly christened the Imperial New Energy Research Division of the Iron Hills.

But Dr. Saadoun could not save Zach's undergraduate program in international and area studies. The elves required the students switch to majors they deemed useful, like engineering or environmental science. But Zach was completely inept in the lab. Dr. Saadoun probably saved him from being executed as a waste of oxygen by finding him work for the goblin allegedly interested in opening a recreational equipment shop just across the street from the Biomedical Science Tower. The professor's true motive for protecting Pitt was for the students who could not get home or had no home to go back to.

That and sabotage. To the elves, he touted his fellow Ph.D. holders' research on renewable energies. When they were out of pointed earshot, he laughed at how many peer-reviewed publishings were ninety-percent bullshit. "I'm in the work of keeping you all alive, not giving the elves something that works," he told his most trusted students.

Zach was dragged back to reality. Literally dragged by Gyo'neri once the two elves left. His boss snarled, "Michel and Nolan are bringing back the first round of cargo. You ain't leaving 'til you got it all catalogued."

"We're doing business with elves now?"

Gyo'neri giggled. "Greedy rats, scraping a bit of cream off the top of the pudding. And if rationing's to be like the Nurianel brat says, we'll be swimming in moolah."

***

Michel and Nolan arrived with three crates, arguing as they dragged them in through the Buffalo Street back entrance. Their loud arguing was a normal occurrence. Gyo'neri was always baffled by it, no matter how many times Zach explained that Michel was a former linebacker from Pitt, while Nolan had been a tight end at Penn State.

"They can't be panthers and lions," the goblin puzzled. "They don't got no shapeshifting energy in 'em."

Meanwhile, Zach appreciated that even an elven occupation could not squelch the football rivalries.

With the heavy lifting done, the jocks left their nerdy coworker to his ritual. He always began by calmly circling each container, feeling the change of equilibrium as new magic filled the storage room. For large drop-offs, it normally took two or three laps. This time, it took five. He hated to give elves any credit, but Deriyan had rightfully talked up the value of his goods.

He ran his hand across each crate. The energy was fairly evenly distributed, which was good. Packing magic in a tight space could be disastrous. A strong artifact could shatter weaker containers and set off an ugly chain reaction. Once he was satisfied that it was safe, he went to work with the crowbar.

Each item was nestled in egg crates and draped in bubble wrap. A few sat in cast-iron pans or had a spoon taped to the outside. The iron in kitchenware kept the magic settled.

Still, he did not rely on those to identify their potency. Magic artifacts could be mislabeled or come with forged documents to get a better price. Assuming an artifact was safe might have been what killed Bretti.

Setting each of them upon a specially-made desk with an iron plate surface, he inspected them one at a time. Mirrors. Jewelry. Porcelain figurines. Boots and slippers. Bones — only animals this time, thankfully. Flasks stuffed with herbs or mysterious liquids. A Faberge egg and a fiddle with blood-red varnish numbered among the more unique of this batch. The egg was magic. The fiddle was not.

If it had no magic, he set it aside. Gyo'neri would choose whether to market it as magical anyway. Upholding honesty fell above Zach's pay grade.

A month ago, after the lightning storm, he had noticed a nervous energy hovering close to earth. His dorm mates said the elves in the lab were whispering and getting distracted. Rumors spread that elves closer to the lightning's origin had been wiped out.

He gave it little thought until that night when he opened one of his advanced French textbooks out of boredom. He just wanted to practice root words. Instead, he slammed the book shut, opened it again, shuffled to random pages, then began to scream. His head throbbed so much that his vision nearly went black, and yet, he could read every word.

Dr. Saadoun sat nearby while he puked into a bucket. "Don't let them know anything about you has changed," he had whispered.

Two days later, the professor was "promoted" to chair a new research institution somewhere southwest and was dragged out of the lab by two orcs. And so, the occupation stole away Zach's real family and surrogate family.

But Gyo'neri sussed out his secret, and when he began picking up enchantments in items, he got his own promotion from shelf-stuffer to employee of the month with unrestricted access to the back rooms with the less legal but more profitable merchandise. There was no raise, but it meant fewer punches in the head most of the time.

He kept a set of wrought iron stakes on the desk, which he tied to anything that hadn't come with its own magic dissipator. He re-wrapped each in an additional sheet of tissue paper, color-coded. The dangerous ones got bundled in purple. The "not innately dangerous but might activate if you shake them" he bound in red.

In an odd way, it reminded him of Agnes explaining the difference between "deadly" and "dangerous" animal classifications when she held a part-time job at the Cincinnati Zoo. Even during the most monotonous part of his work, he could not help but recall memories of her.

Afternoon passed in this manner, broken up only by a sandwich delivered by Michel. He worked until he could only make out gray outlines of the shrubs along Buffalo Street through the small window. It was also too dark to see inside the last crate, so he did not realize at first that he had grabbed an old leathery satchel. It looked like what an old-time mailman would haul.

Scrolls rolled out onto the desk.

"The hell did these come from?" Peeling back the edge of one scroll revealed a language he had never studied. But without any trouble, he read the Greek letters: "...tame the beast, and bring it to my aid. Amen."

The scroll was ordinary papyrus, and its faded letters ordinary ink. But the few words he had read left his eyes twitching and a lump in his throat. The words had been imbued with pent-up power. If he spoke thoughtlessly, or even *though* thoughtlessly, he might unleash it.

Just to be safe, he hovered his hand over each scroll. Seven in all. Some gave off an intoxicating aura, while others buried shadowy and malicious intent. All except one. Only a weak tendril of its arcane energy remained. Its spell had been used.

He put them all back in the satchel and wrapped it in gold tissue paper. Gold for "uncertain."

He tucked it into a corner cabinet. There were secrets even Gyo'neri did not need to know.

***

The next day, Zach practiced hardening his heart and reciting his rejection in case the customer was another haggard mother. Gyo'neri would never let him get away with two undervalued sales. But the early morning's customers were only interested in real recreational equipment. He found himself holding back a different emotion. He knew that any human with the time for leisure and the money for those snowboards were probably being rewarded handsomely by the Imperium.

Nearing lunch, the bell over the door jangled again.

"Good mor —" He looked up to gray eyes with all the warmth of steel in winter, framed by long blond hair streaked with bluish-platinum.

"Where's the proprietor?" the elf demanded.

"He's out for the d..." Zach could not tear away his gaze. She had the elegance of a classic statue. Her clothes were earth-bought, but on her they looked ethereal. The silver knee-length tunic had a sleek, watery sheen, and her black boots went almost up to her knees. A gray braided belt and a long, blue jacket completed her appearance of ice in a storm. Or a waterspout in the ocean against the backdrop of a cloudy sky. Beautiful, alluring, and terrifying up close.

"We have a, a, a sale for th — the skiing gear and —"

"Don't read your script to me," she snapped. "I know what you got."

Should he make an excuse about finding Gyo'neri and slip out the back door? Did she know of his powers? "I don't know, ma'am. I just work here."

"Deriyan, that two-faced, was supposed to leave me something. Today, I find out he's shipped it here. A brown satchel bag. Give it to me, and I won't tell."

"A what kind of bag?"

She leaned over the counter and gave him the full, dizzying effect of her tremendous height. "I see the goblin left his most witless clerk to mind his store. Just my fortune."

"I'm really sorry, but if you want to come back, when my boss is back. I'll even write you a rain check, and if we have it, I'll make sure it's still here —"

"Shut up! He promised me enchanted scrolls." Her mouth twisted into a bitter smile. "I'm done waiting."

Zach did not realize his hand instinctively went into his pocket for reassurance, but her eyes tracked it. "It's there!" She leapt over the counter and pinned him to the wall, the long fingers of one hand around his throat. She shoved her other hand into his pocket.

"Please…" he gagged.

The elf frowned as she ripped out the safety pin and the swatch of pashmina. "What useless trash you keep!"

"What does it matter to you!" If she carried a wand, he would have been struck down on the spot for raising his voice. But in his anger, he went on. "You don't think we keep mementos of loved ones?"

She pulled a frayed thread off the pashmina and glared at him. For a few seconds, the only sound came from the humming HVAC.

To his surprise, the elf blinked first. "Of course." She almost sounded sheepish. "Items of sentiment, to feel close to the ones lost. Who was it?"

"A sister."

"Sister?" She dropped the cloth. "Was this torn from her… body?"

He reached for the floor. She let him retrieve it. "I don't have Agnes' real shawl. I found this fabric down near the Strip. It looks close to hers."

The elf gingerly pulled a ring off her left hand. "This was my own sister's."

Zach blinked. "Did she die in the invasion?"

She returned the ring to her middle finger. "It's because of her, I need the scrolls. They're my one chance to bring her back. May I at least see them?" Her tone was not exactly plaintive, but it was no longer ruthless.

"If you take them, Gyo'neri can't know they were ever here. He will disembowel me… well, probably toss me in a bag into the Monongahela River, because that's on brand for him." He flipped the sign on the front door to "Closed."

"What's your name?"

"Zachary." He kept it at that. No full name. No nickname.

He was surprised again when she replied with a palm against her heart. "Myretha Er-Koraiyes."

He opened the back door. As she brushed past, he counted his blessings for working late last night to move the bulk of Deriyan's smuggled goods into the locked side room, so that she only saw boxes of tennis rackets and golf clubs. "That cabinet. Top shelf."

It took Myretha half the strides it took Zach to cross the back room. She pulled out the satchel. "Which one is it?"

"What do you mean?"

"At least one of these had its spell already spun. Which one?"

"Well, I think..." Zach clenched the pashmina. "I wouldn't know."

"Do not ever lie to me, Zachary," she hissed. "You knew these were important. You kept them separate."

"I play it safe. Never know what kind of magic is in the air nowadays." Her eyes narrowed, and he gulped. "I'm talking of magic in general. I watched the dragon boats versus the fighter jets from my dorm window. I now know that magic exists."

Myretha patted the satchel. "I may take these?"

"Sure. No charge, ma'am. If they were meant to go to you in the first place, I'm sorry for the mix-up."

She tucked the leather under her arm. His heart pounded as her stormy aura washed over him as she passed, about to move on and out of his life.

Just as she stepped back into the showroom, she reached back and grabbed his collar. Zach stifled a cry as she pushed him into the rainbow edge of the cigarette machine. She pressed a scroll against his face. "Is it this one?"

"I don't know," he gasped.

She unfurled another. "What about this?"

"I don't know!"

She thrust a third papyrus at his eyes. "And this?"

His eyes rolled back. A language he had never heard flowed off his tongue.

Let this spirit be secured by stone, by the power of the Zeus, keeper of oaths.

Myretha dropped the gasping youth to the floor. Her own voice shook when she spoke again. "This is it. Two thousand years, and I found it. This one imprisoned my sister in this forsaken ground."

Zach wiped his eyes. His head was pounding again, and he struggled not to get sick in front of her. "You said two thousand? The war was barely two years ago."

She laughed mirthlessly. "You hadn't heard? Back then, we ruled your realm. With all our servant races. Long have we waited for your human mages to die out so that we could reclaim our lands. It was during that war that my elder sister, my dear Gormliet, was petrified."

Zach blinked the tears from his eyes. "Well, I already said you can take those. Go get her back."

"We're not done! This scroll can only bind. It lacks the words to undo the enchantment."

"Maybe it's one of the others?"

She tossed the satchel at him. "Read for yourself."

He had already noticed the spells were unrelated. He sensed infatuation in one, talk of beasts in another. "The spell used on your sister is in an older Egyptian language. The others are in Coptic. None of them are originally from here."

"Obviously," said Myretha. "Deriyan could not tell me how they came to Pennsylvania."

"Did he raid a museum? Maybe a college professor's desk?"

"A lot of thieves resumed their search for loot since the..." She licked her lips. "He vaguely mentioned that these gave him trouble. There ought to be a companion scroll that reverses the spell once cast."

He took out his phone and typed an Internet search. "Coptic... spoken in Egypt... around the second century." His eyes lit up. "I have a theory. You have a minute?"

He grabbed the key ring and singled out the one for Gyo'neri's office. "Before we go in, let me apologize for the blight on the eyes."

Myretha groaned as a buzzing red light spilled out the opened door. "What garish adornments!"

Gyo'neri's favorite piece of decor was a small neon sign he'd gotten from New York. He thought it fit his mafia aesthetic. It made Zach think of *Seinfeld*.

While he went around the other side of the goblin's heavy oak desk, the elf sank into a leather two-seat couch and tried to make sense of the *Scarface* movie poster on the wall.

He found the goblin's ledger in the center drawer and flipped to its newest, nigh-illegible entries. Given the recent partnership with Deriyan and Bretti's brief but explosive racketeering stint, Zach's gut told him that Gyo'neri might have been tipped off about the theft. With what little he'd inspected, he had a hunch about the scrolls' original whereabouts.

"Holy shit. Well, emphasis on the 'holy'." He tapped a word he found a few pages back: *Anthony*. "I bet those came from St. Anthony's Chapel. Gyo'neri's been hankering for what's inside of there. He's convinced that it's a gold mine of Old-World magic."

"I might find the companion scroll there?" asked Myretha.

"There won't be anything left there. The pastor hid a lot of it right after the surrender. The rest is probably in the holding den."

"Holding den?" she repeated.

"People in the business usually get this stuff in two ways. They prefer a direct partner, but a lot of goods get put up for auction. If Deriyan's not fully onboard with my boss, he might've taken some stuff to the den to see if he gets a better price."

"Where is this holding den?"

He flipped to the front of the ledger and spotted an address. "Fuck me."

"I don't appreciate you speaking to me with such profane casualness," Myretha stewed.

"Laurel Caverns! Really? That's the place?"

She stood up. "How long will it take us to get there?"

"Us?"

She dragged him out from behind the desk. "You can detect magic. You are useful."

"I'm still on shift."

Myretha threw back her head and laughed, making Zach realize how stupid he sounded. "I wager that Mayor Mel'kuan's men know that you are magically inclined. If they discover that, they will lock you up or ship you off to their new labs in the west for testing or suppression. Neither is an experience you want to endure. Aren't you happy to have an elf to protect you?"

He swallowed. This was extortion, not protection. "What am I going to do in Laurel Caverns? I don't have any weight to pull."

"Are there any shapeshifting artifacts here?"

"You mean..."

She bounced on her heels, not unlike a teenage girl, and he did not like how it clashed with her stormy tenor. "Zachary, now wouldn't you like to see how it feels to be the boss?"

***

Thirty minutes later, he stared at a map inside a Lexus speeding southbound down Route 43. Myretha was annoyed that he did not know the way to Laurel Caverns. He struggled to explain that he was a little kid when his family visited. Grumbling, she grabbed the map at a visitors' center and tossed it into his lap to read out the directions.

"Why was St. Anthony's Chapel a 'gold mine'?" she asked him.

"The place is pretty famous. Back in the 1800s, Europe went through a bunch of civil wars. Borders changed. And sometimes, villages switched from Protestant control to Catholic or vice versa. It was pretty common for armies to desecrate churches. One priest traveled the continent collecting relics and other holy stuff before the armies got to them. And then he brought them all to Pittsburgh."

"These relics must be quite powerful?"

"Um…" He shifted in his seat. Knowing nothing about St. Anthony's current pastor, he had heard many priests were part of the human resistance. He did not want the arrest of a reverend on his conscience. "Relics aren't magic. I'll, uh, temper your expectations. The priest hid the relics but left the scrolls. Catholics like to keep bones of saints. I think there were a couple cities in Italy that fought over one saint's head —"

She cut off his gabbing with a curt question: "They're sentimental?"

"True." He shrugged. "What I'm saying is, the priest didn't think these scrolls mattered."

"At a time when their magic would not manifest," Myretha pointed out. "That priest may not think so now."

"True," he said again. "Too late for him. Lucky for you, I guess." He was breaking the same rule he scolded customers for in the shop. Don't ramble. Easier said than done while stuck two feet to her right and doing eight-five down the highway. "Did your family live in Egypt two thousand years ago?"

"My house is a vassal to House Nurianel," she said icily. "Even during the elves' first reign."

"What do you think of them?"

"And what would you do with that information?"

"I'm not in the business of information," he insisted. "I'm curious, seeing as they're moving up in the Protectorate."

The car rumbled as it veered off the road. He flinched while she wrenched it back into the lane. "The last one who had anything to say about them was my sister, and her words left her like this."

"The Nurianels that bound her. Not humans?" Zach shuddered. "Then freeing her is committing treason."

"Aren't I fortunate to find you, then," she sniped. "So deep into the smuggling business."

"I don't know a goddamn thing about smuggling *people*."

The Laurel Caverns sign zipped past. She cut off a car in the right lane without using her blinker. "Do this right, and they'll never know. All I need from you anyway is the companion scroll."

"And then we part ways."

She smirked. "Once we find it, I'll reevaluate if I need you for anything else." She pulled off to the side of the road.

"What are we doing?" he said fearfully.

"Dressing you up." She reached into a bag at his feet for a lump of blue tissue paper. Blue meant 'safe to use'. "How well will they know Gyo'neri down there?"

"He usually sends associates rather than go out himself. Most evenings, he's in his office watching movies."

"Then you must make up a reason he would visit in person." She unwrapped a pocket watch, an artifact he had reluctantly taken from the storage closet. Reluctant because, unlike the scrolls, he had logged this one. Which meant Gyo'neri would notice it was missing. *No way I pull this off*, he thought as she dropped it into his hand. For the love of God, he could hear something broken and rattling inside.

"Magic boy," she chirped. "How does it work?"

"I only feel magic. I've never used it."

"You never wanted to try?"

An elf encouraging a human to use magic was ludicrous. Was this all a set-up, an entrapment to make him drop his cover? Then he noticed how she anxiously twisted the ring on her left hand.

"I have to picture him, the way he moves. This is going to be tough. He's, what, three feet max? And bow-legged."

"I didn't drive you all the way here to give up. To give up on *my sister*."

He closed his eyes. She drummed her knuckles against the steering wheel.

"Uh... say hello to my little friend?"

"What?" Myretha looked around as if she expected a dwarf or other "little friend" to pop out of the back seat. Zach felt like an idiot. There was a reason he wasn't a theatre major.

"I said, 'Say hello to my little friend!'"

A loud clicking, like a winding key, jerked his attention back to the pocket watch. He addressed the next movie quote to the artifact. "'You mean funny like I'm a clown? I amuse you?'"

Myretha jerked away. "Your face!"

"Is it working?"

"It was until you talked like yourself again. It moved like molding clay."

A steady tick came from the watch. He turned to the rearview mirror just in time to see his face turn a familiarly unpleasant shade of grayish-green. The corners of his ears sharpened and turned out.

"What do you know, kiddo?" he said with a forced chuckle as Gyo'neri's favorite suitcoat molded around him. "Let's go in and give them a show."

"I'm most certain *you* will," she said.

"Not coming with me?" he asked. "I'll make up something. You can be a classy patron."

She sniffed. "As if I'd dirty my boots down there." But don't even think about going off and doing whatever you want. Because I'll be listening."

He grimaced as she dropped a pendant into the pocket of the suitcoat. The watch wasn't the only thing she'd made him steal from All-Seasons Outdoor Surplus.

"Damn, you're good," he said. "Hey, bucko. You got any money?"

"What did you say to me!"

He threw up his hands reassuringly. "I'm staying in character, I swear. But if I'm going to get my hands on this reversal spell, y'know, I ain't gettin' it with chump change."

***

Within the hour, wallet laden with Myretha's cash, he traipsed down the wooden stairs into a stone tunnel. There was no need to stop by the visitors' center. Laurel Caverns had been shut down to tourists by the elves within days of the surrender while they searched for resources to fill their reserves lost in the short war. Sandstone was no use to them, so they made it a temporary barracks for orcs until they were reassigned to the midwest territories. Smugglers swooped into its twisted passages with filched copper, illegally-grown hot house tomatoes, and — lately — arcane antiques.

The temperature dropped quickly. Flapping bat wings broke the silence. He smiled at the sound. Before the war, he hadn't been particularly attached to the caverns. But the pilfering of the natural wonder had struck him with a pang of sorrow. It warmed him to hear the signs of resilience in the commonwealth's landmark. Then he cleared his throat and adjusted his posture. He could leave no dents in the charade.

A few colorful lights from the spelunking days remained. Distant voices swelled until he arrived in the first of the roomier chambers.

Based on Gyo'neri's words, he'd anticipated a stage with a podium for an auctioneer — human or supernatural. Instead, the atmosphere was like a bazaar.

Humans, goblins, dwarves, and a surprising number of elves gathered around tables or rugs full of antiques, forged ration tickets, and boxes of dragon scales.

He hung near the back of the crowd and took it all in, running his hand down his new pointy goatee. The conversational energy held little of the desperation of the common man he usually worked with. These creatures loved the black market. Whatever they paid for the goods down here, they expected to make back five times back in their various towns. A few surrounded themselves with a cadre of bodyguards. Sellers told potential customers the tales of what dangers they braved to secure their loot, all the more justification for charging top price.

But that was not all that charged the atmosphere. The caverns teemed with magic. How had the elves not noticed?

A gnome chuckled behind a nearby table. "Mister Gyo'neri, showing your face in these parts?"

Zach shrugged. "Eh, a man's got to do what a man's got to do." He leaned his fists on the table. It was surreal to have to look *up* to see its contents. Geodes. Obviously snatched out of a gift shop. Not a drop of magic in any of them. The gnome was probably selling them as cure-alls. The little machines on the other end of the table were far more useful, clicking smoothly thanks to the gnome's natural crafting capabilities.

He continued, "What with Bretti putting himself out of business, I felt it was time I got a proper feel for the times. The 'observation,' and all that."

The gnome said. "I heared the magic infusion got into his merch that used to be inert. Built up over the month, then boom! Nearly took the whole Strip with 'im."

"Amateur move," Zach answered. "Y'know, I took precautions soon as I seen the old magic waking up. I made one of my little human twerps go back over every inch of the inventory. Kept him on twelve-hour shifts for a week, making sure we didn't have a ticking time bomb."

"Ain't no one missing Bretti, though," the gnome laughed.

"No one but his elf benefactor." Zach leaned forward and whispered, "That pointy-eared freak showed up looking for a new front man. Now, I'm more than happy to start doing business with him. But the fucker ripped me off on the first day."

"Which one?"

"Deriyan."

"Oh, yeah. You gotta watch out for that one." The gnome ran a finger across his neck. "He'll talk real sweet and then slit your throat to save his skin."

"Claimed to have loot outta the relic chapel down on Harpster Street. So, I pay 'im real good, and he just 'forgot' to pack that in with the rest of the goods. Buddy, I'm missing 'bout three hundred grand."

"Well, you're shit out of luck. If you find what's missing down here, you can try hagglin' a new deal, but you'll be putting down more money on top of what you paid."

"What I paid don't need to get back to the customer." Zach traced a geode's purple interiors. "With rationing what it is, I might get me better clientele than the mongrels coming to me now all whining about their lot in life. People still used to livin' nice and good. They'll cough up the dough, no problem."

The gnome looked around grimly. "It's a double-edged sword. All that magic wakening up that been dormant for years. More stuff moving down here, and what's in the store rooms powering up. It's a volcano fit to blow its top. I'm half a mind to pack up my humble shack and go somewhere, before it all goes up like Bretti."

"Yeah, take care of yourself," Zach answered. "A guy told me one time: don't let yourself get attached to anything you're not willing to walk out on in thirty seconds flat, if you feel the 'heat' around the corner."

As he extracted himself from the gnome, he scoured the chamber for exit signs. Were there ever exit signs? He couldn't remember. But the energy and the gnome's warnings made him feel claustrophobic.

"Have you found it?"

He held back a groan. The listening pendant was still in his pocket, but Myretha's voice sounded like she was whispering directly into his ear.

"Please give me time. This place is huge. And another problem. The caverns are a ticking time bomb with all the magic."

"Then pick up your pace," she answered through the pendant. "Find Deriyan's other sellers. If he's waiting on the auction, follow the magic to where it's stored."

He pulled on his collar. Should've known she'd offer no help.

Why not escape? He could dispose of the amulet, then slip out a back exit. She didn't know her way through the caverns. He could thumb a ride out of town while she was still getting her bearings.

Seeing another goblin who scanned the crowd in a way that suggested he was security, he scurried forward and tugged on his jacket sleeve. "Hey, Tony, why the auction taking so long to start?"

"Fuck off before I throw your ass out," the goblin said. "Go back and ask 'em yourself."

Thankfully, the first of the goblin's two angry gestures indicated the direction to go; the follow-up middle finger, he just brushed off. He skulked further in, past a twisting wall of floatstone.

He turned down a narrow passage and came face to face with a dead man.

"Shit!" He clamped his gnarled hand over his mouth to muffle the involuntary cry. The empty eyes stared up at the bulbous ceiling. Purplish impressions across his throat and bruises on his knuckles suggested a struggle, but the burns in his abdomen indicated the killing instrument. An elf wand.

"God, Zachary, what are you doing?" he said to himself.

The sound of a box cutter interrupted his self-reprimand, followed by a boyish giggle. "Told you we'd find something good."

He took cover behind a column.

Just around the next bend, like vultures hovering over roadkill, four elves huddled in a crevice stuffing their pockets with vials from emptied cardboard boxes.

One of them, a young man dressed like an Abercrombie and Fitch model, swirled a jar of green liquid. "I hope these are love potions."

"Working yourself too hard?" said his friend with a similar expensive taste in dress. "Or not hard enough."

"They're not for me," Abercrombie said angrily.

The next voice, Zach recognized. Tereilen, heir to House Nurianel, scoffed. "Since when did Auturiel ever lack for a girl on each arm?"

"The ones who throw themselves at our feet were whores before we arrived," Auturiel said. "It's always the prettiest ones that keep saying 'no.'"

The fourth elf said, "You sure we should take them? Sooner or later, someone will let slip to Deriyan how you helped yourself to his profits."

"And what would he do? Complain to the mayor's court in front of my father?" Tereilen laughed.

Zach whispered into the pendant. "Myretha?"

"Did you find it?"

"Tereilen's got it. I can sense it in his coat."

That was all he got out before a hand clamped down on his mouth.

Seconds later, he, Tereilen, and his elven friends, were enveloped in a light so bright that the cavern fully disappeared. It was followed by a tinnitus-like wail in his ears.

The spots cleared in time to see the blinded elves shamble off the ledge in a tangled heap. Two men in armor swooped in. The butts of their rifles came down on the elves' skulls.

"Cuffs, hurry," said a black man with a buzz cut. He and his companion, a pale man with a scruffy red five o'clock shadow and freckles up and down his muscled arms, whipped out zip tie cuffs.

"One wand, Sarge." Redbeard scooped the glowing rod off one of the four. He patted down Tereilen. "Sweet! This one's got a dragon scale undershirt."

"Is it heavy?" asked the man called Sarge.

"No, actually pretty light."

"Take it. We're limited to what we can fit in one box, so make it count."

Zach grunted as the third man, whose face he could not see, wrestled him down. "Get on the ground and don't move."

"Careful!" said Sarge. "I don't think he's with them. And if he's part of the guild, we'll be in trouble with the Master Artificer for roughing up one of our own allies."

"His watch!" Redbeard said. "It's magic."

"Take it."

The hand left Zach's mouth and plucked the watch out of his pocket. Magic sloughed away, leaving him cold and shaky.

"Oh my god, it's a kid," Sarge said.

"The hell are you doing here?" said the man who had assailed him.

"Lex, give him a break." Redbeard fiddled with the watch before turning a piercing gaze back toward Zach. "You can sense it, too. Did the storm wake up your powers?"

It took him a moment to remember the rebels' moniker. "Are you... Fianna?"

"Not sure what you're talking about, kid," said Sarge. He did not lie very well. "Why are you dressing up as a gnome?"

"Please, I will be killed if I don't come out with what I was sent to get. And you better get out of here, too. The whole place is roiling with magic."

"Sarge, we can't let him go his own way," said Lex, the one still holding him. "He's seen us."

"I swear I won't tell anyone."

"Shut up, or I'll knock you out, too."

Zach stopped struggling. He took a closer look at the one in charge. "Sarge... Wilson?"

The three men froze. Redbeard and Lex looked uneasily at their leader.

"Mr. Wilson, I'm Zach Bourassa. I was at Pitt, same class as your son. Ramsey, right? You invited a bunch of us to your church potluck after orientation. I probably didn't thank you for it. I haven't seen Ramsey since the invasion. Is he alright?"

"Kid..." Lex warned.

Wilson became very interested in his rifle rather than look at Zach, who quickly got the message. "I'm sorry, sir."

The sergeant nodded slightly. "Can't be dwelling on the past now. Not except for what drives me to a better future.

"Zach, huh?" said Redbeard. "Since names are going around, call me Nate, but that's as much as I can tell you. You need protection? Can we give you a lift?"

"You're going to take me for my powers."

Lex directed a bit of saliva to the stone floor. "We should. You'd be useful."

"Can you quit scaring the kid?" Nate snapped. "Only if you volunteer first. The more people, the more humans can mount a resurgence. And if you're one of the ones waking up, think of what you can do."

Was this the escape route he'd hoped for minutes ago? The rebels might get him away from Myretha. But what would they make him do next? Working for Gyo'neri was risky, sure, but the goblin found his power too critical to throw him into danger.

"I'm not resistance material."

"But your power —" Nate protested.

With the rebels, his power would guarantee he'd be put in danger.

Lex grunted. "He doesn't care. He's just gonna let us keep living under the elves' boot."

"Get a grip," said Wilson. "I get it. Kid wants to stay alive one day at a time. Most people default back to hunter-gatherer in times like these. Hell, I've played enough apocalypse video games to know it's easy to just be scavengers. But it probably means you're not cut out for our line of work. Whatever you want, if it isn't what we came for, we'll let you go."

Zach nodded gratefully at the sergeant, although being called a 'scavenger' left a sour taste in his mouth. He asked, "You heard about the raid on St. Anthony's in Pittsburgh?"

Lex perked up. "I've been friends with Father since I was your age. Don't call it a raid. It was sacrilege. Still, we didn't go a straight forty-eight hours packing up relics to let looters get away with anything worth shit."

"What's this worth?" Zach unfurled the scroll.

Nate leaned in for a better look. "Don't need my magic to know what it is. Just my minor in theology. You got yourself a Coptic papyrus spell. Father Mollinger might've brought it along with Egyptian relics."

"What spells did they have?"

"Whatever you wanted. Love spells. Help conceiving. Summoning animals or scaring them off. They were popular for centuries, and you can tell because they invoked gods from whatever religion was dominant at the time. Osiris, Juno, Yahweh. Egypt was a melting pot of belief systems." He gave the scroll another glance. "I can't read this with its magic used up."

"It's supposed to have a companion. And it's on him." He shifted toward the unconscious Tereilen, keeping one wary eye on the rebels' nearest rifle. To his relief, the men focused on collecting their own trinkets. As he plucked the scroll from a pocket inside the elf's coat, he marveled at how fast they wrapped artifacts in burlap and stowed them into one box.

"Seal it up," said Wilson. "Let's roll out."

Nate looked back at Zach. "Sure you're not interested?"

"Nate, we gotta go," Lex urged.

"Give it some thought," Nate added quickly. "We got caught flatfooted because magic was never on our radar. But now it's on our side —" He stopped in confusion, as his offer was met with an expression of fear. "What?"

"Something in this room," Zach whispered. "It's spreading out. It's calling."

They all turned to the elves. Zach should have realized that Tereilen would carry a beacon to summon aid if he was ever in danger.

Nate jolted. "On your six!"

The Abercrombie elf Auturiel was awake and holding a vial over his head. "Eat this, motherfuckers!"

Zach yelled, "Not in a room this small!"

The elf ignored him and lobbed the vial at Lex's head. The rebel's reflexes were good, and he batted it away with the muzzle of his AR.

It dropped into another box half full of artifacts. Whatever it landed on, Zach knew by the overwhelming stench of pent-up magic that the two were never meant to interact.

"Get out!" the sergeant yelled.

"Get the kid up front!" But by the time Nate yelled it, there was no chance. They'd crammed into a tunnel exit so narrow they had no choice but to move in a single file with Zach trapped at the rear. Smoke thickened around him. Sparks singed his pant legs, and an acrid taste hit his tongue.

The last thing he saw was Nate turning around. He was being squeezed, and his ears clogged up. All three men were screaming commands he couldn't make out.

He felt like he got smacked in the back by giant's hand. Sharp pebbles battered his head and neck. A rumble gave way to a roar. Then dust. So much dust.

He came around just as someone pushed rocks away from his head.

"Zachary?"

With one tug, Myretha heaved him free.

Nate slumped against a wall. The circular stains on his green shirt were like points on a map marking where the shrapnel had hit, but the blood quickly spread into one dark, sticky mess down his arms and abdomen.

"We need to go," said Myretha.

"We need to get him a medic." Zach tried to wriggle away, but his arms wouldn't obey. He searched for Mr. Wilson or Lex. Had they escaped the tunnel in time? Were they buried nearby?

Myretha pointed at the blood pooling around a deep gash in Nate's chest. "There's nothing you can do. Tereilen's still alive back there, barely. His security beacon is still flashing. His guards will be on us soon."

One of Nate's eyes cracked open. "Kid," he muttered. He was barely able to lift his hand to point.

Zach looked down and, for the first time, saw the reason for his inability to move. With seconds to spare, the rebel had thrown Tereilen's dragon scale undershirt over him. He bore scratches on his hands and wrists from the shattered stone, but the light armor and Nate's arms had blocked lethal damage.

Nate smiled weakly and then closed his eyes.

Myretha led Zach over rubble. Potions flowed from smoldering vials. Tereilen whimpered on his side with one leg mangled beneath him. The only sign of any other elf was a hand jutting out of the stone, long fingers broken and still.

The two barely managed to leap over a "Do not go past this point" sign and into a side cavern before the crowd streamed inside. A minute later, they heard the harsh barking of humans with the Imperial guard, followed by the thumps of their rifles against the craniums of bystanders who were not fast enough to clear a path to House Nurianel's heir.

They followed a winding path until it tilted upward and reached a thin opening. Soon, Zach was shimmying through what had been the cavern's original entrance a couple centuries ago.

The goblin suitcoat had vanished and left him in his regular clothes. He scrounged into his jeans. "No!"

"What?" she asked.

He pulled the pocket inside out. The safety pin had come unhooked again. The pashmina was gone.

Her lips fluttered with a slight tremor before she rendered her face unreadable. She brushed small rocks from Zach's hair. He pushed his pocket back in and shrugged his jacket over the chainmail. "I'm fine."

"You sure?" He could hardly believe how softly she said those two words. It was a full reversal from every interaction since their first in Gyo'neri's shop. The storm at sea had lost its fury.

He handed her the scroll. "I got it."

She hugged it to her chest. "My sister languished for two thousand years. I won't make her wait any longer."

Back in her Lexus, the growing aches glued him to the seat. Myretha pulled into a gas station. While the car refueled, she ducked into the convenience store and returned with a bottle of water, which she tossed into his lap.

"Sorry I'm making a mess," he sighed.

She fit the gas nozzle back into the bay. "I would rather you use it to drink than to wash up. Your nerves are in a state. We've a long way to go." She slipped the ring off her finger and held it up to the windshield. "But we're nearing the end. My sister still sleeps in her enchantment. Her pulse summons me. I have no authority to ask a dragon rider to fly us there, and the airships are being restaged as a precaution for renewed combat. I hope that your airport has a flight going that way."

He brought the bottle down from his dusty lips. "Wait. Where was she locked up?"

"Near Alexandria."

Zach spluttered, "E — g — gy — gpt?"

"We talked about this!"

"That's... all the way around the world." Did she not appreciate the concept of distance? Or passports? Who was he kidding? She would not care one iota. He didn't even know if Egypt existed as a country anymore. It was probably the domain of another elf lord — probably one that started out low-level before the invasion and let most of his or her superiors get slaughtered by the Israelis before leaping into the leadership void.

***

Cruising altitude 33,000 feet

14:46 Eastern European Time

They said nothing while she bought tickets at Pittsburgh International Airport. At least Myretha paid for first-class. With the adrenaline long gone, he nodded off.

Until she poked him. "The stewardess brought out dessert while you slept. I made sure she left you some."

"Thanks." He tore the wrapper off a brownie. Sweets were getting scarcer down on the ground.

"What did you say your sister's name was?"

"A — Agnes."

"What was Agnes like?"

He shook himself. Myretha fiddled with her own sister's ring while she waited for his answer.

"A bookworm. And a good singer. She sang in the choir at her college."

"She studied music?"

"Geology," He played with the now meaningless safety pin. "Getting her master's. She used to talk about being a river surveyor. Back when we were kids, she'd wade out into the creek behind our house and catch salamanders."

"You still had salamanders?" Myretha asked. "Even with magic suppressed?"

"These weren't elementals. Just regular old animals. Her dream pet was a hellbender, but Mom made her settle for an iguana. Named him Nicky Carter." His voice caught in his throat.

"I'm sorry. I shouldn't dredge up such memories."

First, she'd asked if he was fine. Now she was apologizing. Zach never thought he'd heard that from an elf. "I don't mind. I wish it was the memories I could focus on. Instead of my imagination going into overdrive."

"What do you imagine?"

"What happened to her. They found her car on twenty-two after the surrender. It was torched. One bloody handprint on the backdoor, another on the driver's headrest. I don't even know if it was her blood or not. There was no sign of her body, so maybe she tried to run when traffic snarled up. Maybe she was carried away or captured." He pressed on the pin, drawing a bead of blood.

Myretha pulled his hand away. "Don't do that. You can choose to imagine she's alive. She might have found shelter. Perhaps injured and lost her memories, but alive still."

He sank back into his chair. "Home is in Ohio. The rest of our family lives to the west. There's no reason for her to drive east to Pennsylvania in the middle of a battle. Except if she was coming to get me."

She had no response to that, so she looked back out her window. "There was a lake not far from our own house. Gormliet and I used to play on the shore. Building castles, whole towns, in fact, out of sand. Imagining a kingdom of our own, not under House Nurianel."

"You built sand castles?"

"Well, she built them. I was so young, I knocked most of them down."

He grinned in spite of himself. Myretha saw it and gave an uneasy smile back. "Little towns in the sand," she continued, "That would wash away with no fuss. No mess. No blood. What I wouldn't give to see the world like that. I think Gormliet might have been like Agnes, if she's like how you describe."

"Do you mind me asking? What did she do that made House Nurianel seal her away?"

"A petty slight," Myretha sniped. "A comment made in jest about their heir. He stewed over it for years. And in the middle of the Great Sundering, while we focused on the human uprising, he saw a window. He bribed a human mage to petrify her."

"Was it Tereilen?"

"No! Tereilen is a second son. His older brother lost his life to the insurgents a week ago. I heard it was a nasty way to go, but it took great acting on my part to shed tears." She tossed her blond and platinum-blue hair to emphasize her point. "Not that I expect any of your sympathy, but there are oaths that go back to before your lifetime that I cannot escape. House Koraiyes has little love for Nurianel. But Tereilen is more weak-willed than his brother ever was. A part of me believes he won't even care if I break Gormliet's curse."

"You don't suppose Gormliet will lead a coup against them?" he asked.

She hurriedly looked around first class. "Do you talk of treason with so many people nearby?"

He whispered, "But you took his..." He stopped. Don't ramble. Don't ramble.

But her eyes narrowed. "Took what?" she demanded.

He stared at her jacket's deep pocket. "You took the elf's wand from the human man."

She frowned and reached into the pocket. Zach tried to shrink into his seat. He'd done it now. She would leave him like the corpse in the cave, with a hole blasted through his chest. She might let its magic tear through the fuselage and doom all the passengers.

But instead, she handed him a cloth bundle. "I was going to give you this after this was all over, and my sister was cared for. But I see no harm in giving it to you now."

Zach gave the bundle a squeeze. He felt no magic. He unwrapped it, and found it to be a small gold-rimmed case. A tiny piece of bone, no bigger than a fingernail, sat in the center of a reliquary. In an equally small label, in Latin, he read *S. Agnes.*

The lump in his throat grew, and a couple tears dotted his lashes.

"As for the wand, better to take it than leave it buried," she said emotionlessly. "I can only channel so much magic, but given I don't know what awaits us, I'd like to be safe."

He cleared his throat and grabbed his plastic cup of Dr. Pepper. "Here's to the best of outcomes."

Myretha looked puzzled, but she clinked her own cup to his.

***

At Cairo's rental desk, Myretha's syrupy charm came out in full. Between that and her status as an elf, they did not have to wait long for a jeep. She even bought him a scarf to protect his face. It was cheap and did not feel like the pashmina, but he was grateful for it.

The roads were too bumpy for them to talk. Zach nearly jolted out of the seat until she stopped. He checked that the satchel of scrolls was still secure over his shoulder. "Is something wrong with the car?"

"We're nearly here."

He saw nothing but mountainous sand dunes. "I thought we had another hour to Alexandria."

"I said she is bound *near* Alexandria." She narrowed her eyes when he, too, scrambled out of the jeep. "You don't have to come. I can do this on my own."

"I'll bake in the sun if I just sit."

She sighed. "The desert chills quickly when the sun goes down."

He tripped on his first step, but steadied himself and flashed a sheepish smile. "You ever been to Alexandria in its golden age?"

She sniffed. "Strange you think it ever had a golden age. Noisy port city. Good for nothing but rabble and rioters. If any elf set foot there, you wondered what they did to be punished so."

"Still, it's where Julius Caesar duked it out with the Ptolemys. Did you ever see the Pharos lighthouse?"

"I did not." She pressed her fingers, palm down, across her brow and scoured the barren landscape.

"One of the seven wonders of the world," he continued. "Three stories tall. The king forbid the architect from putting his name on it. He only wanted his own name on it. So, the architect secretly carved his signature into the stone underneath the plaster. He knew the plaster with the king's crest would chip off over time and reveal his name." He stumbled again when sand shifted under his boot. "I guess that's a lot like our world now. Your people's mark was always there, and we're seeing it again."

Myretha held up her hand, her sister's ring catching the glint of the sun. "Or, perhaps, problems never go away, no matter how well you think they're covered."

Suddenly, the elf broke into a run. As her long hair and shirt hem billowed behind her, she looked all the more like the storm he had first pictured. He staggered further and further behind, nearly lost sight of her in the wriggling heat waves distorting the horizon.

The hum of magic washed over him.

The elf's hand was raised, the wand held aloft. Sand whirled around her imposing silhouette. Zach found a dune to take cover and pulled the scarf tighter as the fine particles beaded his brown hair and tried to push under his eyelids. Myretha seemed unbothered by it all, eyes only on the hole yawned open at her feet. With each gust, another layer of a stone pillar was exposed. An obelisk, well-weathered over the centuries, stood in the Egyptian desert.

Its ancient inscription read *A traitor's reward.*

Myretha slid down into the hole and punched through the base of the obelisk. The darkness of a hollowed-out crevice greeted them. "Help me out, if you're going to just gape," she called.

Zach slid down beside her and helped clear away the shards. His hands fell upon the now familiar touch of papyrus.

"There's dozens. Might be a hundred. They're packed so tight."

Myretha's eyes flashed with pain. "But where is Gormliet? I came all this way!"

Zach ran a finger up the obelisk's sanded surface. Magic radiated outward, writhing and digging at his chest, as if trying to wring his heart like a used rag.

She thrust the two scrolls into his hands. "Well, stop staring and read it."

"Me —"

"We're so close! Have confidence. If there's hope for your sister, there's hope for mine!"

He backed away from the frantic elf and unspooled the papyri. His hands shook so much that all he saw were blurry black squiggles.

Agnes, if you're there, help me.

He pulled the scarf back up to his nose, breathed deeply, and then rested the two scrolls against the surface of the obelisk. His vision blurred again, but his tongue moved freely.

"I call upon you, Zeus, in the clouds, who freely took the shape of a shepherd, a swan, a shower of gold, who turned Baucis and Philemon into trees to guard for eternity their lands condemned by flood, to watch over new gardens. Let this spirit be secured by stone, by the power of the Zeus, keeper of oaths." Then he read the second, "Draw back your hand. Repent of your command. What you bound before, set free."

At the last word, a crack tore the obelisk top to bottom. Shards struck him hard enough to send him staggering. It was only by some miracle that the debris missed his head.

All but the base vanished in smoke, and a lithe woman took shape in the gray wisps. Hair blond like her sister's, but eyes were a vibrant green rather than gray, which matched her gown. Just like her sister, she wore the clothing of her times. But her time went back two thousand years, and so she looked like an ancient Greek maiden in a loose chiton, decorated in gold brooches and tied at the waist by a gem-encrusted girdle.

"Gormliet?" he said.

"Who?" She coughed. Her hands wavered as if she were still in a seizure. She looked cold with her bare arms, and Zach thought of throwing his scarf around her shoulders.

"It's alright," he said. "The one who did this to you is dead."

Her brilliant eyes scanned upward, past him. "The one who did this... stands here."

She threw herself into the sand, taking him with her. He felt a bolt of heat, and pain seared up his shoulder. His shirt sleeve was in blackened tatters. The blast had come within an inch of his arm and blistered the skin. It would have killed him if it had made contact.

Gormliet hauled him up by his armpits, pushing him between herself and the wand hovering overhead. "Why did you return?"

Backed by the setting sun, Myretha's eyes blazed brighter. "Finishing old business, *sister*."

"But —" Zach said.

"Shut up! It was pleasant, the last couple millennia, without your boot-licking. It must have left a real mark on Tereilen. After all his lovers, he still remembered you trying to nuzzle into his good graces. Soon as he talked of bringing you back, I knew I must beat him to you."

"Still jealous?" Gormliet scoffed. "Your lies, treacherous deeds you blamed on me, still ring in my ears as if told yesterday. What fresh accusations have you concocted to call down a more terrible punishment?"

Zach struggled, but Gormliet was too strong, and his feet slid in the sand. "You can't have come all this way to kill her!"

"I only had to come all this way because she left me behind," Myretha declared. "Cozying up to the Nurianels, exchanging sickening odes of adulation for jewels and leaving your kin with scraps, like we were dwarves or another subservient race." She flung the ring into the pit before raising the wand again.

Gormliet pushed Zach in front of her. "You'll have to kill your pet to get to me."

Myretha smiled. "Pets are easy to come by. Sorry, Zachary. You should've stayed back there. I might have let you live, since I could have just told you the spell failed to work after all these years. But now you're a witness."

Zach prayed to every god in every scroll in the obelisk that he would not feel the pain before death.

What he felt was a punch in the gut. He and Gormliet sprawled once more in the earth.

"What?" Myretha stared at the wand.

A fist-sized hole smoldered in his shirt, but Nate's parting gift, the dragon scale shirt, was unblemished.

With a roar of rage, Myretha flung herself down at her sister. They kicked and spat and cursed one another as they traded blows. Sand streamed down in a small avalanche, burying Zach's legs. He could not crawl away. The scuffle disrupted the ground beneath him. He was going to be sucked down and buried alive. He wrenched the satchel so hard that the old leather strap broke.

Gormliet let out a soft gasp. Elven blood dyed the front of her gown around the hilt of her sister's dagger.

Myretha pulled the blade free and struggled back to her feet. He could see how the spellcasting had weakened her, but that would not save him from her physical weapon. "No witnesses," she repeated with a growl.

He ran his hand over the scrolls, isolating the particulars of each spell. Finding one, he unrolled it and began to chant its spell, this one in Coptic:

"You shall trample upon the lion and the serpent. I shall not fear the scorpion's sting, for you give it into my power. Tame the beast and bring it to my aid. Amen!"

The ground roiled. It was Myretha's turn to stumble. A shadow covered the hole, but the outline of a giant stinger against the orange sunset made its identity clear. Far from the small arachnid Zach had expected to skitter forth, the scorpion looming overhead was roughly eight feet long.

Myretha drew the wand, but no searing light came forth. She had wasted her magic with a miss into the sand then a blow blocked by armor.

Having nothing else, she fumbled with the dagger, but the scorpion had already latched a claw around her and dragged her out of the hole. Her screams turned Zach's blood cold. He looked away and covered his ears before the first of her limbs was torn away. It was over in a minute.

Sweat poured down his head and arms by the time he freed his legs, which had sunk up to his knees. The scorpion snapped its claws, but it did not attack.

He crawled to the other elf. She cradled her stomach. Her hands shimmered with sticky blood.

"Stay calm," he said. "I'll call for help."

"H — hurts," she muttered.

He dug his fallen phone out of the sand. It still worked, but it had no signal. He sat upon the bloodied bank for a few seconds, exhausted. Then he took off his jacket and folded it into a cushion for her head. "It's okay. I called for help. They confirmed they're on the way."

Gormliet's lip trembled. "So pointless. Why she did it..."

"I'm sorry," said Zach. "I didn't know."

The light dimmed. He knew he should get back to the jeep. But as long as Gormliet breathed, he could not find the will to leave her. The scorpion settled down like a dog and waited with him. Other than the elf's ragged gasps, it became silent. He rarely experienced this kind of silence in the city.

"You see the stars? Here. I'll move your head so you can see them. This place must be beautiful at night, without all the light pollution."

"Why are you here?"

"Waiting for help to arrive."

"Why are you here?" she insisted.

"I didn't come all this way to leave you, sister." Keep talking, he told himself, for as long as she has. "Remember how you built sand castles by the lake? Think back to those days."

A tear mixed with the dirt across her pained face. "They... washed away."

"But they were beautiful every second they were there."

"Little castles," she whispered, keeping her gaze on him until the last flicker of life left. He clasped her hands, elbows slightly bent in a reverent pose.

Then he went back to the obelisk and packed every scroll into the satchel. He climbed on the scorpion's back. At his command, it swept the sand back into the hole, fully entombing the pillar and Gormliet before Egypt's nocturnal beasts came looking for meat. His hands were covered in so much sand and blood that he could not wipe away his tears. He closed his eyes and trusted the scorpion to carry him to Cairo.

Unable to see, he listened to the whispers of magic in the satchel.

***

Six months later...

Back room of a noodle shop on Sidney Street, Pittsburgh

Zach ran his pen down the newest list in his ledger. Good old-fashioned paper, jotted with handwritten notes. It was refreshing after scanning antiques all morning. A lamp burned warmly on the table. The smuggled kerosene oil had arrived that morning. Still, he would need to conserve it. Sure, Myretha's wallet still held a lot of coin, even after buying the empty store and hiring a brother-sister duo with dreams of opening a Chinese restaurant to serve as his front. But a good racketeer knew not to bank on the next shipment arriving on time. He could have kept a light spell, but they were needed. Winter in the Alleghenies had been bitter and long.

His new assistant, a bushy-haired kid knocked once before slipping into his office. Kid? Who was he kidding? It was two years' difference between him and Yiannis. They could've shared a college class together. *Guess war really does make old men*, he thought to himself.

Yiannis wagged his thick eyebrows. "The last batch has landed. I bet we'll see flying trucks and bikes next week."

Zach hated to rain on Yiannis' parade, but he'd feel no sense of accomplishment until the flight and projectile incantations were off the scrolls and the rebels were taking to the sky. If it worked, he would savor the thought of a conjured ice blast spewing down a dragon's throats.

Maintaining his disguise was the other reason to control emotional outbursts. He'd been practicing for so long, he thought he made for a more impressive goblin than his old boss ever did.

But deep down, he still felt empty most days. Wasn't committing to a side supposed to give him purpose and passion? He sighed. He would need to learn to enjoy the spots of victory in between hunkering down in the proverbial fox hole.

Still, he faked a light smile. No way was he going to treat his subordinates the way Gyo'neri had treated him.

Yiannis said smugly, "We should celebrate. We got a case of spirits to open up."

"Oh?" He needed to work with his assistant on how not to sound conspiratorial. "Spirits" had nothing to do with drinks or phantoms. It was their code for a visit from someone high up enough in the Fianna to know Zach was no goblin.

He invited their guest into the back for a bowl of miso soup. Thin from the rationing, but Patrick and Xue Liang always made it tasty. "Some new guys showed up," the gaunt soldier said between greedy slurps. "Claiming powers like invisibility and other shit. I'd like you to look 'em over, see if they're the real deal."

"Gotta check my calendar. Couple boxes to get out the back door first. Y'know what I'm saying."

"You may not have a choice. I also heard from someone real eager to meet you. Deep undercover. She 'works' face to face with HL in Philly, so she doesn't make trips like this too often."

HL? The High Lord.

Zach's stoicism failed. "Wh — why me?" He made the same face as back in Gyo'neri's shop, eyes screwed up toward the cruel but beautiful face of an elf.

He looked back at the reliquary of St. Agnes, which he'd given a place of prominence on his desk.

The rebel messenger finished his soup. "She took down a dragon ship in the invasion's early days. Now, with all this magic popping up everywhere. Seems like a good thing, but we better know what we're dealing with. So, buckle up. She wants you ready for the next fight."

Seventh Son

by Lucas Marcum

HELLO. I PRESUME YOU'RE the court-ordered social worker to determine 'competency'. It's about time you got here — I really can't stay much longer. To answer your next question: Yes. I realize I'm in federal custody. I also realize I'm in handcuffs, and a restraint system keeps me in the chair. No, neither of these will stop me when it's time to leave.

So, let's get down to it. You're here because the government thinks I'm crazy, but also suspects me of a crime. Several crimes of a rather serious nature, if we're being precise. Crimes that the fae may be interested in.

It's fine. I've been accused of crimes before — some of them I've actually committed. I'm not sure how the elves view mental illness and criminal behavior, but they seem content to let humans run things when it comes to law enforcement here in California, so I'm going to presume that you will do things as they've always been done — at least until they get here, so we have a little time to speak. I will start at the beginning, as that will make it easier for your documentation. After all, if you don't write it down, did any of it even happen?

May I ask, will you be using the standardized competency assessment instrument or the Minnesota Multiphasic Personality Inventory? I prefer the Minnesota — I find the questions more engaging. The standardized assessment is so very tedious. Before we start, can I have one of those Wintergreen Lifesavers in your pocket? You might wonder how I knew they were there. That's a very good question. Perhaps I can see through your clothing and into the contents of your pocket and briefcase — or perhaps I can smell it on your breath.

Good luck quitting smoking, by the way. It's very hard and if you slip a time or two, it's OK. Everyone relapses once in a while, but *I* believe in you.

Thank you. That's very kind.

Let's start at the beginning. As the file in your briefcase has probably told you, I have an extensive record. Some of it is even true — That sticky note about a third of the way through the file is a great point to start — that's where it gets interesting.

Oh, don't look so surprised about the sticky note. I told you that I can see through things — or maybe it's' just at the point that everyone who's ever done this has put that note because it seems to be where things change.

Can you please stay focused? We're getting off topic — and if you keep letting me surprise you, we're never going to finish in time. Just remember, I'm crazy and you're a trained crazy person wrangler. Yes, I know we're supposed to call it 'seriously mentally ill' or 'behavioral health', but we're both professionals here. Call it what it is — I'm crazy, so with that said, let's begin.

My name in your files is Charles Edward Langford, Junior. It says I was born an only child in Pasadena, California on December 26th at 6:00 am, Pacific Standard time. It says my mother and father are Charles and Rebecca, who both still live at 1095 Fair Oakes Drive, Pasadena, California, 91105. They live in a ranch-style house in a quintessential California neighborhood. You can visit them if you like. My father is a mid-level film executive for television documentaries, and my mother is a sound technician for the movies. She was part of the sound mixing team for *Jurassic Park*. They got an Oscar for it. They are lovely people — and my mother's peanut butter blossom cookies are the best in California.

I see you raising your eyebrows at that 'my name in your files' line. That's OK. I said that because it is just the name in your files. My actual name is Anthony Michael Collins, and I am the son of a coal miner from West Virginia. My whole family is from West Virginia. I have a very big family. I have six older brothers and six uncles, each with a plethora of children of their own. My whole family is from West Virginia, specifically, Marshall County. I was born on June 21st, 1982 at 5:17 pm, Eastern Standard Time. The cabin where I was born was located about a hundred yards from the Grave Creek Mound, in the Kanawha Valley. It's a very interesting part of the world — there's a lot of latent power there. It's been inhabited for almost ten thousand years, you know.

You're giving me that look again. Why would I lie about that? Who claims they're from a dirt-poor family of country bumpkin coal miners when you could say you're from a well-off family that works in Hollywood? No one, what's who, and why you should believe me.

We're getting off topic again. Why are you so easily distracted? I suspect it's because you, unlike most other social workers, actually have an imagination. You can almost see the truth behind it.

Behind what? Oh, you'll see. Anyway, back to the medical history. I suspect you have reviewed the files, because you seem diligent about your job, so you know that I was first reported to start having behavioral issues when I was about thirteen. The record reflects that I assaulted a teacher at San Rafael Elementary and that I hurt her badly enough to force her retirement.

I would like to correct the record on that. I did not assault a teacher. I *defended* myself against a creature that was there to hurt the children. She was there to suck their energy, and when she tried to do it to me, something about me caused her disguise to drop momentarily. This allowed me to see her for what she was — a creature that feeds on the misery and tears of humans, using the power of psionic energy to feed itself. She tried to feed on me, and I *saw* her. She was about seven feet tall, with long, slender arms with hooked fingertips, flowing crimson robes, and where her head should be was a nightmare of black, pupilless eyes and tentacles. Where her mouth should have been was the beak of a squid. I was terrified — what thirteen-year-old wouldn't be? I lashed out, and not knowing my power, I threw her quite hard and injured her badly. They said her injuries forced her into retirement, but that's not true. There's no record of her after she left the school system. She vanished as if she never existed at all. You can go look, if you'd like.

I will tell you this, though — if I knew then what I know now, I would have finished her off right then and there and revealed them to the world... but I didn't. Children don't naturally want to hurt people, and I tried to tell the doctors and school psychologists that — but no one believed me. Eventually, more of them came, and I tried to fight them. The next few years were rough. I was in trouble constantly at school, because I was irritable and on edge, waiting for them to show up. I could hear them whispering to me, telling me that they were hunting me. Even when I tried to sleep, they whispered and peered in through my windows, but they couldn't enter my parents' home. My parents, being good Hollywood liberals and/or reliable blue-collar country folk, took me to the pastor and to counselling.

The result was that I was diagnosed with schizophrenia spectrum disorder at sixteen. The creatures were still around — one of them made an attempt on my life in junior high, but I was ready for them by then. Somehow, I had known it was coming for me and I was prepared. I hit it with a stick I'd been preparing for several years. It was a pretty good stick. I'd been polishing it and had added a large piece of polished quartz I found near the burial mound and iron rings I'd salvaged from an old bedframe I found in a junkyard down in Martinsville. When the creature started trying to drain my energy, I was ready. I pointed the staff and poured all my willpower into it. It knocked the creature down, but didn't hurt it. It got up and came at me, and was going to drain all of my energy, so I improvised and swung the staff as hard as I could. That took it down. I don't think it was dead, but it was very still. The authorities came for me again. The cops said it was 'assault with a deadly weapon', but I was found not guilty. I think you know why.

I was sent to an inpatient treatment facility for that one, then after I convinced them I wasn't crazy, I went to juvie. That was bad. There was a group of boys in there that tormented me terribly. Hitting, kicking, spitting, and generally abusing me as they wished. Two of them even took me into the bathroom and... well. I don't want to talk about that. I cursed them all — curses only a sorcerer of great power can conjure; terrible curses of conflagration and death, but they only laughed and beat me more — and as their blows rained down, I saw their ends in flame and agony. Again, I foresaw what was to pass. Some years later, Jeffery Talen was cooking and severely burned himself in oil. He died in the hospital a month later. Alan Dearborn rolled his car while drunk driving and was burned alive in the wreck. Darren Michaels was burned in 2006 when his Humvee hit a bomb in Iraq. Jalen Anderson died from electrical burns as he was trying to work on his house in 2010. A strange series of coincidences to occur to a group of cruel men ruthlessly tormented the seventh son of an Appalachian coal miner wouldn't you say?

I endured that place for two years. I was released the day I turned eighteen and because my criminal record is sealed, suddenly I was a free man. Thank you to the modern California liberal for *that*.

That brings us to the next part of things — the part where that sticky note is in that file. To you, it might look like a litany of arrests and hospitalizations, consistent with a sudden decline in mental health, and I'll give you that. It does — frankly, if I were you, I'd think I was crazy too. Attacking random homeless people in the street, breaking things, and ending up as a psych hold in the emergency room multiple times a year — I get it. I've read all the records and they all say the same thing. 'Acute psychotic episodes in the contest of poorly controlled schizophrenia spectrum disorder'.

Oh, don't look so surprised. California Health and Safety Code 123000 makes it mandatory for all patients to be allowed to review their complete medical records. The events are all accurate — but they don't reflect what *I* was seeing and doing, just what *other* people saw. They saw an assault on a random homeless man, and I saw myself as protecting the public from one of *them*. They saw a ranting patient in the padded room in the ER, but I saw myself using incantations to drive away the horrors disguised as the sick. They saw me carrying sticks with junk glued on them and muttering, I was working on using what power I could muster to make weapons against the horrors that lurked in plain sight.

This went on for several years. The creatures would come, I would drive them off, get locked up or drugged to my eyeballs. Then, when I had settled down, I would eventually be let out, and I'd continue trying to protect the public from the enemy they didn't see.

I can see your pencil flying — let me help. 'Subject continues to demonstrate complex delusions with persistent audiovisual hallucinations with schizoaffective elements, consistent with previous diagnosis of schizophrenia spectrum disorder.'. I told you. I have read my chart.

This is all boilerplate at this point. You can copy and paste my history as well as anyone. Let's skip forward to May of 2015.

You might ask what was happening then, and that would be a good question. The answer is all sorts of stuff. The US Government caught some Chinese spies and was trying them. Tom Brady was busted using deflated footballs and fined by the NFL. An Amtrack train derailed in Philly and hurt a bunch of people. There was a big boxing match — Mayweather versus Pacquiao on which I lost ten bucks on to Tom, who was another person like me who could see *them*. He went missing back in 2010. *They* likely got him.

No, that stuff was all going on, as life does. What was far more interesting was what *wasn't* happening. What wasn't happening was that I wasn't seeing *them*. They weren't on the streets. The ones in the police force and on the staff in the ER were gone. The ones in the preschools and old folks' homes were gone. The ones that preyed on the homeless teenagers in Ventura Beach were gone. Just... vanished.

At first I was glad — because I had been finding and fighting the monsters all over the Valley for almost twenty years, and I was tired. My body was growing weak, and the mental strain was incredible — even for me. Then, I began to worry. Where had they gone? They had everything they wanted here. Power, authority over their little kingdoms and plenty of defenseless and unknowing humans to feed on. I made it my mission to capture one of them and ask.

I can see the pencil has stopped moving. You likely don't want to feed into my delusions. That's OK. I'm going to finish this story, then I'm leaving. Walls cannot hold men like me. I'm only here because if the local cops didn't catch me, the elves would be suspicious, and I don't want them knowing what I've been up to.

Anyway, back to my story. I tracked down an elusive one of them I'd been hunting for some years to a low-end daycare center in Los Altos. I waited until the children were released for the day, then entered through a rear window. I caught *it* as it was finishing paperwork alone and subdued it. Well — I say 'subdued', but we had an absolutely brutal fight. It ended up with a rather dramatic end with a transformer station blowing up around us and the power of our clash causing an earthquake. I see the raised eyebrows. You're free to look up anything I say. The US Geological survey records will back up my claim. You'll find it everything I say is quite factual.

As the creature lay defeated amid the showers of sparks from the destroyed transformer station, I pointed my staff at it and demanded that it answer my questions. I must have been quite the sight — unshaven, unwashed and with a wild look in my eye from the battle, pointing my staff at a defeated foe as the sparks and actinic white light from the electricity arced around me. In my mind, it is quite cinematic, I assure you. Answers, I demanded! Well. Let me tell you. I got an answer, but one that I wasn't prepared for. The creatures were fleeing. They had been feeding on our world for millennia unopposed save a very few like myself — but now something was coming. Something dark and beautiful, elegant, inhuman — and cruel beyond measure. The creatures that I had feared for my whole life were fleeing, as children flee from the howls of a wolf from the darkness. If these incomprehensible tentacled horrors that fed on the fear and pain of the vulnerable were fleeing in abject terror, what could be coming? What abomination awaited our world in the darkness? The creature then faded from our world, leaving naught but a stain of greasy earth and dirty crimson rags.

I spent many weeks afterwards wandering aimlessly around the Valley, lost in thought, the dread growing in my heart. On the rare occasions I slept, I dreamt of coming dooms: fire and war, conquest and slavery. I saw mighty nations humbled, and humble people rise. I saw treason, bravery, greed, lust and sacrifice. I saw the fiery death of the old world and the rebirth of the new from the charred ruins, like the phoenix of legend. When I woke, the world was as it always was — *they* were gone as if they had never existed. Was I mad? Were the doctors and social workers right? Had *they* ever existed at all? Had I? I found myself questioning my own existence — indeed, the existence of the world.

As I pondered, I found myself in Griffith Park, at the Observatory. I sat and looked long out over the City of Angels, with her in all her glory — the mix of glamour, violence, glitz, filth and considered jumping — then the portals opened. The invasion had begun. I felt a surge of power coursing through my veins, energizing me as I'd never felt before. The doubt, the fear, the anxiety over being hunted for my whole life melted away as if someone had turned the wattage up in my brain — and I could *see*. For the first time in my life, I could see! There were glowing lines in the sky, radiating out of the portals, soaking into the ground, trickling into everything around them. It was... intoxicating.

I was so euphoric that I almost didn't notice the creatures of darkness and beauty until they were almost on top of me. I fought them with fury and precision, honed by long years of combat against the horrors. These were the creatures *they* had been afraid of? These... faeries? These wisps of insignificant power? With but a little time to learn to channel my new power, I could learn to dominate them — to drive them out of our world, to save humanity and to fulfil my destiny!

I can see your skepticism growing in your face, but why should it? We no longer live in a world of science, not since the fae forced their way back into our world and demonstrated that our vaunted science is nothing against the power of magic.

Perhaps that is why the fae are so interested in people like me. Because we see the world as it is, not as we want it to be. I'm sorry. I am getting philosophical. Our time grows short. Three elves and their human lackeys are pulling up outside the prison as we speak in a dark armored Suburban, so let me tell the rest of my tale. I think we can drop the pretense of the competency assessment — unless you still believe me to be 'avoidant'.

I know you doubt the story I've just told. That's OK. I'm not sure I would believe this either — after all, what proof have I offered? Just events that a reasonably intelligent person could have retroactively built into his deeply ill worldview; an attempt of a broken mind to understand what he saw and lived through as his neurotransmitters and damaged cognitive processes tried to process the pain he endured.

Or... perhaps it's all true. Perhaps I'm the seventh son of a seventh son, born on the summer solstice in a nexus of power; destined to protect our world from the eldritch and the fae and whatever evil lurks in the mists and illusions of our reality — or I maybe I'm the mentally ill only child of a well-to-do family from Pasadena, California.

Once that cell door closes behind you, you will have to decide for yourself.

Going Native

by Jason Kyle

Fall, 1811.

Northern Idaho

Kaelith ne'Che'tin's heart pounded as she bounded down the hill and through the strange woods as silently and swiftly as she could. A dozen elves, her former kin, were so close in pursuit she could hear the occasional curse and snapping of dead sticks in the distance. She glanced fearfully up at the sky, noting the sun's position. If she could just elude them for a few more hours, it would be dark, and her chances of escape would increase dramatically. If they caught her, the best she could hope for would be a swift execution for desertion.

A wide river cut across the landscape, broken by a long, thin sandbar. Maybe, if she could make her way across this river, she would be safe, she thought. She looked behind her, half expecting to see the silhouettes of her pursuers advancing on her, but they were too far up the steep hill. She turned back around and gasped, nearly jumping out of her boots. There by the water's edge was a large animal with shaggy gray fur. It was similar to wargs, back home, but smaller. From a previous visit centuries past, Kaelith recognized it as a wolf. It was scarred, and missing a bit of one ear, and when the elf burst from out of the woods, the creature lifted its head, as startled to see her as she was to see it. Its ears flattened back, and it snarled at her, baring its jagged teeth.

She froze and her stomach knotted up at the sight of the ferocious-looking beast. "Nice wolf," she said, soothingly. Sweat trickled down her back as her mind raced with courses of action. Her bow was already in her hand, along with three adamantium-tipped arrows. She might be able to nock, draw, and loose an arrow into this beast before it could attack her, though she didn't like her odds. Worse, if the wolf even yelped, that would likely only draw her pursuers down on her.

Kaelith stared into the wolf's amber eyes as it regarded her. She was desperate to get moving, but her fear of the more immediate threat posed by the wolf outweighed her fear of her pursuers, for the moment. The stand-off continued for a few more heartbeats, then the wolf's ears perked up. It looked past the young elf woman in front of it and sprinted away. Kaelith had only a moment to process the wolf's behavior before realization hit her. She cursed and dove to one side, just as an arrow zipped past where her head had been a second earlier and landed harmlessly into the water.

The scout drew an arrow and rose out of the brush. An elven scout in leather armor and green clothing similar to her own was stalking down the hill toward her. She had no desire to kill a fellow elf, though the others seemed bent on forcing her into it. Her arm shook from the strain of holding her arrow drawn, then she snarled and loosed her arrow. It whistled through the air, landing inches in front of the man. She just couldn't bring herself to kill him. Not yet, at least.

He swore and leapt behind a tree. "Stop this foolishness, Kaelith, and return with us!" he called out. "It's not too late to put all this behind us!"

"Because House Che'tin is famous for its kindness," Kaelith scoffed bitterly, then swore as she saw the faint shapes of other elves clad in greens and browns skirting down the hill. They tried to be quiet and hidden, and to an uruk or dwarf, Kaelith supposed they would have been successful. She was neither, and an excellent scout herself, and so she marked their progress warily.

"Just let me go. Go back without me. Nobody will miss me. I don't want to have to kill any of you, but I am not letting you take me back!" She warned, pleading, but determined.

"Kaelith, this is madness." This new voice was Hartu Taranath, the scout leader of this excursion. "What will you do? Live in this wilderness until some predator eats you? Try and live among humans? Look how that worked out for our kind before. Elves and humans cannot coexist in peace!"

A dozen responses crossed Kaelith's mind. None would matter to them though, she decided, and she had to act quickly before she was completely surrounded. So as she planned her escape route, she gave the group a final warning. "I'm staying here. Go home. The next time I loose an arrow at you, Velandir, it won't be a warning shot."

Even as she delivered her warning, Kaelith drew another arrow, nocked it, and slunk away into the woods. Not far away, she saw a large, rotted out tree and thought to hide herself within it, but as she made her way there, a voice cried out, "There she is!"

Kaelith hunched down and broke into a sprint. An arrow hit the spaulder strapped to her right arm, and glanced away, though the force of the impact caused Kaelith to hiss in pain. She spun around, sighted on the green-clad figure chasing her, and loosed her own arrow. It penetrated the elf's cuirass deeply enough to injure him though not enough to kill him, and he slumped to the ground, cursing in pain.

An arrow flew past Kaelith, biting into the back of her thigh. She cursed as a burning pain coursed through her leg, but she ran on and moments later she reached the large, rotted tree. Another arrow buried itself into the trunk in front of her, accompanied by the sound of footsteps pounding toward her. She whirled around, drawing a short sword at her hip. Her attacker drew his own, similar blade, and the two became a blur of motion, stabbing, slashing, and parrying. Kaelith fought frantically, knowing that every second spent fighting this elf could bring the rest down on her. She needed to end this fight, *now*!

The moment came when her opponent overextended himself after she side-stepped a sloppy thrust of his blade and she lashed out, kicking the side of his knee. It buckled, but she gave it one more kick, making sure it was broken before she fled, as he screamed in pain. Cries rang out, and Kaelith realized she was boxed in. A line of figures came down the steep hill toward her. Panic began to take hold of her, so she turned westward. There was the large, winding river before her. She'd wanted to avoid the water, if possible. It was wide, and fast-moving, and if she were spotted, evasion would be nigh impossible. The water might protect her from the group's arrows, but Hartu Taranath had some magical ability, being a true scion of House Che'tin that he was. She had no better ideas though, so with no further hesitation, she dropped her bow into the current, dove into the icy cold water and swam for all she was worth. She surfaced only long enough to gulp quick lungsful of air, then submerged again.

Her skin burned from the cold so badly that the numerous cuts she'd sustained thus far were barely even noticeable now. The water's current made it impossible to swim directly across, and she was further hampered by her clothing, boots, and the light armor she wore on her upper body and arms. Her sword, dagger, and the quiver she still wore strapped across her back did her no favors either.

In optimal conditions, she could have swum the width of the river in maybe two minutes with little difficulty. Under the present circumstances however, she had to pause to catch a breath several times. Every second felt like an eternity, but eventually she did make it across and slowly crawled out of the water onto the opposite embankment. She began to shiver, almost uncontrollably, the moment she cleared the water, but forced herself to look back across the river.

In the woods, she saw at least two figures walking south. She might have sighed with relief if she weren't shivering and panting so heavily. She knew she couldn't stay on the riverbank though, and willed herself to move into the woods, glancing back every few steps. If she were spotted now, she was well and truly screwed, she knew, for she was in no shape to run or fight now.

Kaelith needed to get completely clear of her former companions, and she needed to get warm, she knew, or she risked dying. That actually made her chuckle, if only weakly. *Wouldn't that be ironic?* she mused. She'd bided her time for centuries, ever since the horrors she'd witnessed in the wars against the dwarves, hoping for an opportunity to return here. She'd been allowed on one previous expedition, with House Lhandriel, over fourteen hundred years ago to a place called Britannia. She'd loved it, and had thought more and more of escaping back to this realm. Now, she'd finally managed to go on this scouting mission to this wilderness and just two days into it, she was on the verge of death.

Kaelith trudged on, and by walking as quickly as she could, up the even steeper western side of the river, her shivering subsided just a bit. She stopped after a few minutes, when she decided she was deep enough into the woods that there was no chance of discovery, and slowly stripped out of her dripping wet gear. Her hands fumbled at the buckles that attached her cuirass and she cursed in frustration, but eventually she got her boiled leather armor off. She pulled off her ankle-high leather boots and poured a bit of water out of them. Next came her padded, knee-length tunic, trousers, and undergarments. She wrung them out as best as she could and shivered when a light breeze hit her nude body.

Before putting her damp clothing back on, Kaelith checked on her various injuries. Her armor had saved her from taking too many, though her left forearm had a deep cut and both legs had some cuts. She cut a strip from the hem of her tunic and wrapped it tightly around her arm, and another around her leg, then glanced around again, still wary of being found.

"It would be just my luck to be found while I'm naked," she muttered. She grimaced as she slid back into her damp clothing and donned her weapons and armor, hesitating when she picked up her quiver. Several arrows had apparently been lost to the current, she noticed, and she no longer had her bow but decided that her remaining arrows might still prove useful, so she slung it across her back, and moved out again.

All around her, the woods teemed with life. Birds cawed, and small furry creatures with cute, bushy tails whose names she didn't know scurried about. As she walked, she warmed up, and her clothing dried off in the fading afternoon warmth. Periodically, in breaks in the trees, she paused to look around, partly to watch for danger, partly in awe of the sheer beauty of the landscape. The trees were brightly colored yellow and orange and red leaves and the sun felt good, shining down on her from a nearly clear sky. It was a stark contrast to the harsh climate of her home.

"There's not even any dragons to watch out for here," she mused. That much had been clear when her group had been briefed on what to expect on this side of the temporary portal they'd come through — no dragons, or magical creatures of any kind in fact. Though Kaelith's ability to harness magic back home was unusually weak, she was nonetheless good at detecting it at least. That was something else about this world that felt... off. She could sense magic, but it was faint. Very faint. Almost like catching a whiff of something on the wind. At that, Kaelith frowned, and sniffed. The elf realized that she actually was picking up a barely noticeable scent of... something. She continued walking, not intent on anywhere in particular, but determined to get as much distance as she could from the Hartu and the rest of their group. As she climbed, the smell became stronger, until by the time she finally crested the hill, she was able to identify it. Woodsmoke.

Curious as to the source, Kaelith began walking in a wide arc until she identified the direction — due west. She proceeded on cautiously, stopping once to watch yet another small creature go by. This one had comically large ears, a small, plump body, and rather than run or fly, it leaped around on large, hind feet. The thought crossed her mind that she might need to try and kill one of these, though without her bow, she wasn't sure how successful she would be. They moved about so quickly!

Another hour went by and the woods thinned out, revealing a massive expanse of wilderness. Kaelith trekked up and over one more small hill before pinpointing the source of the smoke she'd been smelling. Hints of the smell of cooked meat reached her nostrils now, too, causing her mouth to water. The sun was nearly touching the distant horizon and she saw several thin, barely visible trails of white smoke, emitting from what seemed like a mere shadow across the land. Only after moving closer, did she realize that an entire valley had been hidden from her previous vantage point.

"Whoever these people are, they really know how to pick a camp site," she said with a nod in appreciation.

Kaelith considered her options. She had been told her whole life how terrible humans were, but with every battle she'd participated in during the long war against the dwarves, she'd grown increasingly suspicious of that narrative. She was disgusted by how the slaves were treated, as she grew older, and felt that deep in her heart, she just wasn't like so many of her kin. Her father had said as much more than once. Her caution warred with her curiosity for a short while. In the end, her curiosity and growling stomach won out, and she walked the last couple hundred paces to the ridge that overlooked the valley.

Conscious of being spotted by the inhabitants below before she was ready to reveal herself, Kaelith sat down under a small tree and stared down in rapt fascination. Within the valley were a dozen conical tents made of hide, bristling with poles that jutted out from the crowns. Two more structures had also been erected. These were much bigger — big enough to contain as many as two dozen people, she figured. Racks of meat were set up outside. These were what Kaelith had smelled, she determined, and again, the sight and aroma of the meat made her mouth water and stomach growl. All about, bronze-skinned people with long, black hair moved about, talking, working, or performing various tasks.

Some smaller variety of wolf roved about the camp, and it intrigued Kaelith to see that they appeared to be tame. A small herd of another, much larger type of animal was contained in a fenced area near the encampment. Horses,

Kaelith remembered then. She'd seen these before, on her last visit to this realm. Humans rode them the way elves and orcs rode the large wargs back home.

She watched this settlement of humans for awhile, noting the sun's disappearance with unease. She wanted to observe them longer before making herself known, but she was very hungry, and these people struck her as similar to the uruks back home. If they were, then her showing up at their village after dark might be perceived as rude at best, deeply suspicious at worst. Considering that it was also growing colder practically by the minute, Kaelith gritted her teeth and decided to walk down to the village. She strode down boldly, but casually, guessing that someone would spot her in short order. She fidgeted with a ring on one finger — one of the very few magical items she carried, and would be very useful, hopefully, in the next few minutes.

Within two minutes of walking, she felt like she had eyes watching her, but when she looked around, she saw nothing, nor did she hear anyone. She kept going, at a steady pace. If she hesitated, or acted suspicious, she figured, these people might just decide to kill her and not take any chances. Her own people might do the same, after all.

Once Kaelith got to within a hundred paces of the village, she saw that these people were indeed aware of her. The women and children mostly went about their business, playing and working, but several men stood at the perimeter, watching her. Two or three had bows in their hands, others had spears, axes, or clubs. Most of these were stone, she noticed, but a couple were steel. Not that this made much of a difference, she thought, trying to remain calm. Her armor might deflect one or two stone-tipped spears, but if they all attacked at once, she would die, without a doubt. They stood still, patiently, and watched as she approached, making no aggressive moves, but neither welcoming, either.

"Hello," she said respectfully, looking at the oldest-looking man in the group, when she could identify no obvious leader among them. His braided hair was streaked with gray, but his clothes seemed no worse or better-looking than any of the other men. If he wasn't the leader, she figured he was at least elder among these people.

The men looked at her with astonishment.

"How do you speak our language?" one man asked.

"Who are you?" another demanded.

Unsure of what gestures of supplication these humans used, Kaelith clasped her hands together and dipped her head. "My name is Kaelith ne'Che'tin, formerly of House Che'tin of the El'dori. I am able to speak your language through the use of magic," she said, hoping that this admission may impress them. "I am simply traveling through. I smelled your food, and hoped I might trade something in exchange for a meal and maybe a bed for the night? I can be gone in the morning," she added.

The men glanced around at each other, a bit warily, but none made any show of aggression. Neither did they seem overly intimidated, however.

"Greetings, young woman," the older man said. I am Running Wolf. These are my people," he gestured behind him. He looked her up and down, taking in her disheveled appearance, and her weaponry, then gestured to her face. "Your appearance is... curious. You have black hair like us, pale skin like the traders who have begun coming more frequently to our villages, but your pointed ears and violet eyes are unknown to us."

"My people are from distant lands, though there are more of my kind here," she replied. She hesitated, then added, "If they catch me, there will be trouble."

The man cocked an eyebrow and looked past her for a moment, then shrugged. "You are here, and show respect. Come, join us for a meal and let us talk. You will be safe with us while you are our guest."

He spoke with a mild confidence that piqued Kaelith's ever-present curiosity, so she quickly complied, falling in step behind the man. A couple small wolves sniffed cautiously at her, and several children stopped playing to openly gawk at her. The elf giggled, and made a face at one of them, eliciting a burst of laughter from a little girl.

The group made their way to one of the two, long hide structures and ducked inside. Three hearths were arrayed along the center, and the smell of freshly cooked meat nearly overpowered Kaelith. There were a dozen other people inside — men, women, and children of all ages. At one fire, a young woman sat stirring a pot of stew and humming a melody while she nursed an infant at her breast. In another spot, an old man bound the fletching on an arrow with a child mimicking his task on another arrow.

Running Wolf guided Kaelith over to an open area of the lodge, where a woman about his age greeted him warmly. "This is my wife, Morning Mist," he told her. "She can tend to your injuries. Then you can eat." He winked at her as her stomach rumbled at the mention of food.

"Who is this strange, wounded woman you've brought me?" Morning Mist said with an exaggerated look of suspicion at the two of them.

Kaelith introduced herself as she removed her armor and the bloodstained bandage around her arm while Running Wolf examined her discarded cuirass. He rapped it with his knuckles. "Buffalo hide?" he asked.

"Uh, I don't know what a 'buffalo' is — it's manticore leather. Lighter than mail, but nearly as tough," she replied.

"Hmm. I wonder how it would hold up to my son's new musket," Running Wolf mused.

"I've no idea what that is either," Kaelith admitted sheepishly.

"The cuts to your legs don't look bad," Morning Mist cut in. "I can give you a poultice to rub on them tonight. And I can give you buckskin leggings to wear, rather than what you're wearing if you'd like. They're rather torn up."

Kaelith looked around at the light tan, soft leggings the people around her wore with approval. "I'd like that," she said with a smile to the matronly woman.

Once the elf was patched up, Morning Mist served her a bowl of stew, which made Kaelith's eyes roll back as she ate her first bite.

"Oh gods, this is delicious! I haven't eaten since yesterday evening!" she exclaimed.

"What did happen with your people, by the way? Why do they hunt you?" Running Wolf finally asked.

Kaelith grimaced, and took another bite as she processed how to answer. "My people have been at war with the dwarves... another people from my homeland, for generations. When I came of age, I became a scout in the army of my house, and saw how terrible that war was..."

Visions of the atrocities her people, even members of her own family whom she'd grown up with, played out before her as Kaelith described what she'd seen, and even done herself, over the years.

"The final straw for me was when our mages destroyed the dwarves of Blackstone Mountain... I had to leave. I just couldn't be a part of it all anymore," she said. Her eyes gleamed with unshed tears, and she focused on eating the last bit of her stew.

"And these people are here, now?" Running Wolf asked.

"Eleven others, though I wounded two of them when I left. I tried to slip away last night without them even noticing. I wasn't clever enough, and they chased me down. Humans have forgotten my people even exist. They prefer to keep it that way, for now."

"Ah," Running Wolf said. He ate his own bowl of stew, then pointed at Kaelith's quiver of arrows, lying nearby. "May I see those?" he asked.

The elf withdrew an arrow and passed it to him. He examined the arrowhead and the fletching with keen interest. "I know the arrows of the Schitsu'umsh tribe, Blackfeet, the Shoshone, and others. I have not seen arrows like these before." He tapped the tip of her arrow, and his eyebrows rose in mild surprise. "Very sharp," he said with approval.

"Adamantium. One of the best alloys in existence," Kaelith replied with some pride, then it slipped and she cleared her throat. "Dwarf slaves showed us how to make and use it," she admitted.

"And all of your people have such arrows?" Running Wolf asked.

"Yes. And our leader has magic. That's much, much more dangerous than simple arrows."

"I see," Running Wolf mused thoughtfully.

"I know that look, husband," Morning Mist said from nearby, studying her husband's face. "You plan on walking the warpath against these... elves."

"I think we may have to," Running Wolf agreed. "We shall see."

"No, you don't!" Kaelith said, raising her voice in alarm. Several people around her paused in their own activities to glance over at her. She ignored them. "You don't want anything to do with them. They're cruel, and vicious, and I should never have asked for your hospitality —" Kaelith protested until Running Wolf raised a hand, silencing her.

"You said you are part of a scouting party, yes?"

"Yes," Kaelith replied.

"Scouts are only sent where more plan to follow," Running Wolf stated flatly. "I think if we do not deal with these few now, we may have many, many more to deal with later. We shall see, if they come onto our land, but I shall not seek out a fight."

The trio talked for the rest of the evening, eager to learn more of each other's culture and homeland. Others in the lodge came and listened as well until eventually, one by one, the lodge's inhabitants began rolling up into their furs and going to sleep.

"You may sleep on those furs over there," Morning Mist said, as she also handed a pair of soft, buckskin pants to Kaelith.

Kaelith took the gift with a smile, bid her hosts goodnight, and was asleep nearly as fast as she stretched herself out on the pile of soft furs.

***

The elf woke up to the sound of children giggling and the smell of food cooking. She cracked her eyes open to see a group of half a dozen children gathered around and staring at her. She slowly sat up, yawning, and gave the children a friendly wink and a smile. Morning Mist noticed her up, came over and shooed them away, giving Kaelith a chance to pull on her new buckskin pants in addition to her long, green tunic. Once she'd finished dressing, the older woman handed her a wooden bowl of food — dried berries and slices of meat.

"Come," Morning Mist said. "Running Wolf wanted to speak with you outside once you woke up. Your people came to us earlier this morning."

At that, Kaelith nearly spit her food out. "They what?" She gasped.

"Three... elves? People like you with pointed ears, wearing green clothes and armor like yours came to our village. Our men stopped them and talked. They said they know you are here and demanded that we give you over to them."

"Clearly you told them no... but why?" Kaelith asked as they continued outside. "I'm not one of your people. Why would your village risk a fight with the other elves to protect me?"

By now the two had walked to where Running Wolf and a lean, muscular young man in his twenties, who Kaelith guessed was his son, were standing at the edge of the village, looking out into the trees. The elf looked curiously at an odd, long object the younger man had in his hands.

"We told them no for several reasons," Running Wolf answered for his wife. "We have offered you food and lodging. It is not our way to hand over guests to an enemy to be slain, as they made clear was their intention. Also, my son, Silent Bear saw your fight yesterday with the other elves and was impressed. You were brave, but also honorable. He also saw how you interacted with the wolf. You showed him respect, even as you fled from your enemies. We appreciate that."

"They'll be back," Kaelith warned. "They're probably out there now, waiting until dusk. I was hoping they wouldn't even cross the river. It was certainly miserable enough for me!"

If Running Wolf was alarmed by Kaelith's warning, he didn't show it. Silent Bear even smiled. "They traveled south a few miles to a decent fording site. My son followed them a ways, then returned here after they made camp, east of us. They are watched now. We will know if they come back."

Kaelith gaped as she processed this information, and her respect for this old man who stood casually beside her with a hide blanket draped around his shoulders grew.

"My son retrieved something of yours, by the way," he said, gesturing to the younger warrior. Silent Bear beamed and produced an object that had been leaning unnoticed against a nearby tree.

"My bow!" Kaelith exclaimed, taking the proffered weapon and examining it for damage.

"Beautiful weapon. I replaced the bowstring, otherwise it works fine," Silent Bear said. "We also retrieved two of your arrows."

"Thank you! Now we have at least one weapon that will certainly pierce their armor, if and when the Hartu's group returns," Kaelith said, lightly tapping the silvery arrowhead of one of her arrows.

"We might be more ready than you think," Running Wolf said with a sly smile. "Why don't you loose an arrow into that tree down there?"

Kaelith looked and saw a lone tree that the old man pointed at, and in a smooth motion she nocked, drew back, and loosed an arrow into it, then looked back at Running Wolf expectantly. He in turn nodded to Silent Bear, who poured a measure of black powder from a horn he wore slung across his chest down into the staff's metal tube. He fiddled with a couple of other pieces, then brought up his peculiar metal and wood staff, tucked the wider end into his shoulder, and squeezed a small, metal spike. She heard a light 'click', followed immediately by a very loud 'BOOM!'. Flame spit out of the staff, along with a huge plume of smoke.

"What is that!" she shouted, incredulously, as the ringing in her ears died down.

"That is a musket. It's a new weapon we got for a few furs from some white traders that visited us last summer. It shoots these metal balls," Running Wolf said, holding one up for her to see. "Go. Look at the tree."

She did, with the two men right behind her. When she got close enough, she saw in astonishment that while her arrow had sunk about two inches into the tree, the ball fired by his musket had sunk twice as far, and shattered the wood around it. She stuck her finger into the hole, amazed at the damage.

"Will that penetrate your people's armor?" Running Wolf asked.

"Yes, that should," Kaelith said with a gulp and shuddered at the thought of what such a weapon could do to a person.

"That is good. We have never fought elves before, but we can learn of them through you. I assume your people have never fought the Nimiipuu before?"

"No," Kaelith replied.

Running Wolf nodded again. "Then would you like to learn to shoot this, until your... Hartu returns?" he asked, carefully pronouncing the elven word.

"I would love to!" Kaelith grinned with excitement. She unstrung her bow and set it back down against the tree, then reverently took the musket from Silent Bear.

***

Kaelith spent the morning learning to load, aim, and fire Silent Bear's musket, but was happy to call it quits when he informed her that they had to conserve the rest of their powder and shot. Her ears hurt, her shoulders were beginning to ache, and she was eager to understand more of the Nimiipuu and their culture. The day flew by, and before she knew it, the sun was getting low in the sky. About fifteen men, she noticed, had armed themselves, and painted colorful markings on their faces and torsos, for those that didn't wear shirts. Some also had feathers protruding from their hair.

"One of our scouts returned a short while ago. The elves are on the move. They will be here in an hour," Running Wolf said. He too was armed, and his face was covered in red and black patterns. He had a large, hide shield on one arm, a spear in his other, and an axe was tucked into his belt. "We will intercept them and give them one chance to turn around and leave. If they do not, we will kill them."

Kaelith winced, not savoring the idea of killing her former kin, but understood the situation. "Agreed," she said at last.

The group ate a light meal, then departed the village as the women, children, and a few elderly men waved them off. The region was rugged, and heavily wooded, so the group went on foot, though he boasted of how good their horses were. Twenty minutes later, they spread out and took up hiding positions, just on the far side of a long ridgeline that separated the Nimiipuu village from the elven camp site. Elven scouts prided themselves on being able to move quietly and conceal themselves when needed, but Kaelith was astonished at how quickly and efficiently these natives did so.

A short while later, ten figures, walking single-file, made their way up the steep, wooded hill where Kaelith and Running Wolf's warriors hid. The second in line was Hartu Taranath. She gestured to him, so that Running Wolf and the others could identify him as their primary target. Then Kaelith stepped out of her hiding spot and intercepted the group, fifty paces away.

"Hartu," she called out.

Instantly, the elves broke out of their file and into a loose wedge formation, nocking arrows as they did.

"Kaelith. We were just coming to collect you. Have you finally decided to spare everyone the trouble and turn yourself over to us?" Taranath asked. Unlike the others, instead of a bow, he had a long sword in one hand. His other remained empty.

"I already told you, I'm will not let you execute me. This is your last warning, Hartu. Turn around, go home, and don't come back," she warned.

"This conversation is a waste of time," Hartu Taranath snapped. "Kill her," he ordered, and immediately, the elves under his command brought up their bows and loosed a volley of arrows at Kaelith. She was prepared for that outcome however, and the moment their bows began to rise, she sprang to one side, jumping behind a large tree. The arrows tore through the space where she had just been, and a shrill, animalistic yell echoed through the woods. Arrows from Running Wolf's warriors showered down on the elves, and two fell, dead. Three more cursed as arrows penetrated their armor, but not deeply enough to kill them.

The elves took cover and loosed their own arrows. One unlucky Nimiipuu warrior staggered back and collapsed to the ground with a strangled cry, shot through the throat. Another warrior, barely out of his teens, rushed the elves with a battle cry, raising a club high overhead. Two elves shot arrows into him, though his momentum propelled him forward into one of them. He smashed the elf in the face with his club as he fell, dead.

The loud roar of Silent Bear's musket cut through the chaos of the fight, and for a moment, every elf paused, startled by the sound. An elf who had just stepped in front of the Hartu rocked backwards as a musket ball slammed into and through his torso. Hartu Taranath spotted the warrior, only partially hidden by a tree, pulled out a wand from his belt, and brought it up.

"No!" Kaelith shouted and charged him, but she wasn't quick enough. A jagged streak of lightning shot out from the wand and struck Silent Bear, knocking him backward. He landed hard on the ground, a blackened, smoking wound on his chest marking where the bolt of lightning struck him.

Kaelith loosed an arrow at him as she ran, but the elven patrol leader twisted, and it deflected off his armor. Around her, Nimiipuu warriors loosed arrows or charged the elves, fighting them in hand-to-hand combat, but she was intent on Taranath. She drew her sword and slashed at him in one fluid motion but he weaved away from the strike and brought up his own sword, deflecting the blow.

The two fought furiously, as one by one, the elves fell dead, either riddled with arrows or cut down by axes or spears. Desperately, the Hartu pointed his wand at her but before he could activate it, she slashed at his outstretched hand. The wand, and the elf's fingers, went flying, and he screamed in agony. Kaelith closed in but Taranath wasn't out of the fight yet. In a flash, he launched a series of cuts and slashes at her. She dodged or deflected all but one. His sword pierced through the space between her cuirass and the spaulder protecting her upper arm. She cried out, and dropped her sword as pain shot through the right side of her chest and down to her fingertips. Then she was kicked to the ground.

"This is the reward for your treason!" he hissed as he pulled his blade back for a killing strike.

The blast of the musket sounded again then, and from her prone position, Kaelith saw Hartu Taranath stagger back, a pained, confused look on his face. A hole that had suddenly appeared in his chest trickled a stream of blood, and the Hartu dropped to one knee, gasping and grunting in pain. Kaelith looked over and saw Running Wolf, slowly lowering the smoking musket. Even through the red and black paint distorting his features, she saw the pain and rage there. Running Wolf dropped the musket and drew the axe from his belt. Wordlessly, he strode over to the elf, who screamed a last, defiant curse at the human warrior before the axe came down, splitting his head open.

Looking around at the bodies strewn around, Kaelith saw one elf stagger to his feet, look around in alarm, then take off running. "There's one left!" she cried, and despite the throbbing pain in her right shoulder, she scooped up her sword in her left hand, and gave chase. The angry whoops behind her let her know that the other Nimiipuu warriors still alive were right behind her.

***

Velandir ran as fast as his wounded leg would allow him. Bile rose in his throat as he heard the dying scream of Hartu Taranath. He had to get away from these woodland demons! A portal would be opening at noon, in two more days. If he could lose them, then hide out until then, he could still get home and report the news. Glimpses of movement, and the sounds of running feet to his left and right informed him that he was being surrounded. He cried out in fear, and turned to look over his shoulder. This caused him to trip over a rock, and he was knocked to the ground. The painted warriors were on him in an instant, but they did not kill him, as he expected. Instead, one snatched up his sword from where it had fallen nearby, and they encircled him, not saying anything.

His eyes darted from man to man, expecting to die at any moment. But they did not attack. Instead, the group broke apart, and an older man, accompanied by the traitor, Kaelith, approached him, slipping on a translation ring.

"Do you understand my words, elf?" the man asked in a deep, menacing voice.

"I — I do. What are you going to do to me?" Velandir asked, trying to suppress his fear as his heart threatened to burst inside his chest.

"Your people killed my son," the old man growled. "I would prefer to kill you, slowly, then let the wolves feast upon your corpse. You are lucky though, and will not die today. Instead, you are going to go home. My warriors will see to that. Do not return to your camp. The two men you left there are dead now. You are going home, and you will warn your people to never return here. If they ever do, we will be ready."

The old warrior nodded to his men, who helped Velandir to his feet.

"Kaelith has told me that your kind live very long lives," Running Wolf continued. "Maybe you think your people can wait until mine are dead before returning. Don't. Our memory is long, and no matter when you return, if you are foolish enough to do so, we will be ready, and your people will die. Tell this to your leaders."

Running Wolf removed the ring and returned it to Kaelith. "Take his armor and clothes and release him. Let no harm come to him until he has gone home," he told two of his men, who nodded.

The group roughly tore away Velandir's armor and clothing, despite his cries of protest. As Kaelith watched him flee, naked through the woods, she turned to the older warrior, teary-eyed. "I am so, so sorry for the loss of your son. And for the loss of your other men. I'll be on my way now, as I said I would. I've done enough damage to your village."

"This was not your doing," Running Wolf sighed. "It was theirs," he said, gesturing to the pathetic form of Velandir. "If you wish to stay with us, you may. You will be accepted among us."

"I think I'd like that," Kaelith said, and together, she walked back with Running Wolf and the remaining Nimiipuu to collect their fallen and go home.

The Sword in the Stone

by J.F. Holmes

My name is David Kincaid. I suppose that was all you could call me now, but in my former life I could add, "Major, United States Army, 1st Special Forces Operational Detachment–Delta." But that was then, before the Invasion, and for a time afterwards. This was now. The 'now' that I was in well, I was a refugee, like so many others since that day in August when the Fae opened portals into our world.

We had been on the tail end of the first winter of the Occupation and the insurgency I had been fighting in the New York City area was slowly being hammered down. Friends killed, my chain of command destroyed, the people fighting alongside me scattered to the wind. America had surrendered and now, well, I was sitting, alone, in an old mine in the Catskills with my hand grasping the hilt of a sword set in a stone. Yep, a sword in a stone. I had tried to pull it out and there it still sat, six inches of blade and an ornate ivory hilt with a silver lion's head.

I had come to this cave after our raid on the Fae dragon pens at Mohonk Mountain House, cut off from my friends and driven into the mountains. My own sword had been taken from me by some kind of unkillable mercenary, by orders of my friend Father Michael Feradach, Society of Jesus and spymaster for the Resistance.

"For the best, I suppose," I said to the sword in the stone. It hadn't actually been my sword. I guess since the original owner, Giaus Julius Caesar. was two thousand years dead, it belonged to whomever held it in their hands, and that wasn't me anymore. Good thing, because with it gone, I could see where it had been driving me crazy, obsessed with, not beating the Fae, but conquering.

"It 'twas for the best," said a voice from behind me, and I almost jumped out of my skull. My flashlight sat on a ledge, burning steadily, and my pistol sight settled on the center mass of a man who had apparently snuck up behind me. Losing my touch.

He was of shorter stature, dressed in high boots, a vest and blue overcoat, topped by a powdered wig. If I had to guess, it looked, I don't know, colonial? He was clean shaven, looking at me without a hint of concern in his eyes. In one hand he held a pipe, which he proceeded to light with a match and puff on. On his hip was a long, thin blade, probably some kind of rapier.

If you had told me a year ago that I'd be sitting in a cave in the Catskills, pistol aimed at what was probably a ghost and having a conversation with it, I'd have laughed. Since then, I had seen shit that would blast your soul from your body, if you let it. I didn't laugh. Not anymore.

"I thought you'd look more... Dutch. Short, bearded, longer pipe. Floppy hat."

The apparition smiled, a bit sadly. "I know of whom you speak, but they are currently residing far deeper in the mountains. Captain Hudson and his crew have their own burdens to bear and are biding their own time as to when to confront the Fae."

I holstered the pistol and sat down. Fuck it, what was I going to do to a spirit? I wasn't Father Feradach and my faith was at an extreme low point. "So what are you, the ghost of Christmas past?"

"Christmas?" and a puzzled look passed across his face. "There is so much I don't remember, and so much our Savior has denied me as I walk the Earth. No, Maybe the ghost of revolutions past, perhaps."

I peered more closely at him and then it hit me. "Arnold. Well, I'll be damned."

"You may very well be, Kincaid, as I am. You came very close with that Roman sword, but perhaps I can give you some redemption, even if it's too late for me."

"What do you mean?" I asked him. Screw it, I was probably hallucinating and slowly dying from some kind of bad cave gas, so I might as well pass the time in conversation.

"I mean that you're making a hash of this war you're fighting."

"No shit, Sherlock. Kind of funny coming from a traitor like yourself. What do you give a shit?"

My words seemed to strike home and he actually faded for a moment, to the point where I could see through him to the tunnel entrance that led outside. Then with a grimace of pain he came back into full view.

"I may have not played the best political hand, but you will have to agree that my tactics were sound. George was always better at seeing the larger picture. "

"Then why," I asked, "isn't he here?"

I almost heard him sigh. "George has passed on, as he well deserved to. Perhaps in the time of our country's greatest need, I may find some redemption and salvation. But if you're worthy, as the story goes, you may have something of his," and he gestured toward the hilt of the sword sticking out of the rock.

"Tried that, as you probably saw. Maybe I'm not that man. No army, my soldiers dead, chain of command gone." As I said it, I felt my own spirits sink to a new low.

"Perhaps, but someone thought you may be and I was called."

***

"So," I asked the ghost, "what makes me worthy?" I asked, though I think I already knew what it might be and why this apparition was here.

"Ah, what does? I was worthy once, then I wasn't. Though I thought I was doing the right thing, on the right side." The ghost seemed to drift off and I snapped my fingers. "Right," he said, and the world fell away from me.

BLINK

It was summer, and we stood on a road. In front of me was what I instantly recognized as the main gate to Fort Knox. because the deactivated M1 tank still sat up on its brick podium. Well, deactivated and melted into slag and ceramic. Vindictive fuckers, the Fae were, and kinda dumb too. I mean, a statue, come on. Piss poor target selection.

"What's this about? I'm sure this place took a hell of hammering in the Invasion."

Arnold's ghost shook his head. "Not initially. Took the Fae a few days to get here, over the mountains. I did what I could to help, but you know how it went."

"So why am I —" but then I stopped. A roar that I instantly recognized tore at my ears and shook the ground, and an immense black dragon thudded onto the ground in front of us. It reared its' head backwards, getting ready to spit fire or acid over whatever this kind did. "JESIS CHRIST!" I yelled, and got ready to die. Arnold just stood there as the cloud of poisonous gas swept over me.

He looked up and laughed as a golden dragon, smaller than the other but with a wild haired young woman on its back, dove out of the sky. It blazed with a fire that was like drops of liquid sun, raking the black one and burning off its scales. She arched it over and up, and I actually heard her exultant yell of triumph, accompanied by what could only be singing from the dragon.

"That... that's Harley!" I sputtered, clawing for my rifle.

Arnold put his arm on me. "She can't see or hear you."

BLINK

It was raining, a light drizzle that seemed almost to be a fog. I knew where this was, too. The Pacific Northwest, I had spent plenty of time there at Joint Base Lewis McChord, getting soaked by that deceptive, non-stop rainy drizzle.

We were up on a rail bridge, looking down at a forest road passing underneath. A man ran down the road, clad in a ragged army uniform and dragging leg irons. Behind him, an elven lord, dressed in hunting leathers, was almost mockingly following him. His bow casually had an arrow knocked, and it was obvious that he was playing with his quarry. Following the elf were three knights in full armor.

"We have to do something!" I said urgently. "Screw this spooky shit!"

"Wait. Look," was the only reply.

So I did look, with my trained eye, and could barely make out an almost gigantic figure blending into the scrub that grew up around the bigger trees. What gave it away was the long, angular line stretched out in front of it. I recognized a sniper in a ghillie suit, or thought I did.

The elf drew even with the hidden figure and, from a distance of about forty feet, the unmistakable BOOM of a Barrett Fifty rang out, almost deafening. Though the magic armor protected him, he was thrown to one side like a rag doll, crashing into the embankment. A split second later a stream of tracers reached out from directly underneath where we stood, beneath the bridge, hammering the knights.

"Oh, I love this part, I wish we had such things back in my day! Though grape wo —" but his words were cut off by a tremendous CRACK that I recognized instantly as a claymore mine. It had detonated less than ten feet from the armored figures and what was left of them was splattered against the closer trees.

Three men ran out from the bridge, well, two men and a woman. Hard to tell through the smoke and the rain, but one had hair in a long ponytail. Each had a shotgun in their arms and they ran past the elf, hammering what I assumed were slugs into what was left of the armored figures, not taking any chances.

The elf started to get to his feet, struggling to draw a wand from where it hung on his hip, and a fucking BIGFOOT, the sniper with the Barrett, stepped down from his perch and punched the shit out of the Fae, knocking him backward and out cold. The Sasquatch picked him up, made a loud call and the entire team took off running in a different direction from the ambush. The supposed weak prisoner ran away from under us with an ancient water-cooled Browning cradled in his arms.

"Roberts," said Arnold, a bit smugly, "couldn't have done it any better."

BLINK

We were on a wind-swept plain on a summer evening, Oklahoma I guessed, maybe North Texas. The first stars were coming out but the sunlight still lingered in the west. Although I grew up in New York, I had spent plenty of times crisscrossing the country, even done a spell teaching some lessons learned at Command and General Staff College at Leavenworth. This had the same feel, but dustier. As if to confirm it, on the other side of a two-lane road sat a battered doublewide with derelict oil pump in the front yard and an older pickup truck. Yep, probably Oklahoma.

With a rumbling roar a long stream of motorcycles crested a low rise off to our left, streaming northward. In the lead was a huge orc astride some kind of monstrosity of a bike, a human woman sitting behind him, hair streaming in the wind. Behind him came a caravan of bikes and pickup trucks, most of the bikes ridden by humans wearing motorcycle leather cuts, showing several different club logos. The pickups were tacked with both orcs and humans, with more than one having a heavy automatic weapon jury rigged onto it. There were hundreds, and they streamed past me in a thunderous cascade.

"OK, what the hell is that?" I asked Arnold.

He smiled. "Let's just say that the Fae control things much less than they think in certain parts of the country. That orc, Tukor, is about to lead his troops into battle against the local lordling. It's almost like Saratoga, with the local militia streaming in for the kill. Ah, that was glorious."

"So," I asked, "is all this happening at once? What's going on?"

The ghost looked at me and then —

BLINK

This place I knew well, our safehouse on Long Island. Well, safe estate. We stood in the main dining room, at the end of the long table where we had laid so many plans for our failed insurgency. At the further end sat two women, facing each other, ones instantly recognized.

Before I even think I yelled, "Shannon!" and ran down the length of the table towards her.

Arnold was there before me, holding me back. "David, she can't hear you!" he said urgently, but when he did, both women's heads whipped around in our direction, Shannon's hand going for her missing gun and... Elarissa for her non-existent wand. Their movements were eerie mirrors of each other, as if their minds were working together.

We held still, and after a moment both returned to eating the food in front of them, precise motions that again seemed like reflections in silver glass. Cut, fork, put food in their mouth, chew.

"OK, what the hell is going on here?" I demanded of my guide.

He moved me away, looking troubled. "There is much here that I do not understand, other than that powers of great evil have been worked on both women. Though I think the danger to them has passed. Nay, the elf maid has come unwilling from a place far, farther away than my soul has ever roamed. And I do not know why you were shown this, maybe to give you some hope?"

BLINK

It was a small farm, somewhere in the mountains of the northeast, I think. Vermont? The Berkshires? It was fall though, with the colors of New England.

There was a man out front of the house, chopping wood, with his back to me. The front door to the house opened and a woman stepped out, holding a young baby in her arms, calling out, "John! Dinner!"

I knew them both instantly. Master Sergeant John Clark had been my team second in command and my friend until he was wounded on the Bear Mountain Bridge. The woman was Staff Sergeant Gina Hollis, another of my soldiers and, unknown to me until just recently, they were a couple.

"Is this the future? If not, that baby is kind of really premature."

The spirit shrugged, "How am I, a ghost of the past, to know what is the future and what isn't?" He said it with a grin though, as if he were enjoying himself. Smug ass.

I started to move down towards them. If anything was going to happen, it was with my 2 IC, one of the smartest tacticians I knew. He had had my back in dozens of close calls and I needed him.

The hand on my arm felt like a blood pressure cuff from a frozen hell, a grip of ice that stopped me in my tracks. "This isn't their fight anymore. Sometimes soldiers have to understand what they fight for. It's not for each other, it's for the child. Tell me, Major Kincaid, have you ever been to Venice?"

I knew what he was talking about. "The Tempest."

"La Tempesta," he replied.

"Snob."

"Of course. Giorgione, the soldier and the woman and the baby. In the end, it's what men like you and I do what we do. Not for Duty, Honor or Country, not for glory." He smiled and actually laughed. "Well, maybe a little bit of glory."

BLINK

It was dark, though there had once been streetlights. These were shattered or bent over, as were most of the windows on an old factory. This was a rough part of town, whatever town it was.

"What's this?" I asked. It was no place I knew.

A door opened, letting out pulsing red light and a large figure was thrown out by two big humans in black suits. The orc, for that's what it was, skidded though the puddles and mud, winding face down. He slowly rolled over, sat up, and vomited on himself. After a moment, he got up and stumbled to the door, pounding on it. "WANT MORE!" he yelled in rough accented English. I could see in the street light that he was shaking, a nervous twitching.

A small window slid open and a voice barked, "Fuck off, orc tweeker. You get more drugs when you bring back more gold. Go steal it from your elf lord. Bring us his head and you can have all the coke and meth you want." The window slid shut with a bang and the orc slid down onto the street, sobbing.

Slowly he rose to his feet, unsteady but with purpose. "Kill my lord!" and he barked a weird laugh, drew his sword and charged down the street, cackling maniacally.

"Interesting," I said, momentarily forgetting the ghost next to me. "Looks like they're as corruptible as any other troops.

"More so," said Arnold. "The life they lead is a horrible one, a defeated people who are ruled by spell and lash, their baser emotions for violence and warfare exaggerated in service of the elves. The powders that the humans are selling, though, are just as evil."

I nodded. "Tough bastards, even so. I'd rather not fight them if I have a choice, and if they get corrupted by drugs, so be it."

It seemed as if time sped up, a faint hint of dawn rising in the East when the orc showed again. He stumbled in rapid motion, time slowing down again as he banged on the door. The window slid open and, in the light from inside we could see that he was holding up something.

"Good enough," came the human voice, and the door opened to let him in.

The tossed the object over his shoulder and it rolled to where we stood, landing at my feet. It was the head of a small elf child, eyes wide in terror, staring out into eternity from beneath blond bloody locks.

"Well, that's one less you have to fight later," said Arnold, but I had already turned away.

BLINK

We stood in green space, looking out over the East River. I recognized the park immediately, Brooklyn Bridge Lookout at the ferry terminal, and it was just before dawn. In front of us stood the bridge, still shattered from the stand of the 69th. The bodies were gone, of course, but the East tower was still pockmarked from thousands of bullets.

To my left, across the river, stood Manhattan, now the city of the elves. If anything, the towers seemed taller, with sorcerous webs that glittered like diamonds strung between the highest floors. The sunrise was slowly working its way down and when it touched each strand they blazed into crimson light. Dragons spread their wings and flapped, waking up from their perches on the tops of the buildings.

"What are we waiting for?" I asked, kind of disheartened by this display of Fae magic and might.

"A sword-day, a red day, ere the sun rises!" said Arnold. I looked at him and he had a grin on his face. "Great lines, from a master poet. It was almost as if he had watched me charge the barricades at Saratoga!"

"Narcissistic nerd," I muttered, and turned back to watch the sun caress the buildings. Lower, lower, and it touched the western tower. From it flew the black and silver banner of House Tavor, the Fae Rulers of New York. A bitter taste was in my mouth, gunpowder, fire and blood and death and defeat.

"Are you trying to piss me off?" I snapped. "A lot of good men and women died here."

He waved his hand as if to shush me, still looking at the tower in front of us. I waited, the light slowly creeping down from the banner, and suddenly...

"Mother of God, it's beautiful," and my heart soared.

"I know," he said simply. "Your man Waters did it one night, a great deed, and they've stopped trying to take it down. Not even dragon fire can touch them, and I have no other explanation than that the hand of the Lord Jehovah protects it. Surely it's a message from Him."

There, high on a makeshift flagpole, where I had once used an American flag as a decoy to take down a dragon with an IED, high above the battlefield, was Old Glory. Battered, a bit shredded on the end, but flying defiantly in the morning breeze. Beneath it, as was right, flew the green and gold of the 69th Regiment colors.

BLINK

We stood on a rooftop, about three blocks from two eighteen wheelers backed up to a loading dock in bright moonlight, a large parking lot surrounded by a chain link fence. Men were coming in and out of the back, carrying long boxes and crates from the warehouse to the trucks. I instantly recognized military tough cases, things used to transport weapons and munitions. One of the men had his back to me but I knew from his sheer size that it was Isaiah Jones, former Marine and one of the people who had been closest to me when planning and executing our raids. Next to him was the bald head of the Serbian gangster and weapons dealer Sasha Zivcovic. Sentries covered the entrances, armed with some seriously heavy rifles.

Well it was good to see that someone was still doing something. Then I caught, from our elevated point of view, a glimmer of something metallic in the darkness in the moonlight down a side street, rank upon rank of armored figures. Ahead of them dark green clad figures flitted from dark space to dark space, scouting ahead. They moved stealthily, stopping to examine places where trip wires or IED's might be hidden. Whatever had happened, the Fae had learned. Similar scouts leapt from rooftop to rooftop.

"Oh boy, this is gonna suck," I muttered.

My guide said nothing, just watched with me. Experienced soldiers, we both knew what was about to happen. One side or the other was going to get an ass kicking.

An elfin woman, wearing barely anything, leaned out around the corner and motioned to the sentry closest to her. He laid his rifle on the ground and walked over as she stood with arms raised in his direction, welcoming him into her arms. He embraced her and they kissed passionately; I almost felt his fear as he started to sag then, I saw his body melt away like a deflated blowup doll.

"Shadukai!" I muttered, and went to start forward, but then stopped myself. Zivcovic's head had snapped up, looking right towards where the sentry had been. He immediately started shouting orders and every man there dropped what he was doing, scattering into the building or down an alley, out of sight.

Only Jones stood, taking out a two headed axe and pulling off his jacket to reveal a coat of mail. He knelt and put the butt of the weapon on the pavement,

With a blare of horns the Fae company charged into the yard as the elven special forces followed after the fleeing weapons dealers. Seeing Jones, they spread around him in a circle and let a noble step through their ranks. He was clad in mirrored plate mail, carried a shield with the sigil of House Tavor and a drawn long sword that crackled with energy.

"This is a setup," I said. "No way Jonesy is going to sacrifice himself just to let Zivcovic get away. They had to have planned for this."

The knight stepped forward with a shout and swung his sword. It passed through Jonesy and the elf, expecting resistance, spun around and lost his footing, crashing to the ground.

From the higher rooftop behind us, I heard a laugh and then Jonesy's voice yell, "SURPRISE MOTHERFUCKER!" One of the trucks, followed a split second by the one next to it, shattered in a series of small explosive charges that released a gray cloud of fog into the air. Some of the Fae started to cover their mouths as the knight clambered to his feet.

"What is —" Arnold started to say, but I instinctively grabbed his arm and pulled him down onto the roof.

It was a good thing we were spectral, because this was one of biggest fuel air explosives I had ever seen. The building crumbled under our feet as the blast wave swept over us.

BLINK

"Take me back to the cave," I said, sure in my purpose now as the inferno roared around us.

"Take me back to the cave, Major General Arnold, please, sir."

"Don't push it," I said, "it's going to take more than doing me favors to cancel out your court martial."

***

I sat there and looked at the sword hilt protruding from the stone. It looked pretty contemporary, kind of like the Army NCO swords from the civil war era or a Marine Corps blade. Not like the handle of some ancient iron thing from post-Roman Britain. The pommel was a silver lion's head and the hilt looked like bone or ivory, with a simple small crossguard.

"So, not Excalibur. And I don't think it's been here long. Though if it's a magic sword, who the hell knows, could have been here forever. But this rock is limestone; a few thousand years and it would be buried. Plus rotted away."

Arnold snorted. "Analytical, a good quality in an officer. But yes, it's magical, in a way. Faith makes magic. I lost my faith, and lost my magic, so to speak."

"So, whose is it? Does it have a name?"

"No, George was far too practical a man to name a tool. But he had faith in his weapons, and his men. As for how long it's been here, well, I had someone steal it from the museum at Mount Vernon just before the Fae showed up."

"Mount Vernon... George... fucking... Washington?" I exclaimed. I had started to reach for the hilt but jerked my hand back, almost feeling like it was burned. Arnold seemed amused at my cursing. If I remembered right, he had been a soldiers' soldier, a true grunt who could probably lay down some language with the best of them. And a merchant sea captain too, maybe swore like a sailor.

"Yes, this is his cuttoe. Carried it all through the first part of the war. Oh you should have seen him outside Boston! He walked in front of the troops while they built the barricades, and I'll be damned if everyone didn't worship and fear him. He was tall, you know, and that blade is longer than anything I carried. I really admired him and considered him both a friend and a mentor. Until..." and he started to fade out. He looked with great fear over his shoulder and I could swear that I heard some kind of faint, hissing screech.

"I... I... I betrayed him, I betrayed them all..." he muttered, then started heaving great sobs. Sheets of ice started to creep up his legs and he babbled, "No! Not yet! Not yet!"

"Hey!" I shouted at him, reaching out and slapping him across the face.

Arnold swam back into view, the look of fear replaced with anger. "Damn your eyes!" he yelled at me, getting up and walking away. "I should have you shot!"

I ignored him and let him rant for a while, remembering that he had been well known for his temper. An idea had started to form in my head and I reached out, put my hand on the hilt and pulled. The blade slid out as if it had been oiled and put in a sheath yesterday.

That shut Arnold up. He walked over and sat down next to me as I examined it. "It's made for slashing from horseback, I don't know if you want to get into a duel with one of those armor-plated Fae bastards."

"I've done it before, and if I have to, I'll do it again. But you weren't exactly one to lead from the back, were you?"

"Of course not, but I didn't have the fate of humanity weighing on my shoulders," he almost smirked.

"Neither do I. What we need are some big goddamned heroes. And you're going to find them for me."

More From the Fae Wars

Get the full series!

Onslaught

What would you do if America and the world were invaded tomorrow by a relentless and brutal enemy? In an alternate 2015, a US Army Special Forces Team, part of the legendary black ops unit "Delta", is in midtown Manhattan to take out a Chinese spy and his handlers, sending a message short of outright conflict. All goes smoothly until they find themselves in a full blown shooting war through the canyons of the City. Portals from another world have opened in Central Park, making a way for figures out of historical nightmare to invade. The

Fae, creatures banished from Earth thousands of years ago and now only part of our legends, have returned with Dragon fire, spell and sword to conquer and take revenge. The first volume of The Fae Wars covers Team Three, G squadron, Special Forces Detachment (Delta) as they fight their way off Manhattan and then join the defense of the refugees as the Fae assault the bridges. The fabled 69th Infantry puts up an epic fight against superior weaponry and then the war descends into the asymmetric hell that the Delta Operators know so well. Along the way they find new allies and old powers that come to their aid.

The Fall

For the first time in two hundred years an enemy has stepped foot on American soil and war has come to our cities. The US military is rocked back on its heels and driven into a fighting retreat as each defense line falls. The foe is unstoppable and ... Fae. Creatures from a legendary past who have come to reclaim the Earth in the name of magic and revenge. In the hills of Pennsylvania a ragtag, devastated army prepares to make a last stand against dragon fire capable of melting an Abrams tank and wizardry that stops fifth generation fighter jets in mid-air. Inevitably it comes down to shining steel verses human will, and Sergeant Oliva Acevedo transforms from a hospital clerk to a hardened fighter. Volume Two of the best selling "Fae Wars" follows the fighting retreat of the US Army as the Fae establish control of a shattered America.

Futures Past

Two thousand years ago the Fae were banished from Earth and they've spent that time plotting return and revenge. When their portals open around the world and start crushing the human's military with spell encased steel and dragon fire, it becomes a massive struggle between technology and magic. When the Fae Invasion hammers the West Coast, Captain James Powers and his California Army National Guard artillery battery is caught on its way home from Annual Training. In a running battle the unit is smashed by combat with orcs and elves, leaving their commander struggling to keep his people together and alive. Along the way a dying priest with a strange ability to see the future manipulates people and events to bring Captain Powers to his true calling as a Seer. As they run and fight, the humans gain new allies, Fea tinkerers who love all things mechanical and hate the elves. With their help they begin to take the war to the enemy in a brutal mayhem of ambush and assassination. Book Three of the Fae Wars series following the bestselling "Onslaught" (set in NY City) and "The Fall" (Pennsylvania)

Tales From the Occupation: A Fae Wars Anthology

Wars end, enemies are defeated and territories are conquered and the combatants have to return to a life changed. America and the rest of humanity have fallen to the Fae, ancient mortal enemies of mankind. After building their strength for two thousand years, the Elves have claimed their vengeance and now rule Earth with an iron fist and dragon fire. Down but not out, a human resistance is building, but first daily life needs to be lived. An anthology of stories exploring life during the Occupation in the best-selling Fae Wars universe.

Insurgent

Wars come and wars go. Eventually even the most belligerent of combatants will arrive at some kind of living arrangement, either through exhaustion or slaughter. Kill enough, down to the last child, and there will be no more war … until the next one, of course.

In August 2015, the war started, portals opening up between their world and ours, allowing the Fae to return to our (or their) home world in blood, fire and magic. Conventional forces fought back as well as they could, but the invasion had been planned to hit us in the middle of our civilization. America's military was scattered overseas or concentrated in large bases that were quickly overwhelmed by forces that were dropped right in the middle of their units. The fighting was brutal and horrific, magic overwhelming technology. It took six weeks, and the President surrendered to spare the civilian population. A puppet government was put in place and the Fae started to divide the conquered lands into principalities run by their Great Houses, slowly turning America into a land of feudal slavery. Thing is, though, the Fae had lived in their exile for thousands of years, fighting wars among themselves and against various races that populated their new home. Pitched battles where there was a clear-cut winner and loser. They had never fought an insurgency and had no idea how bloody it could get. Major David Kincaid. United States Army 1st Special Forces Operational Detachment–Delta, soldier of a defeated but unbroken nation, was going to show them. If, that is, he can keep the faith. The follow up novel to the bestselling "Fae Wars: Onslaught" by J.F. Holmes.

Ghost

There are wars, and then there's War. The all-encompassing thing that is fought on many levels, and with many kinds of weapons, many kinds of warriors. Even ghosts.

Alex was no one, a man just trying to get by at his paperwork job at the new Homeland Security. A man grieving for his wife, who had died in the Invasion. Someone just trying to keep his head down while the elves appointed him to do the paperwork of putting their boots on the necks of a conquered American people. Thing is, even a nobody paper shuffling clerk has a weapon, one that had lit the fires of revolution in America hundreds of years ago. His mind, and his words. The internet was still up and running, somehow and someway, and Alex takes to his keyboard. Inspired by his hero Patrick Henry, soon the words of the "Ghost" start inciting attacks on the Fae and the District of Columbia rings with explosions, gunshots and cries of Freedom. The Resistance notices, and Alex is soon assigned a bodyguard and a handler, an ex-police officer who is running from her own hidden past. Together they work to keep the flame of resistance alive and escape from the tightening net of the Fae. The consequences are, as always, Liberty or Death.

Northwest Front

Fae Wars returns on a new front as war rages in the Pacific Northwest!

Corporal Erik Doherty isn't some kind of special operations super soldier; he's just an infantry grunt trying to get by in what was once the United States Army, now an enforcement arm of the Fae overlords. When orders come down from a chain of command more interested in boot licking their new masters than protecting American citizens, he has to make the choice. To serve and live, or run and die? Ashleigh Greene is a teenage girl with a price on her head, the Fae looking for retribution for the killing of one of their nobles. As her hometown burns behind her, she flees into the mist shrouded forests of the Pacific Northwest, her family killed by dragon fire and her world destroyed. On separate paths, each human comes face to face with a haunting legend that has lived for thousands of years. One that has been waiting, watching, and hating the old enemy that has finally returned. Together, they bring war to the Fae in a battle for honor and revenge. Book seven in the best-selling Fae Wars series!

Vendetta

The echoes of the Fae Invasion have died out in the Midwest when a new thunder rumbles across the plains. Tukor, former warband leader of the Red Arrow Clan, now rides with a motorcycle club of humans and orcs against his former masters. It's hard to tell which challenges Tukor more though; being the new chief of all the orcs in the free city of Wichita Falls, Texas, or being engaged to the tough and lovely human woman Misty.

Throw in an elven duke that's still pissed at Tukor for murdering his sons, a motorcycle club that'll follow the chief to hell and back, and a newly arrived orc matron determined to prove Tukor and Misty wrong about their future. The Fae occupation of the Midwest just got way more bloody.

Featuring orcs on choppers, magic ammo and a whole crew of Army SpecOps, the tale of Tukor and Misty is a front seat view of the occupation in the Southwest that no one expected, least of all Tukor himself.

Relics of Empire

In a world shattered by elven conquest, where magic crackles and dragons soar, the Navajo Nation stands as a defiant refuge. Living there is Ben Yazzie, a battle scarred Marine veteran who wants no more war—until a brutal encounter with elven oppressors at a remote gas station ignites a spark of rebellion. Alongside Maria Hernandez, a grieving widow fueled by vengeance, and a band of unlikely allies, Ben is thrust into a fight against an empire wielding arcane power and ruthless ambition.

As ancient ley lines awaken, unleashing chaos across the American Southwest, Ben uncovers a legacy of resistance tied to his ancestors and a mysterious relic from a forgotten era. Magic surges and the earth itself stirs, forcing Ben to embrace his destiny as the Coyote, the elusive and mysterious warrior leading a desperate stand against an otherworldly tyranny.

From the dusty trails of Arizona to the neon-lit chaos of Las Vegas, *The Fae Wars: Relics of Empire* is a pulse-pounding tale of courage, sacrifice, and defiance against overwhelming odds. Will the old ways and a warrior's heart be enough to reclaim a shattered land?

The rebellion begins here.

Harley's War

In the tale of years, counting from the day the Fae returned to Earth, the war was done in six weeks. Fighting stuttered on for two years afterward, as the Great Houses assumed control and built human society into their liking. Or ignored it. The shock troops and great armies of the King were withdrawn, to leave the conquerors, the conquistadors, to send back tribute to the Old World.

The Event, when the Demon Core made its presence known on this world, changed the nature of everything, allowing t he magical Paths of the Way to be accessed by Humans on the level of what they had known of old, before the closing of the portals in 528 CE.

However, throughout the ages between that date and the Event, despite the closing the Ways by the Magus Concilium, there have always been wild magic users. Some haunt humanities legends as heroes, some paid a high price and were burned at the stake. When the Fae returned and our technology failed, they were often the fire that kept our resistance burning. Hereafter is the tale Harely Osman, the woman who was to become famous as The Dragon Rider throughout the war-torn lands of a defeated county.

~ Major James Bognaski, Unit Historian, United States Army Mage Corps
Excerpt from "Spelljammer: The Corps Monthly"
Issue #271, Vol 1, August, 2046

Authors

John Holmes

J.F. Holmes is a retired Army Senior Noncommissioned Officer, having served for 22 years in both the Regular Army and Army National Guard. During that time, he served as everything from an artillery section leader to a member of a Division level planning staff, with tours in Cuba and Iraq, as well as responding to the terrorists attacks in NYC on 9-11.

From 2010 to 2014 he wrote the immensely popular military cartoon strip, "Power Point Ranger", poking fun at military life in the tradition of Beetle Bailey and Willy & Joe.

His books range from Military Sci-Fi to Space Opera to Detective to Fantasy, with a lot in between, and in 2017 two are finalists for the prestigious Dragon Awards.

In 2018, he launched Cannon Publishing, www.cannonpublishing.us specializing in military science fiction, fantasy and thrillers, with an emphasis on works from up and coming authors.

Lucas Marcum

Lucas Marcum is a critical care nurse practitioner and an officer in the US Army Reserve. When he's not working, or performing his reserve duties, he can be found hiking, reading, attempting to perfect his soft pretzel recipe and spending time with his family.

James Copley

James Copley is a former Non-Commissioned Officer of the U.S. Army, having served over twenty-one years in both Active and Reserve/Guard units, variously trained as Infantry, Communications, and Ordnance specialties before finally retiring from the Army National Guard in 2016. During his service, he deployed four separate times, twice to Iraq and twice to Afghanistan.

He is currently working as a software engineer in Central California with his wife, two children, and two dogs. Reading was his number one passion from a very young age, and more recently he decided to try writing his own. Feel free to join him on his writing journey!

Charli Cox

Charli Cox is a best-selling Military Sci-Fi and Horror Comedy author. She also writes Sci-Fi, Alternate History, and Military Fantasy stories.

If you enjoyed Fae Wars: Northwest Front and want to see more stories about Ash and "Gunny," Cannon Publishing has you covered. Burnt Mountain and Sasquatch will be coming to your Kindle later in 2025. Also, please be sure to leave a review!

Representing #teamandmore, Charli's first published short story is in The Phoenix Initiative: First Missions from Chris Kennedy Publishing. She has stories in Bureau 42 and Express Elevator to Hell, also from CKP.

Look for Whistles of the Wendigo, an Alternate History/Military Fantasy novel set in the Joint Task Force 13 universe from Three Ravens Publishing, due to release soon.

Charli's previous experience has been as a Realtor, HVAC Business Manager, IT Office Manager, and freelance bookkeeper. Professional skills such as drafting strongly worded emails transition surprisingly well into writing fiction.

An animal lover and #boymom, she lives in SW Oregon with her Leg husband, two sons, an Arabian mare, and two Husky mixes who think they are hooman.

Learn more about Charli and sign up for her newsletter on her website. Hang out with her on Facebook, Instagram, and/or TikTok.

Jason Weiser

Mr. Weiser has been a government contractor for the last eleven years, and before that, a writer working odd jobs trying to get by. He has a BA in History from CUNY Brooklyn. Mr. Weiser released his first novel in 2025, with Cannon Publishing, but before that, released a short story in their 2018 Spring Military Sci Fi Anthology.

Mr. Weiser is also an avid wargamer and has been published quite a bit in the hobby, having most recently run "Military Miniature" magazine as it's editor in chief from 2021-2023. Before that, he wrote for EpochXperience (a division of SJR Research) as a contributing writer for their blog on wargaming and military history topics from 2020 to 2021.

He also wrote two scenario books on Cold War wargaming topics, "Red Star, Burning Streets" and "Red Star, White Lights".

Mr. Weiser encourages all his fans to visit Cannon Publishing at their website

Brian Gifford

A military veteran with more than 25 years of service in the U.S. Air Force and Army (in an order that would surprise you!), Brian is a lifelong science fiction and fantasy nerd of the highest order. A student of the hard sciences and the arcane arts of cybersecurity and IT alike, Brian has spent a lifetime accumulating his unique view of the world, which he now insists on sharing with everyone else. He is a husband in awe of the magnificence that is his wife and the proud father of three awesome sons, and looks forward to retiring from the military in the near future to focus on his family and his writing.

ML McIntosh

ML McIntosh is a part time rock star, part time vengeful essence of femme wrath. She works the always shift in unapologetic science fiction, dream fiction and urban fantasy. Follow her Instagram @ml_mcintosh and stay weird.

More from Cannon Publishing

Join the Crew!

Sign up for our newsletter for the latest news on new releases and more.

Follow our authors at their Amazon Pages!

Shane Gries (Dragon Finalist)

Lucas Marcum

Al Hagan

James Copley

Jason Kyle

G. Scott Huggins

Michael Morton

Charles Hackney

Jon LaForce

Jason Weiser

Kal Spriggs

Brian Gifford

Charli Cox

Dan Kemp

Jonathan Shuerger

J.R. Wise

Steven Vickers

David Hensley

More Books from Cannon Publishing

Irregular Scout Team One

In July of 2016 a plague swept the world, and the civilization collapsed and fell. For a lone National Guard sergeant, a veteran of the wars overseas who had settled down to a new life, the nightmare began on a hot summer evening at the barricades. Orders and chaos, gunfire and being overrun, his unit dwindles away in the face of the infected. Months later, living in the ruins, the thud of helicopter rotors followed by a crash and the rescue of a downed pilot leads Sergeant First Class Nick Agostine back into the arms of the US military. From his experience comes the idea of teams, military and civilians experienced in dealing with the undead and barbarism of the wilds. The first Irregular Scout Team leads the way for Task Force Liberty to advance down the Mohawk Valley in Upstate NY, making contact with survivors and clearing out the infected with stealth and firepower.

Volume 1

Volume 2

Volume 3: Civil War

Volume 4: Bad Company

Volume 5: End of Days

The Line

When the world descends into chaos and anarchy with an unbelievably swift plague, turning victims into ravenous maniacs, the soldiers of America's storied 1st Infantry are asked to hold the line. From the brutal streets of urban combat to the bloodied, desperate defense on the plains of Kansas, they fight a war against an unrelenting enemy who used to be their fellow citizens. As civilization falls, can they hold the line?

The Thin Dead Line
Dead Storm Rising
The Big Dead One

Fallen Empire

What's a soldier to do when the war is over? When he's only known conflict his whole life? Since time immemorial the solution has been to find another war, this time for pay. Whoever has the credits and wins the high bid gets the experienced fighter. Sometimes, though, the credits aren't enough to cover the price. Empires rise, but Empires also fall. The Terran Union has spent five centuries under the control of the alien Grausians, like a barbarian tribe under the thumb of Rome. Now, after almost two decades of civil war and succession struggles, the formerly subject races have settled back in their ancient territories to lick their wounds and re-arm, leaving hundreds of settled planets to exist in a political vacuum. Into that space steps the free companies, mercenary units that fight for gold, honor, power and glory. Veterans who can't get the wars out of their souls, new recruits looking for adventure, corporations with their own agenda. Join us in a 27th Century that echoes history.

The Irish Brigade

Overrun

Silent Violence

Doom Company

From Book 1: Sandy Decker had a problem. Well, multiple problems. Some good, some bad. Some pretty bad. The good problem is that she was up a whole bunch of credits and the title to an Azelia class yacht called Vagabond King. That was the good problem. The bad problem was that she was in debt to Daresh An-Jaska, Former Princeps in the Golden Legion, Grausian exile, and the biggest gangster in the sector. Not a money debt but a favor debt, one that she paid principle on doing favors in return. Dirty deeds that never seemed to pay enough, of course. That was until yesterday, when she found a line she couldn't cross.

Today, faced with a brutal and violent death at the hands of Jaska, Sandy did what any good former spy would do. She told a story and sold a secret. Operation Marconi and the missing Terran Union battleship *U.S.S. Resolute.* Now it's good news, bad news.

The good news: Jaska bought the story.

The bad news: Jaska didn't trust Sandy as far as she can throw a grat. So the mob boss put 'controls' in place to ensure her compliance. The kind that blew your head off if you didn't do the job.

Now all Sandy and the crew of the Vagabond have to do is follow a decade old trail to the *Resolute*, salvage the mission package for Operation Marconi, and find the objective—a secret location where the Old Empire produced their greatest weapon.

Vagabonds: A Fallen Empire Novel

Athenaeum, Inc

The Professor has problems, and not just what decades of soldiering did to his back and his knees. His boss just died, leaving him as CEO of the extremely discreet intelligence contractor Athenaeum, Incorporated. His old buddy the Operations Director is a highly skilled Army Ranger veteran but his finance chief is slightly unhinged and spends her money on highly inappropriate work outfits. The surviving old men on the Board of Directors are stuck in the 1970s. Running Athenaeum out of an old Cold War bunker and keeping their roster of experts together is expensive, but the government contracts are drying up or going to bigger, flashier corporate players.

Door Number Three

Doubling Down

When nuclear war erupts on Earth, the American colony in the Alpha Centauri system is left stranded. As the new day dawns, a furious attack by the native inhabitants threatens to overwhelm the colony's defenses. It's left to the thin red line of the US Army's 9th Regiment to stem the tide and ensure humanity's survival in this harsh new world. From two time Dragon Finalist and author of the best selling series "Irregular Scout Team One" and "Invasion" comes a new tale that tells of the struggle for survival on a brutal planet.

Offworld: Ragnarok
Offworld: Expeditions

Cannon Fodder: Tales From the Gun Crew

Fifteen stories from Cannon Publishing Authors, each taking from the universes of their novels to bring you perspectives and deepen their world. From 27th century mercenaries fighting on distant planets and young soldiers riding with Arthur to defeat Saxon hordes, to enchanted weapons dealing damage in hands of Fae, we bring you the best of Science Fiction and Fantasy!

Valkyrie

Humanity engages in a desperate struggle with an alien species for this side of the Orion Arm. Space ships die in instantaneous bursts of light and turn into vapor, but on the ground Marines scream and lie wounded in the mud and blood, praying for the Valkyries to come save them. They aren't wishing for death and a Nordic goddess to take them to Valhalla, the wounded are praying for the men and women of the '348th Field Hospital MEDEVAC to dive through fire and hell to come save them. Because they know that ...Valkyries never die!

Valkyrie
Valkyrie: Rebellion
Valkyrie: Attrition

High Caliber Awards

The Cannon High Caliber Awards are an annual contest for new writers. In it we ask them to submit a novella length story of Science Fiction, Military or Fantasy genre to challenge their skills.

2024

2025

The Wishkiller Saga

While on patrol Captain Aethal Paaling discovers evidence that an ancient terror has reached the rich soil of his home: the Lotus, a prolific growth whose addictive leaves devour their victims from within turning their hosts into horrible, terrifyingly violent mockeries of humanity. Created at the dawn of history by the twisted power of a godly relic called the Well, the return of the Lotus may be a harbinger of even more horrors to come. Carrying the fatal news to the capital, Aethal discovers that even in the face of death itself, the Lords Paramount of Verlaen will fight to keep their secrets and their power. With only the guidance of his legendary Greater Rifle and the aid of the Pheonix Lancers, the soldier must find his way through the halls of a forgotten holy order and into deep dens of crime seeking answers. He must find the truth as quickly as he can, because the Lotus may have already taken root among those he loves... and fighting it may cost him everything, including his soul.

A Cold and Mortal Spring
War of the Shattered Moon

When nine out of ten people in the world have died in a brutal plague, what do those who remain do to pick up the pieces? Does the creed, "Duty, Honor, Country" have a place any more if there's no country left? On his way across the devastated remains of Texas, Marine Corps veteran and survivor Eric Marten rescues a young woman from a vicious attack by men who have turned into savages. As Dani slowly learns to trust him, they try to stay alive in the deathlands that America has become, using all their wits to survive a post-apocalyptic nightmare.

90% Death Rate: A Post Apocalyptic Thriller
Angel of Death: A Post Apocalyptic Thriller
The Bloody Princess: A Post Apocalyptic Thriller
The Devil's Pitchfork

A single train carries what might be the last vestige of civilization through a hellish nightmare. A few hundred alive out of millions, lights going out all across what was once America as the possessed arose from the dead and murdered the living. A few hundred survivors travel across the country in an armored train, seeking some place to shelter in a fallen world. All that remains is a dystopian nightmare marked by rains of blood, impossible horrors, and portals to Hell opening in the skies.US Army Captain Jack Zamora is responsible for their safety, a self-imposed burden that wears on him every day. Fighting off undead, protecting the survivors, keeping the train running and supplied as his team desperately plans their next moves. Starvation and disease threaten. but it gets worse, because the ancient gods have sent their emissaries, horrific beings of myth and legend that walk the Earth. Things that can drain a man's very life essence or even that of an entire city.

Hell Train: All Aboard

Sometimes a hero isn't what you expect, and the one you need comes from the castaways of society. Nearly broken and at the end of his rope, former decorated scout pilot and prisoner of war, Red has finally accepted the inevitable. He and his kin have no future in the Human Confederation of Worlds, being gene mods and barely human themselves. With the help of his friend he flees Terra for adventure and fortune out in the reaches of the galaxy. Along the way he's dragged back into conflict that calls on all his piloting skills and he learns the deeper meaning of Kin, as his crew becomes his family.

Path to Freedom: The Path, Book One

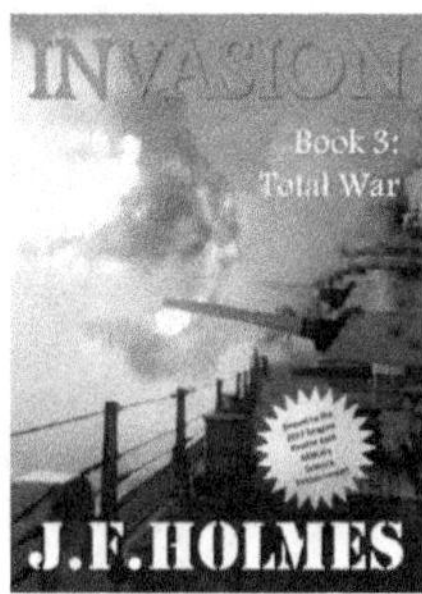

More than a decade after the Confederated Earth Forces were defeated, their commanding general, a boyhood protegee, lives in exile and disgrace. His life on an isolated farm is forever changed when two strangers show up at his homestead, and the war comes crashing back down on him. The problem though, remains the same. How do you fight an enemy that is technologically superior and holds the high ground?

Invasion: Resistance

Invasion: Day of Battle

Invasion: Total War

The military experience is timeless, and echoes down from our past and into our future. Along the way, not everything is as it seems. Thirteen stories from established and new writers in the field of Military Science Fiction and Military Fantasy bring you tales of the terrors of combat and the even greater fear of the unknown in Cannon Publishing's first Bi-Annual Military Anthology.

Fifteen classic Science Fiction stories from both masters of the craft and up and coming new writers! A tyrannical United Nations pulls the strings of its colony worlds, ruling with an iron fist. Corporate interests take precedence, and brushfire rebellions smolder on the edges. One system, home to the only alien species yet discovered, with human allies throws off the yoke and calls itself Independence.

Feedback from the slight pressure of a hand closing sends a powerful mechanical arm smashing into an opponent. A neural link hurls blustering plasma fire from your suit's shoulder mounted cannon. Your reactor levels scream with overload as return fire smashes into your armor, and damage alarms wail while you hurl your twenty ton body sideways for cover. You're a Mecha, a mechanical fighting machine with a human pilot. The guy that the infantry curse at in training and pray for in combat. The machine that the last hopes of your people ride on. The construct that strikes fear deep into alien hearts as they hear your turbines power up. The one able to pass through hell and come out the other side victorious, or die trying.

In the near future, massive empires rule the stars, and west of the Reach, they are battling for control of new systems. In the no-mans land between the front lines, Captain Nate Meric and the crew of the privateer Lexington fight for prize money, and loyalty to their ship and their friends. Beneath it all, though, runs a hidden dream. To see America restored, and take her rightful place among the stars.

Sea of Fire: Demonrise

Brian Corel, former slave, gladiator, ex-fiance to an Empress, exiled Captain of the Taland Royal Guard and now owner of the frigate *Widowmaker,* does the best he can to balance the lives of his crew with his own desire to live life as a free man. Skirting the border between being a privateer and an outright pirate, Corel stumbles into a war with a religious cult intent on corrupting the kingdom of an old friend and has to set things right while grieving over his lost love. Along the way he signs a dragon into his crew and has to risk everything to rescue his brother from the grasp of a demon that has destroyed an entire continent.

Chosen by the Sword

There are some things a PhD doesn't prepare you for, like running two feet of steel through the guts of a flesh-eating monster straight out of a nightmare, while ducking razor sharp claws. Or having the sword critique your fighting style while you do it. Dave Howard had a problem. Last week, he was out looking for a teaching job in the middle of a wrecked job market. This week he was neck deep in green blood and hellfire. Dragged into it by the very sword, his grandfathers' mysterious possessed blade, that was now walking him through hacking up a ghoul without getting his own head cut off. This wasn't exactly what he had gone to school for, and the University he had just taken a job with seemed to be anything BUT an academic institution. More like some kind of monster hunting bunch of weirdo nerds. Maybe his degree in Personality Psychology might be useful there, at least. The fighting though ... as he dodged another swipe of claws and awkwardly tried to follow the instructions the sword was screaming at him, he shot back at it, "Hell, I'm Canadian! Swordplay isn't in my cultural DNA!"

Beyond the Wall: A Novel of Post-Roman Britain

The legions are but a memory, the glory of Rome only a shadow of crumbling ruins and broken walls. A darkening tide of barbarism was washing across Britain's shores and the lights of civilization were slowly flickering out into darkness, only kept burning by the legendary Red Dragons cavalry unit. Led by their Tribune, Arthur, who serves no kingdom but goes where the fight is hardest and most crucial, they wage desperate battles to keep back the tide. The Red Dragons ride the length of Britannia to fight the invading Saxons, Scoti and Picts, wherever they show, from across the seas or down from the Highlands. At sixteen years old Peredur of Gwynedd has listened all his life to the stories of his father Pelinor fighting with Ambrosius Aurelianus. When word comes that his older brother has been slain in battle with the Saxons, his desire for revenge leads him to follow in his father's footsteps as a warrior, becoming a cavalryman with the Red Dragons. Along the way he may either find himself a warrior and leader worthy of Arthur or be left lying forgotten in the dust of history.

Two souls collide in the middle of a deadly war.

Sergeant Sylvie Lyons of Her Majesty's Royal Engineers wishes she'd listened to her grandda's advice and stayed away from the military.

USMC Sergeant Hondo Cassidy wants nothing more in life than being a Marine and fighting. Hondo and Sylvie find themselves thrown together when his artillerymen are assigned to provide security for her engineers deep in the desert of Afghanistan.. Amidst death, destruction, cultural misunderstanding and the inevitable that happens when you mix an all male unit of Marines with an engineer unit that is mostly female, Sylvie and Hondo find in each other a reason to live. That is, if they can survive.

Semper Die

The dead rose expecting a feast. What they got was a firefight.

Sergeant Alex Slaughter and the Marines of Alpha Squad were on a routine training exercise near Quantico when everything went silent. No comms. No command. No clue.

What they find when they return to base is worse than anything they trained for: a bioweapon has unleashed a zombie virus that has shattered civilization, and now they must survive the Collapse.

But as the squad pushes deeper into hostile territory—through the death-choked streets of Arlington and into the rot-stained corridors beneath D.C.—they discover that the undead aren't the only threat. Desperate survivors, rogue military units, and darker truths buried beneath the weight of secrecy will test their loyalty, their mission, and their very humanity.

Written by USMC veteran Jonathan Shuerger and set in J.F. Holmes's brutal and unrelenting Irregular Scout Team One universe, Semper Die delivers pulse-pounding action, authentic military detail, and a terrifying vision of what happens when duty and apocalypse collide.

Lock. Load. Semper Fi. Semper Die.

Troll Hunter

In a world ravaged by endless war between humans and trolls, Gabriel Cullen, a grizzled hunter gifted with the rare ability to track by scent, is captured by the very creatures he hunts.

Bound both by his captors' chains and by an ancient prophecy, Cullen glimpses a chance to end centuries of bloodshed—if he can trust the trolls who butchered his kin. When a sinister force from the deep dark threatens both sides, and even trolls tremble at its approach, the tracker is forced to question everything he believes.

Unaware of her father's changes in hearts, his daughter, Isabo, a fierce warrior driven by duty and vengeance, vows to rescue him, leading an army that wields a devastating new weapon to crush the troll clans. Yet her quest risks igniting a deadlier war. As Cullen allies with a young troll warrior and a blind shaman to confront a demonic evil from a forgotten age, both father and daughter face wrenching choices between peace and betrayal.

In a land where hope is fragile and blood stains every blade, their sacrifices will forge a new world—or shatter it forever. Troll Hunter is a raw, gripping saga of loyalty, loss, and the brutal cost of survival.

More from Irregular Scout Team

Volume 1

In July of 2016 a plague swept the world, and the civilization collapsed and fell. For a lone National Guard sergeant, a veteran of the wars overseas who had settled down to a new life, the nightmare began on a hot summer evening at the barricades. Orders and chaos, gunfire and being overrun, his unit dwindles away in the face of the infected.

Months later, living in the ruins, the thud of helicopter rotors followed by a crash and the rescue of a downed pilot leads Nick Agostine back into the arms of the US military. From his experience comes the idea of teams, military and civilians experienced in dealing with the undead and barbarism of the wilds. The first Irregular Scout Team leads the way for Task Force Liberty to advance down the Mohawk Valley in Upstate NY, making contact with survivors and clearing out the infected with stealth and firepower.

This is a remastering of the best selling Zombie Killers series, combining the 2017 Dragon Awards finalist "Falling" with book 11, "Patient Zero", placing the story in proper chronological order and connecting the stories together.

Volume 2

A year has passed since the plague destroyed most of civilization around the world and the U.S. military is slowly starting to move out into a devastated country. From their bastion in the Pacific Northwest mechanized task forces take the fight for America onto the offensive.

In front of the military, deep into the wild ruins, go the Irregular Scout Teams. A mix of hardened military veterans and experienced civilians who can operate for long periods of time on their own. Checking the road, rail, and water transportation infrastructure, identifying groups of survivors for reinforcement or evacuation, running rather than fighting. The Teams have all the might of their task forces' firepower on call but it's better to be unheard by the infected and unseen by the lawless.

IST-1, the first team and the most experienced, is ordered to operate on their home ground of the ruined Upper Hudson Valley. Sergeant First Class Nick

Agostine, the Team Leader, driven to fulfill his oath to the Constitution and his county while haunted by the memory of his dead family. His fellow NCO and Team Medic, Doc Hamilton, trying to keep everyone alive. Ahmed Yassir, a man without a country or tribe, deadly at a thousand meters with is calm shooting. Isaiah Jones, a giant of a man with a machine gun and a booming laugh, who grew up surrounded by violence. Brit O'Neill, the fiery red head with the ice blue eyes, who is just as ready to take off an infected's head with her shotgun as she is to put at teammate into their place with her sarcasm. Former Serbian soldier Sasha Zivcovic, who is a born killer living in his preferred element, war.

As the eyes and ears of Task Force Empire, it's their job to save the lives of thousands of soldiers by providing accurate intelligence. That's the mission, in theory, but incompetence, the fog of war and politics get in their way, putting the entire teams' lives at risk.

This isn't a book about the Apocalypse. It's a book about the men and women of Irregular Scout Team One and how they lay their lives on the line for each other in the face of incredible danger. A book about how a bad decision or just plain bad luck can put yourself and the ones you love at risk. In the end, though, it's a book about ...

... Hope.

Volume 3: Civil War

Three years after the Undead virus / parasite infected the world, civilization struggles on. The United States is scraping by as a nation by the skin of its teeth, with forty million people crammed into the Pacific Northwest, living in squalid refugee camps. Army units have made inroads into the ruins of the rest of America, working on clearing the major cities.

Outside America, England survived, as did other island nations. The survivors are struggling back to their feet, fighting a long, exhaustive campaign to regain the Japanese Islands and Europe.

On an island in the Hudson River, thirty miles north of the nearest Army outpost, several families have homesteaded. Mixed military and civilian, planting crops and salvaging the land, they are survivors of the Army's elite scout teams. Children are born, old friends mourned, rivers run clean and trees grow in the ruins. The fight, though, still goes on ..

Irregular Scout Team One, call sign "Lost Boys", is working clearing operations in support of Task Force Liberty, designating targets for Close AIr Support. Their assignment is interrupted by the Task Force commander, who gives them an off the books mission that will plunge the nation into civil war.

This book contains the original books four and five of the Irregular Scout Team One series, "Civil War" and "Endgame". The entire series has been remastered and put in the proper order.

Volume 4: Bad Company

The world has fallen, swept away by plague and civil war. In a quiet corner of what remains of the United States, former Scout Team leader Nick Agostine struggles to adjust to peace, wanting to raise corn and kids with his wife. He has a good crop of both growing when the reality of violent war shatters his precious peace.

Called back to active duty, Colonel Agostine is tasked with planning reconnaissance missions for the Scout Teams to take out the leadership of the rebellions Mountain Republic. A final strike to end the last war, but when nuclear weapons become involved, Irregular Scout Team One travels to Florida in chase of a renegade traitor. Disaster overtakes the Team and Agostine sets out on desperate search to find his missing wife.

Through it all, the question runs, what price loyalty, and does the dream of America still live on in the hearts of men, or has it died in the ashes of barbarism?

Volume 5: End of Days

The plague has come and gone, followed by Civil War and the ruin of America. Still, the torch of hope is held aloft by those who haven't forgotten their oath...

As the Federal government battles the remnants of the Mountain Republic, Colonel Nick Agostine settles into a calm life of running a trading post and farm north of Albany. Feeling restless, after the harvest, he sets out with most of IST -1 to explore a long valley north of the remains of New York City, searching for survivors and looking for places where refugees can resettle.

Along the way old hatreds thought long buried resurface and the Team finds itself caught in a brutal ambush. As bullets fly and grenades crack, casualties mount and a shot sends the Scout Team leader spinning to the ground. He awakens to find himself facing torture and death in his most desperate situation yet. It could be ...

The End of Days.